Hilty Defeats Entropy

Also by Thomas Corcoran

Novels

Waiting for V-J Day
Decoration Day

(In Commodore Hilty, Afloat and Ashore):
The Flag List
Commodore Hilty's Second Act

Stories

The Hobbledehoy

Non-Fiction

Afraid of Less: What To Do About the Future

Hilty Defeats Entropy

Wins sweeping victory.
What next for him? World Peace?

A novel by
Thomas Corcoran

Bernice Feigenbaum & Company

Philadelphia ~ 2025

ISBN (HC): 979-8-218-65856-4
ISBN (PB): 979-8-218-65857-1

First printing

This is a work of fiction, set in the imagined past,
occasionally depicting historical figures and places.

Cicada on cover:

Detail from Fontaine KM, Cooley JR, Simon C (2007) Evidence
for Paternal Leakage in Hybrid Periodical Cicadas (Hemip-
tera: *Magicicada* spp.). PLOS One 2(9): e892.
doi.org/10.1371/journal.pone.0000892.

Sources for the epigraphs:

Nathanael Hawthorne, *The House of the Seven Gables:
A Romance (1851)*

Henry James, *Daisy Miller and Other Tales (2016)*

Titus Lucretius Carus, *The Nature of Things,*
translated by E.A. Stallings (2007)

To Linda

In this republican country, amid the fluctuating waves of our social life, somebody is always at the drowning-point.
—Nathaniel Hawthorne

Was a man to sit and deliberately condemn his future to be the blank memory of a regret, rather than the long re-verberation of a joy?
—Henry James

Then death is nothing to us.
—Titus Lucretius Carus

Contents

One

A Roman Triumph

Winter Ivy

Dansby Swanson chased the first pitch, a slider low and away. Sitting alone in the corporate box at Wrigley Field, Bradford Hilty groaned.

Hilty hadn't actually seen the pitch—too fast, too far away—but he knew its shape from hours of watching TV, and of course Swanson's lunge, so deep in his slump, was painfully, boringly familiar.

In fact, despite a winning start to the season, several of the Cubs' best players were chasing these days. Coaches and managers and, sad to say, the players themselves made the usual excuses. But it wasn't the cold or the wind, typical of mid-April in Chicago. It wasn't a bug or two left over from spring training. It wasn't a predictable deviation from the mean—balls hit hard but right at opponents—which would correct itself in time.

No: these guys, the survivors of years of natural selection, with their superior eyesight trained to read the very spin of the pitches, and their superior reflexes trained to respond in fractions of a second, and their powerful, elegant swings trained by the finest coaches and analyzed with every metric, were bound by self-doubt. A vicious circle: indiscipline, excuses, overcompensation. He had seen it all before, in many enterprises.

Or perhaps it was ego. For some of them it was ego, certainly; wicked self-satisfaction fed by too much money. Overpaid, overfed, overcoddled, and over here.

Or perhaps, to be fair, it was his own bad mood. Swanson seemed like a nice enough guy, although he had given his opinion a little too freely as a new arrival last year. He was not so outspoken now.

Luzardo, the Marlins pitcher, threw a heater above the zone, and Swanson couldn't resist that either. He got a piece of it, sending it like a missile to the backstop. The apologists would say that he had timed it perfectly and only an eyelash had kept it from flying onto Waveland Avenue. Hilty knew something about easy excuses too.

Another pitch out of the zone, another foul. With no one around him he allowed himself an expletive—not the f-word of course, he never used that. Everyone else was inside the suite celebrating the latest historic high in the company's share price; drinking too much and eating food too rich and listening to praise full of platitudes. He himself, as Senior Vice President for Quality Assurance, had contributed significantly to that success, but he was repulsed by the vulgarity of celebrating higher profit, and he had come out here both to protest that and also to show his respect for the game. It wasn't the first time his principles had set him apart from his colleagues.

The box that went with the suite consisted of five rows of five padded seats high above the first base line. The Company leased it for the season—twenty-five tickets multiplied by eighty-one games plus the cost of the suite, the booze, and the catering. As an example of corporate waste, this item nearly blew its own whistle. During the latest contract dispute, the labor unions had brought it up more than once—"a boondoggle for people who hardly need one"—but management had held firm. After all, who better to support the national pastime than the nation's leading aerospace firm?

While he watched the game, treating his discontent with what the shrinks would call exposure therapy, a lady slid into the seat beside him; someone he knew by her aura, which had delighted him for fifteen years. She was the wife of the CEO, his disloyal best friend, Admiral James S. "Slate" Greene, U.S. Navy (Retired), who had once voted against his selection to be a flag officer and who just a few minutes ago, in lavishing praise upon other members of the leadership team, had passed him over again.

Swanson took two pitches for balls—no credit to him, for both were in the dirt. Nico Hoerner, on second base, was tempted to steal, but Fortes, the catcher, blocked the pitches adroitly, sending Hoerner back to the bag.

"Nuts," Julia said. "If he'd made it to third, he could have scored on a sac fly."

"Uh-huh."

"But Luzardo's having trouble with his command, isn't he. And his pitch count is high. We'll get a chance against their bullpen soon."

"It won't make any difference if we keep expanding the strike zone. Good Lord!" Swanson had chased another slider for the second out. "You weren't here a minute ago, but he whiffed on exactly the same pitch to start the at-bat. You see how he nearly fell across the plate? The exact same awkward swing, with a runner in scoring position!"

"It's enough to drive a man to drink."

He looked across to expose her for laughing at him. She smiled, trying to appear sympathetic. He turned to watch the next at-bat.

"The ivy's brown on the outfield wall," she said.

"It doesn't green up until June."

"I'd hate to crash into that going after a fly."

"There's a warning track—but yes, I would too."

"On the other hand, the grass looks green and beautiful, like Scotland. And I don't know how they make that pattern with the mowing. The infield is pristine, and I love the white bases. The symmetry and order of it, and of course the skill of the players. No wonder you came out here."

Alone, she meant. She wasn't a fan of sports except as they interested the people she liked. Not that she was false: she had a remarkable gift for empathy.

"Good Lord, now Wisdom's doing it!" he exclaimed.

"How unwise of him."

"If you're going to ridicule this sacred game, Julia, I'll make you stay out here and watch every pitch. Even if it goes into extra innings, which I doubt."

"You mean I won't have to work the room any longer?"

[5]

"He might have said something, you know. Quality deficiencies are at an all-time low. For the first time in years—in years!—our customers have renewed confidence in our products. Air, sea, space, munitions." He shook his head. "I feel small having to blow my own horn, even to you."

Turning in her seat, she put her hand on his shoulder. He was comforted by what, apparently, she saw. For his part he saw an attractive woman of the world who had never lost her authenticity and her kindness. When he first knew her she had worn her hair in a beehive, still popular among mountain women decades after Jackie Kennedy, and had spoken in the soft twang of Appalachia even with her PhD in comparative literature. As an admiral's wife, she had been a little country among the other wives. Now she looked her part. Her shingled haircut had probably cost five hundred dollars.

"I know he's sorry," she said. "He was held back from giving you your due because everyone knows you're his friend, and also there were three or four egos he had to stroke—you know who they are—under the adage of keep your enemies closer. By the time he should have gotten to Quality, he just forgot."

"Did he tell you this, Julia?"

"The crowd has gone home. It's only Slate and Maddy. If you'll come inside I think you'll be pleased."

He would like to be pleased about something. Eventually she led him up the steps and into the suite, not unlike an adult readmitting a child into company after a meltdown.

The suite was almost empty. The staff was cleaning up, working around Slate and Madeleine, Hilty's wife, who were feeding their faces from a platter of brownies and lemon squares.

"Come try these, Brad," Slate said, as if Hilty had been in the room all this time. "The lemon squares are not too sweet, and the brownies have that first-bite crunch that you've always liked."

[6]

"Who's winning?" Madeleine asked.

Slate raised himself from the platter. He was a tall man, though no taller than Hilty, lean and handsome, long-limbed and slim-hipped, with grizzled hair brushed back from a straight hairline in tight waves. Somewhere in their friendship he had acquired charisma—perhaps he had compared himself to the people around him and accepted talent's invitation to lead them. In their first ship Hilty had been his boss, a salty lieutenant lording it over a callow (though smart-alecky) ensign. When next they had served together, Slate had been three paygrades his senior. A four-star admiral, he had run the Navy and commanded the Pacific Fleet, and when he retired, he was a natural for the board of Chance-Stevens-Arrowsmith (CSA), where he'd thrived, becoming its vice chairman and then its chief executive and chairman after a nightmarish time of accidents and scandals and changes at the top.

Six years ago he had brought on his old friend, who, by all objective measurements, and laboring in a black hole of organizational gravity, had transformed the workmanship of one hundred and forty thousand employees operating across five continents. Something of that achievement might have been included today among the praise.

"Let's sit," Slate said, and the four of them moved to a table. After a moment to read his audience, he continued: "Brad, I need your help. I'm supposed to testify to one of the House committees next month, and I can't make it. I want you to take my place."

Madeleine was expressionless, waiting for him to react. Julia was wearing a nearly indiscernible smile that this was the thing she had promised.

"Get a postponement," he said.

"No good. The hearings run up against the primaries."

"Then get someone else. Someone more senior. Frank Townes of Commercial Aircraft. He was the first one you mentioned in your speech. He'll bask in the committee's love: no aircraft accidents in six years."

"That's just one area, though, yes, our most visible. The whole company has a great story to tell. I want you to tell it. You've been the driving force behind our success, and you already have credibility with the members as a truth-teller."

"You mean as a fault-finder."

"I mean what I said. You're our Admiral Rickover—yes, sometimes prickly. But your word is golden. And you've sat with me at these hearings often enough to know the stagecraft."

Not exactly *with* him, however: *behind* him in the first row of seats, ready to supply the handsome witness with any facts required, for which purpose he was never called upon. This was Slate's apology for leaving him out of the praise. He never apologized for the things that really hurt, only for effluvia.

Julia, through her fond expression, was urging him to accept. Madeleine's lack of expression could mean either indifference, which was unlikely, or a desire to counsel him in private.

"Let me sleep on it," he replied. He would not thank him for this small mark of confidence. "I'll let you know tomorrow, though I'll have to do the same as you, rearrange my schedule."

"I'll give the K Street folks a heads-up just in case," Slate said—his way of reminding his friend that a suggestion from a senior officer is tantamount to an order.

A Second Childhood

On the way home Madeleine told him all the gossip he had missed by his hissy fit. She didn't put it that way, but she may well have thought it. The talk seemed a kind of placeholder for the more important conversation she wanted to have when, calm again, he could give her his full attention. Falling silent, she relaxed against the door, letting the shoulder belt hold her and the car take her on and on.

The village of Northriver, where they lived, was a paragon of rural development, with only a line or two still showing from its farmer's tan. Coming off the express-way, he was always amused by its welcome sign, green, chipped, and dented, with its *Pop. 4,238,* a number that might have been accurate in the 1970 census.

Madeleine bestirred herself to follow him into their house, into the historic den, where they often ended their day, as his parents used to do. For this had been his child-hood home. In the one great indulgence of his obsessively self-disciplined life, he had bought the house from the family who had bought it from his father so many years before. Much of it had changed since then, but the den, an alcove off the downstairs hallway, had survived, and he had reprised its look from memory.

The room was a trapezoid, as wide as the hallway on one side with a bay window on the other. A larger chair, of thick brown corduroy—she had put her foot down against the Naugahyde of his parents' day—on the right side of the window looked out upon a small plum orchard, and a smaller chair on the left looked out upon the pool dug by that other family. Between the two chairs was a trapezoidal mahogany table with a lip all around, identi-cal to the old one except for the missing cigarette burns and drink rings.

When the den had been furnished, he had assumed his father's place in the larger chair.

Now she moved the footrest from his chair to her own, putting her feet up and sliding down until she was nearly recumbent. Her eyes were closed and her hands were folded across her chest as if she were meditating. Over the years her lovely complexion had grown downy and translucent. It was one of the first things he had liked about her, that interest in the world—and in people—glowing in her skin like sunrise.

"So what are you going to do?" she asked quietly.

"About the hearing?"

She frowned: his prevarications wasted her time.

"I should pass on it. You can be sure Slate has another reason. There's some contrarian among the members—"

"Your kindred spirit." It was meant to taunt him, but her voice hardly rose above a mumble. She seemed worn out from the celebration. Or—he must be careful here—she might have dined well, as the Victorians used to say.

"Thank you. I'm thinking of someone who will try to sabotage the hearing. Slate knows that if a snuffy like me is attacked, it won't make news in the business journals. Anything to protect the holy share price. He's not doing it for my benefit—not doing it, let us say, to atone for leaving me out of the speech today. I don't trust him."

This, a sad condemnation of his best friend. He should be ashamed to say it if it weren't true.

She sat up with a suspicious glance, and her voice was sharp: "What are you looking at, Bradford?"

Six years ago, he and she had come to the brink of divorce. Their decision to reconcile had been difficult and could have gone either way. Among other consequences, it had provided her with a moral advantage as the lesser offending partner in the crisis. She had been on a lark, relatively innocent—or so she said—with a goofy paparazzo who took clandestine photos of celebrities on private beaches. He, recalled to active duty to command a squadron of destroyers being transferred to Taiwan

[10]

against the near-violent opposition of China, had fallen seriously—though chastely—in love with the woman assigned to him as his assistant/keeper. A lark was a misdemeanor; love was a felony.

The purchase of this house directly afterwards had dropped another weight in the scale, in the form of the ghosts of his unhappy youth, which often haunted him and haunted too her memories of the early years of their marriage. On her first visit, his secret girlfriend, she was three months' pregnant. The visits that followed were a call of duty marked by his mother's soft tyrannies and his father's daily decline into drunken incoherence, not excluding sexual innuendo. She had borne it without any lapse of respectful attentiveness; more than once she had helped him to bed. Afterwards she must listen to her husband's complaints about both his parents. One dreadful morning she had found his mother dead in her chair—the chair in which, constructively, she herself was sitting now—the *Chicago Tribune* still clutched in her hands. Yes, there were ghosts. She had never liked this house.

He turned from the window. "I'm still here. I was looking at the plum trees. People are covering their trees with mesh. The cicadas are going to emerge soon."

"Oh, the cicadas, is it?"

"Brood XIII. Half a trillion of them. It's going to be an invasion. A mess. A cacophony." He smiled at the word; pedantic humor was part of his marital persona. "Believe it or not, Risk Assessment issued a paper about them."

"Do you want to know what I think?"

"Always."

"I think you should do the hearing."

"Oh, the hearing, is it?"

She was leaning across the arm of the chair now, using her hands to make her points. Her eyes were alight, and her cheeks were flushed. "First of all, you don't know that Slate doesn't have a schedule conflict. Julia said something about a pitch to the Chinese. Second, you deserve to be recognized. Besides the actual results—no aircraft

[11]

accidents in six years, and so forth—it says something that the workers respect you so much."

"It does. I'm proud of that."

"You are. The committee should hear what you've done and how you've done it. If there's a naysayer among them, well, you've dealt with people like that before, haven't you."

"Including my own deputy."

"Including her."

"All right, I'll think about it."

"That's my opinion anyway." She said this as simply offering a point of view, without pressure on him to act on it. Their marriage these days involved a great deal of subtle indirection, like the diplomats of two countries with recently restored relations. In the years of their innocence, if either of them had made any kind of suggestion, the other was sure to follow it.

She rose. "I'm going to swim."

"I don't think the cleaner came this week."

"No matter. I'm swimming laps. I'll make a bow-wave."

"Better now than when the cicadas come."

"You're on top of it." She put her hand down on the table to push off with and took an unbalanced first step. He wondered again about the drinking. His father when going to bed had pushed off in just that way.

"It will help me clear my head," she added.

Defending the Share Price

The Subcommittee on Aviation of the Committee on Transportation of the U.S. House of Representatives, for such was its formal name, met in Room 2167 of the Rayburn House Office Building in Washington DC. Holding with damp fingers the leather portfolio containing his opening statement and some key charts and graphs, Hilty walked down the long corridor and through the open doorway.

From Slate's example he looked confident yet respectful, vigorous yet thoughtful. Bill McIntyre, CSA's chief lobbyist, with the kindly manner of a groomsman, brought him to his seat at the witness table and sat in the row behind him. When called upon by the chair, he stood erect and took the oath in a loud, clear voice.

Without seeming to gawk, he took in his surroundings. It was comforting to his nerves that the large room was almost empty. Thirty-nine members were assigned to the subcommittee, and if all had been present they would have crowded the dais before him, as they did whenever the hearings promised to make news. Nothing like that would happen today; instead of thirty-nine, there were eight. This wasn't close to a quorum—even a majority of the staffers had stayed away. Truly the hearing didn't matter. This was why Slate had given it to him.

The chair of the panel, the Honorable Rebecca Tumulty of South Carolina, belonged to that small cohort of extremists in her party who didn't care what they said as long as it made headlines, the more outrageous the better. In daring clothes—former President Trump was an admirer of décolletage—but with a passable assumption of dignity, she went through the preliminaries well. When addressing the witness she was soft-spoken and encouraging.

He delivered his opening statement with generally the right inflection. *Res ipsa loquitur:* the thing speaks for itself, the thing in this case being Chance-Stevens-Arrowsmith's excellent safety record. He stated the facts and showed the appropriate charts. "In short," he said, speaking a little more loudly but avoiding theatrical effect, "during this period, more than seven hundred thousand passengers have flown nearly two billion miles in our aircraft, every mile of it in perfect safety. We're all familiar with that old truism that flying commercial is safer than driving your car. Of course it is. What this data shows is that we have now entered an era in which, even as passenger miles have grown so remarkably, flying commercial is safer than riding your lawn mower."

Tumulty, whose first career had been as a weather girl, hated dead air. As soon as he reached to mute his mic, she said, "Thank you, Mr. ...ah...Hilty, that's a great line. Without further objection—oh, excuse me," as one of her staff handed her a document. "Without further objection, members will be afforded the opportunity to examine the witness, observing a time limit of ten minutes. As chair, I call first upon myself."

She glanced at the document, ever alert to a cue.

"Mr. Hilty, in this very positive account you've given us, which shows the achievements that are possible when corporate enterprise is freed from the crippling burden of high taxes, can you tell me what your company is doing to mitigate climate change? Oh, excuse me"—for the staffer was close upon her again, whispering a correction. "I'm sorry, I meant to say: Isn't it true that all of this growth in passenger miles has had no impact whatsoever on the so-called greenhouse gas myth?"

"I'm sorry, Madam Chairwoman," he replied, "do you mean on the actual concentration of greenhouse gasses in the atmosphere?"

"Well sir, that's what I said. On the myth of it."

"I don't know about the myth. But I do know that our designers and engineers are working hard to reduce the carbon footprint of our own production and of the operation of our aircraft, most of which comes during takeoff and landing. This isn't really my area, however. I would be happy to speak to an expert and provide a more complete answer for the record."

"You can't kill all the cows, you know."

"To reduce methane, ma'am?"

"And you can't fuel all the jets with fentanyl—I mean ethanol," she corrected herself as the staffer started to rise from his seat. "You can't expect anyone to fly in a plane that smells like popcorn popping."

"Ma'am."

"Let me turn to another subject. Your company is doing well, but that's a recent change, correct? Don't you think you would do even better if the president—the right president—imposed a tariff on all foreign aircraft operations? Let's say that every time someone flies in an Airbus, it would cost him twenty-five percent more. Wouldn't your sales increase—I should say, Wouldn't they *take off,* thank you very much." She grinned.

"I don't know, ma'am. Airbus is a fine company, but they are not our only competition. I don't know how we could impose a tariff on countries simply for flying here, but assuming that we could, would you want to levy such a tariff on regional aircraft like Bombardier of Canada or Embraer of Brazil?"

"Maybe not the Canadians, especially if they become our fifty-first state, but any Central American company for sure. And Africans, and Chinese, and whoever makes planes for A-rabs."

When he didn't answer, when silence seemed the only answer, she went on.

"All right, let me ask you this, Mister Authority. Your aircraft are divided into First Class, with fancy seats, and the Hoi Polloi, where everyone is crowded together. Am I correct?"

"Do you mean—?"

"Yes or no?"

"Well, Business Class and Economy are the usual terms. We build our interiors to our customers' specifications."

"So wouldn't you say that your customers would make a whole lot more profit and you could sell your planes for much higher prices if you took out the back half of the Hoi Polloi section and put in SRO?"

"Excuse me?"

"SRO: Standing Room Only."

"Is that a serious question, ma'am?"

"Serious and brilliant."

"What about safety?"

"If the plane goes down, they're all going to die anyway, just like straphangers in a bus that a terrorist bomb blows up. What's the difference?"

"But the passengers wouldn't be safe even in moderate turbulence. And back to your question: who would want to fly that way?"

"Deported immigrants," she replied. "We have eleven million of them to send back."

Scant as the attendance was, this raised an undertone. Bill McIntyre was at his shoulder to whisper, "Just let it go, Brad." He nodded.

Tumulty was pleased with her words and their reaction; certainly here was news. "I have time to ask the witness one more question," she said. "Lemme see here. Mr. Hilty, you say your planes are safe. But are they secure?"

"Certainly, ma'am. In compliance with all FAA rules."

"But *secure* secure? Wouldn't they be more secure if we armed the pilots? And the stewardesses too? They'd take out any terrorist in a South Carolina minute."

How to respond to this? Whatever McIntyre might advise, simple humanity must be heard. "I have to say, ma'am, that the idea of a shootout on an aircraft traveling at forty thousand feet is terrifying to me. The chances of an explosive decompression—"

"*No* chance, as long as the rounds don't penetrate the walls of the plane. And you could reinforce them with Kevlar. Have you thought of that?"

"Will the chair yield?" asked the ranking minority member, sitting next to her. "With respect, may I point out that the time limit has been reached?"

"The chair acknowledges the gentleman's interruption and will cut short her further remarks. I will leave it to other members of the majority to ask the witness whether the American people wouldn't be better served if the Federal Asshole Administration and the National Tea Slopping Biddies were abolished."

One member of the majority did ask about the FAA and the NTSB—or rather he harangued the witness about the uselessness of both agencies and the evils of government generally. Among the minority, three members confined themselves to tempered praise. Only an hour of the hearing had passed, and already people were looking at their watches. The hearing had been routine, unremarkable, boring. It was time to wrap it up.

"Mr. Hastings" Tumulty intoned.

Joshua Hastings, of Minnesota, was that contrarian whom Hilty remembered from the other hearings. It was hard to say what he was after. During Slate's appearances he had asked highly detailed questions whose answers had to be looked up and provided afterwards: missile defense interceptor kill probabilities when decoys were present; the redundancy of propulsion systems of the new Navy corvette being built in CSA's shipyard; the strength of commercial aircraft fuselage panel fasteners across a range of pressures and temperatures. Questions far beneath the normal interests of a legislator and the chief of a major corporation. It was possible that Hastings saw himself as another Ralph Nader, the consumer advocate. On the other hand, it was possible that he saw himself as serving the public.

[17]

Certainly he didn't look like Ralph Nader, glowering, beetle-browed, carried away by conceit. Blond and slender and beardless, he looked like an angel. If he asked for your daughter's hand in marriage, you'd want to agree without first inquiring into his family background or his financial position or, for that matter, your daughter's feelings in the matter.

He nodded several times with evident pleasure to speak to the witness.

"Yes sir, Mr. Hilty. I do appreciate that most positive report. Or should I call you *commodore,* sir?"

Commodore though he had been (by courtesy), he made a show of turning his nameplate around so he could read it. *"Mister* was good enough for Thomas Paine, Congressman: I'm sure it's good enough for me." There were chuckles in the room, but Bill McIntyre coughed. Clever remarks might amuse the onlookers, but upstaging the members seldom went unpunished.

Hastings appeared not to notice the cough or the cleverness either; he had something on his mind. Leaning forward against the edge of the dais, he said, "Quite so. Very good. Your report is encouraging, Mr. Hilty. As I suppose it is meant to be, with billions of dollars in profit at stake, not to mention the CSA share price. We are all encouraged by the data. I know I will certainly be more careful the next time I climb onboard my lawnmower."

The amusement caused by *this* cleverness, and from a man normally so serious, should have let him off the hook.

"Though I do have to ask you, sir," Hastings went on: "what's the reality here?"

A gust of wind blew through his vitals.

"Of course, Congressman, there is a wealth of other data supporting my testimony, which I would be happy to provide. But I do think that what I am sharing with the subcommittee today represents a real success. Fairly and objectively, sir."

"Those charts are about the commercial airplane business, aren't they?"

"Yes sir. That's the most visible thing we do, where the public's confidence is absolutely critical. The data also fairly represents the results we've achieved throughout the enterprise. And more than that, in the past six years we have seen a gratifying renaissance of what used to be called American pride in workmanship; a gratifying renaissance in our own country and which now seems to be the standard in all the countries where we operate."

"Globalization—bullshit!" said Tumulty over her open mic while looking off as if to discover who farted.

"I've seen it myself, Congressman," he went on. "The pride is real too—since you ask about reality."

That answered the mail and without causing offense. Strange to say, he felt a bond of sympathy with this man, zealot as he might be. Hastings and he were after the same things, the righting of wrongs, and it would hurt him to be misunderstood. Truth be told, he wanted Hastings to admire him.

But the angelic face now looked like killing, like the face of an assassin when, Glock in hand, he approaches his victim.

"So you would have us believe, sir. And I must confess that for a number of reasons I want to believe you. But let me suggest a different reality. Let me suggest that your company is just one serious accident away from waking us up from our happy dream. An accident, God forbid, with fatalities—with many fatalities, perhaps—and then, fully awake, we read about all the shortcuts taken in the name of profit. All the skilled, trained, experienced employees laid off in cost-cutting measures or because they believed in the right to organize; laid off and replaced by unqualified newcomers. All the near accidents in manufacturing caused by this. All the men and women on the assembly lines who short their work under the relentless pressure for greater productivity. It's good enough, they tell themselves, only now they need to 'inspector-shop' for someone to sign it off. You're a Navy man, Commodore. Let me assert to you that you're sailing in a deep, forbidding sea and only a thin plank stands between you and eternity."

He looked along the dais, thinking there might be help. But those members who were following the discussion—at least half had their heads down over their phones—simply went on smiling their photogenic smiles. Let the witness twist in the wind as he might, he was on his own.

He took a breath while he nodded his agreement that this public official had a duty to ask his question—indeed, to make his prophesy. There were a dozen ways to finesse the answer. Yet this was the vital moment—the hearing would turn on his response—and it might do some good if he took up the challenge.

"Yes sir, I agree: *Oh Lord, thy sea is so great and my boat is so small.* A thin plank, indeed. But in the Navy, whenever my duties took me below the waterline, I was reassured that my poor soul was being protected by something much stronger than quarter-inch steel."

"You're speaking of—"

"The Lord God," said Tumulty.

"My shipmates, Congressman. Sailors. Talented, well trained, dedicated, and utterly selfless. It was a privilege to entrust my life to them. And now, whenever I fly, I feel equally confident. No one can predict the future, of course. Folly and failure are part of our human condition. Accidents do happen. By the same token, nearly all accidents are preventable, and that prevention is made possible by intelligent processes of job design under rigorous protocols for inspection. As well as, I would emphasize, honest, open communications free of fear.

"Quality assurance is both a science and an art. The science can do a great deal, and the art—sound judgment, pride in workmanship—can do the rest, as much as we fallible humans may ever hope for. The pride I speak of, legitimately earned, founded on actual performance, begins with self-respect and a conviction that the work is important. When I first came to this job, the mantra may well have been *Do it faster, make it work.* With the strong support of our CEO, Admiral Greene, I believe that our company has now changed that to *Do it right, whatever it takes.* And that's the story I have come to tell today and the lesson that I would share with any organization serious about raising its standards of quality."

Hastings glanced at the time remaining. It was clear that he was pondering a response. Bill McIntyre whispered to let him have the last word.

Tumulty asked, "Has the gentlemen finished?"

Hastings tapped the dais as if to get a running start. "Not quite, Madam Chairperson. I would submit to the witness that the glowing report he brings us and his own eloquent testimony represent only a remission in the nearly continuous pandemic of human folly and failure, from wars to bridge collapses to oil spills to airplanes that fall from the sky. And that he will be back, sooner than any of us would like, to excuse the next accident or spate of accidents. And that this subcommittee should regard any testimony like this, however, welcome, as ephemeral—or, if you prefer, ma'am, as the grace of God—and that we should continue to focus our efforts on uncovering and correcting what is certainly still wrong and probably being concealed from us."

"First time as a witness?" Tumulty asked him in the kiss-and-make-up after the hearing. He stood across the dais from her with McIntyre's hand on his shoulder. Now that the klieg lights were off, the members were as friendly as folks at a church social.

"Yes ma'am."

"Wa-all, you'll learn, if Slate Greene lets you return to us. Sorry I had to eat your lunch." Her shapely hands made air quotes; indeed, she was a good-looking woman. "It's election year, stupid. Ha-ha, isn't it just! But it's always a bit much for you debutantes. Next time, instead of the waltz, I'll take you on a nice slow dance."

[21]

Bill said, "Rebecca, you're a hoot."

"And you're a panderer and seducer, but I love you."

Most of the other members were in motion—several gave him a valedictory wave or smile—but Josh Hastings had stayed in his seat. The angel face had no purpose now but amiability.

"I appreciate the Captain's Call, sir," he said.

"You served, Congressman?"

"Quartermaster third class. Enlisted surface warfare."

"What ship?"

Hastings replied with a name notorious on the waterfront as a basket case.

"So you too have experience with things falling apart."

"Oh God, yes! Things falling apart on that ship made me think I could do something more with my life. The book on you is that you're a famous fighter of entropy."

"Always. The sea is salt, and salt corrodes."

"And people do. My division officer committed suicide."

Hilty replied, "That's sad, yes. I remember the case. In my more judgmental days I used to think it meant a failure of leadership somewhere. Now I can't make up my mind about it."

"The same is true in building airplanes."

"Not quite. War is chaotic and wasteful, and the emotional toll can be deadly. But manufacturing and maintenance can be controlled to an actual six-sigma standard. We've done it."

Though he grimaced at his own cant.

"We'll see," said the prophet. "I hope so."

"Anyway, Congressman, you were good to hear me out. I appreciate it."

"And I appreciate your coming. You did well. A, a—"

"Surely not a victory lap," said Tumulty as she passed behind Hastings's chair.

Bill said, "I would call it a mutual cat grooming."

"Ha!" said Tumulty, and she disappeared through the hidden doorway in the wainscotting.

Hastings looked at Bill then at the witness. "I was going to say a Roman Triumph. All honor to you, Commodore, but there should be someone in your chariot to remind you that you're not a god."

"There is," he said with a grin. "My dear wife."

Plaudits

"I just got off the phone with the CEO of Toro," Slate said. "He was calling to compare safety records."

"I'll bet we've got them beat."

"I said in my fine-print voice that the opinions expressed were of the witness and did not represent any position taken by or contemplated by Chance-Stevens-Arrowsmith and its partners, but that I thought you hadn't done badly for a rookie."

His cheeks flushed. "You mean for a debutante."

"A what?"

"Rebecca Tumulty's sense of humor. She promised to be kinder to me the next time."

"Don't let it go to your head. I do think you failed in your primary objective, however."

"In what way?"

"Our share price went up again today. If you become a regular face of CSA, we'll soon find ourselves overvalued."

How good this felt. Over the years he had always been pleased when, Slate having misbehaved, he could correct him, reprising their roles on that long-ago ship. Still, as the world saw it, Slate was the greater man, if not the better man, so the praise was welcome.

"When are you coming home?"

"Sunday night."

"Another day?"

"That's right. You know my two-for-one rule." The rule to spend two days at the destination for every day getting there. Slate did know it, though it was not uncommon for him to spend a day in the air for a two-hour meeting. But then he had made a virtual office of his private airplane.

"So what did Maddy think of the hearing?"

"I haven't spoken to her. I just got back to my room. If she saw it—"

"Of course she did. It was on C-Span."

"If she was moved to watch, she'll have feedback."

"You would have been proud of the way she worked the room at the share-price party. While you were off in a snit."

"I was watching a good baseball game instead of sucking up."

"No, it was a snit. A Hilty snit. Not that I blame you, Brad. I wanted to say something about quality, but in that moment it didn't parse."

This, apparently, was the best he could do for an apology, but even the crumb of it was nourishing. According to the Code of Slate, which crossed and recrossed the bright line of conventional morality, and which made such good use of inspiring words, only deeds mattered.

After getting into bed he phoned Madeleine, taking advantage of the time difference. One of the pleasures of their new marriage compact, when either of them traveled, was pillow talk by cellphone. She should be expecting to hear from him now, especially after the day he had had. But the call went to voice mail.

The next morning his Roman Triumph didn't feel so triumphant. Perhaps the doubter in his chariot had whispered to him while he slept. In the light of day it didn't seem that he had been all that eloquent and masterful. What if Hastings was right and only good luck was keeping those airplanes aloft? Was the quality of CSA's products really so superior? Did so many employees really take pride in their workmanship? When he returned to the office on Monday his inbox would be full of the usual reports of folly and failure, of stupidity, sloth, carelessness, and mendacity that he had denied in the hearing yesterday. What if a plane crashed...today? All the lives lost, the aircraft destroyed—it could happen. Of course he worried: entropy was a fact, things fall apart. Someday the universe would stop expanding, and even his scattered atoms would collapse into the infinite unity. He felt flat, apathetic; this was the morning after a different kind of debauch. He would have felt better if he had talked to his wife.

He had breakfast in his room. The young person who brought his cart was entirely too cheerful. Just as he began to eat someone else came by. "What now?" he asked. A man from the concierge staff had two messages for him, which he took at the door, barely civil. One of the messages was enclosed in a number ten envelope with CSA's letterhead and *Government Operations* underneath. The other, a personal note, bore a return address in Georgetown. He opened it first.

Inside was a card on expensive stock under the imprint of a blue flag with four white stars at the corners and a fouled anchor in the center. The black ink had spread a little into the bond, and the cursive script was slanted to look masculine or at least executive, as if dashed off by a busy official. A busy official she was, and highly placed:

Dear Brad,

You did so well yesterday! I was thrilled to hear every word of praise from the committee. And you looked terrific and sounded like—I don't know, but totally convincing. No surprise there.

If you're still in town, as I'm told you are, can you join me for dinner tonight? I'm having a few people I think you will like, and afterwards I want very much to talk to you, just us.

Ever your friend,

Robin.

Meaning Robin McGill, the Honorable Robin McGill, Secretary of the Navy, former commander of the Pacific Fleet, former commanding officer of a crack destroyer, and a radiant figure from his past. Equivocally so: fifteen years before, when he had commanded the readiness squadron in Norfolk, Robin's ship had made an historically long and splendid combat deployment overseas. He had just been passed over for flag officer. She, charismatic leader that she was, what the sports world liked to call a generational talent, was on her way to the top. When she brought her ship back to Norfolk with its flags flying, in the face of so much glory he had suspected her of a serious breach of Navy Regulations and had tried, notwithstanding her celebrity and his personal admiration, to prosecute her. This had led to a moment that might have ended her career had not Slate Greene, at the last possible moment, tasered him. In the years since, he and Robin had treated the conflict as a family quarrel healed by time. She had entered his life again—he had actually served under her—during the Taiwan adventure. But he never forgot that the former question of her culpability had gone unanswered.

What on earth did she want to speak to him about? On a second reading the note, despite its breezy style, seemed to have been written carefully. His mind ran from a belated confession to a call for help to an offer of employment. She was not unkind. She had always returned his admiration. Still, and despite her flattery here, it must be something she wanted, not something she wanted to do for him. The note provided her number, and a little tremulously he phoned her to accept, happily leaving a message when the call went to voice mail.

Inside the other envelope, from Bill McIntyre's office, was a scrawled note—*A star is born! Well done, Brad!*—enclosing a ticket to a performance that afternoon by the New York City Ballet at the Kennedy Center. Thus was his empty cup filled to the brim, another argument for the power of positive thinking. The hotel lobby backed upon a mall, whose convenience invited him to shop for something more appropriate to wear for the dinner. After all, she wanted to see him—alone. Tie or no tie? A Washington insider would know. It seemed reasonable that on a weekend the mode would be to dress up a little.

When he had belabored this decision sufficiently and had had a spot of lunch, it was time to meet Bill's car. He went out to the curb with a slight pang of guilt for not having tried his wife again; though she, of course, could have called him back. His father used to say, who never called or wrote after his mother's death, *Your arm isn't broken either, bub.*

Their seats at the dance were simply astonishing. Here presidents sat for performances of state.

"Where did you get these tickets?" he asked Bill.

"Oh, that was Slate. Nice, eh?"

People were looking at them, wondering who they were.

The music started. He wanted to be open to a new experience, but in this case that meant chromatic discord, garish costumes, ungainly poses, and the annoying thud of heavy-footed landings on the boards. *De gustibus non est disputandum:* there is no accounting for taste. Very well: his taste did not extend as far as Brutalism. He couldn't wait for the performance to end.

The last piece was *In the Upper Room,* choreographed by Twyla Tharpe. Expecting something like the earlier dances, he was still wondering about Robin when the figures on the stage eclipsed all other thoughts. One pass interrupted another, unrelenting: the tension built, tightened, tightened beyond enduring. The dancers were so beautiful! What they did with their bodies was so incredible, and they kept doing it, adding ever more complicated, difficult, and powerful combinations until he seemed to hold not only his breath but his life, and the stinging tears ran down his face. Two male dancers turned a female through a somersault, passing her from one to

[29]

another as if by levitation, a movement more precise and graceful than he had ever seen in sports; and that modern thing that Twyla Tharpe was saying, whatever it was, broke him completely, and he put his hands to his face and sobbed. Bill McIntyre was crying too. The two men looked at each other and laughed. All the way home they talked of nothing but *In the Upper Room.* "The hell with my masculinity," Bill said. "That was beautiful."

He himself felt chastened and cleansed. More than forty years of marching in step, including long service to his country, now seemed like a waste...or perhaps like a preparation for some supremely creative new phase in the time remaining to him. He must go home and finish a history he had been toying with. He must write something just as beautiful—poetry, perhaps. He should study music and throw off capitalism and leave the military-industrial complex and go work at a dance company. Madeleine would know if only, chancing her ridicule, he could find the words to describe what he was feeling now. And that was this: that death doesn't matter if you've really lived. *Mors nihil refert ad eum qui vere vixerit.*

In the Upper Room

None of the men were wearing ties. One woman, or perhaps a woman transitioning to a man, was wearing a bowtie. When he arrived at Robin's house and went upstairs to the drawing room, he saw at once that he was overdressed. His tie began to choke him.

Robin, vividly beautiful, brightened when she saw him. "My dear friend," she said, giving him more of her person than hospitality required. He met her embrace halfway, and as he did so the sweat rolled under his arms. "Come with me," she said, taking his wrist, a hold likely calibrated between the intimacy of the hand and the formality of the elbow. "Let me introduce you."

That done, she asked if he wanted to wash his hands before dinner. In the powder room, inspired by the disposable towels (the nice absorbent ones with the waffle texture), he stripped down to his waist and wiped his armpits. The lump of the tie in his pocket would be incriminating: he hung it on the back of the door. If he forgot it he forgot it, though it had cost, with tax, a small fortune.

By the time he returned, the guests were going downstairs. The house, built in the nineteenth century, had been designed according to the Victorian model, with the kitchen and dining room on the ground floor, the public rooms on the floor above, and the bedrooms on the floor above that. The Victorian tradition that each gentleman lead a lady down to dinner wasn't observed, nor any conscious regard to precedence, but Robin and the other VIPs went first and sat at the head of the table. On her right was Senator Williams, the ranking member of the Armed Services Committee, and on her left the Under Secretary of Defense for Policy, from which position, if he were able enough, as one official had been, he might mislead the nation into invading another.

[31]

He himself was a few places down the table, between a junior network correspondent on the Pentagon beat and a Catholic priest who ran a homeless shelter in the District that had once been patronized by Michelle Obama.

He began to feel dangerously important himself. This was not unlike those corporate dinners at which the other guests all seemed second-rate. Then too the epiphany of the ballet, the exhilaration of knowing that he was called to make a change in his life, was still operating on him. Then too he was excited to watch Robin at work, giving full play to her personality within the tranquil demeanor that her high rank required. Yet he knew her. They had a past. He had seen her beset by trouble.

They were twelve at the table, too many for general conversation. The junior correspondent, even as she enjoyed her dinner, pumped him for a scoop. When he didn't give her one—say a massive coverup of airplane deficiencies—she asked who would win the next mega-contract from China.

"If I tell you, I couldn't do insider trading," he replied.

"Which rookie quarterback do you like better?" asked the priest, leaning into the conversation. "Your Caleb Williams or our Jayden Daniels?" Here was real tact, the facile touch of a pro. He had probably charmed Michelle Obama by asking what her daughters liked to study.

"It would be bad manners in a guest," he replied, "to diss the hometown hero. If I'd been drafting, I might have drafted Daniels first. But let me tell you both what I saw this afternoon at the Kennedy Center: the Twyla Tharpe ballet. A life-altering experience—life-altering, I mean it! The two of us who went, two big strong men, wept like children. Truly, I'm reborn!"

As it happened, the talk around the table had lapsed into one of those coincidental silences, so that he seemed to be confessing his salvation to the group. Instantly the others shook themselves into life. Robin beamed. Half a dozen wits vied to respond to the confession.

The quickest among them said, "Reborn were you? Nice work, padre!"

"Tell us about it, Brad," Robin said.

How he wanted to adopt her tone, that cool, cultivated diction of those Washington sophisticates who always spoke for the record. A plethora of possible answers gave him the equivalent of writer's block. Finally he said, "Well, it was just spectacular. The dancing."

The dancing: how insightful.

Senator Williams raised his hand a mere inch or two, and the table fell silent.

"Oh yes, *In the Upper Room,* very good! It had its vogue when Twyla first staged it, in '86 I think it was. Lord, so long ago! I was a callow young man from rural America, simply overwhelmed by the big city. Have you seen the reprisal, Robin? No? Excellent!—I'll take you. Tell me, Commodore, did Delgado dance the last two sections?"

To this he replied that he wasn't quite sure. But that wasn't the whole truth, and since he wished by now to complete the act of self-mortification, he added, "I don't know who Delgado is and wouldn't have recognized her—him or her—on the stage. This was my first ballet, ever. I was just trying to describe how I felt. It doesn't matter."

"Straight talk with no self-advertising," Robin offered. "His many friends know that Commodore Hilty is the opposite of a show horse."

She looked about the table to change the subject, and the talk resumed. He leaned back from its flow. All the joy that Twyla Tharpe had given him was gone now, as if a second glance at some remarkable sight had revealed it to be an ordinary thing. Gone too was the feeling that he could— that he should—do something wonderful with his remaining life: something as beautiful and powerful as that moment, something deserving of all the time and effort preparing for it. The ballet, like so much of art, was just an illusion.

❧ ❧ ❧

The dinner ended with coffee and tea, port and liqueur, men and women together: then everyone walked upstairs to the drawing room. Williams waved Hilty ahead of him then stopped him on the landing. "So you testified yesterday," he said. "Becca Tumulty said you did well, a Roman Triumph."

"Along with that naysayer who says you're not a god."

Williams laughed. "Who was that?"

"Joshua Hastings of Minnesota."

"He's a strange one, isn't he. I wonder that he feels comfortable with his party. He's convinced that only his ideas are right, and he would rather lose a bill than compromise on it."

"That seems to be a common attitude."

Williams ignored this. "The thing that saves him is longevity: they love him in the Fifth District. I see him, someday, running for president on a third-party ticket."

"Like Ralph Nader without *Unsafe at Any Speed.*"

"Or Ross Perot without EDS. What was his nay-say?"

"That I don't have his gift for prophesy."

"Sounds about right. Worry not. You're well liked on the Hill, across the aisle and in both chambers. Perfectionists always are. When Robin told me you were coming tonight, I was happy to hear it. Yours will be an easy confirmation."

"Confirmation?" he asked, but by then they were in the drawing room, and Williams had moved beyond him. *Perfectionist?* he might also have asked. But that was an old charge, and not displeasing.

The pheromone floated through the drawing room that it was time to thank their host. Being required by their lifestyle to go to dinners, these people prized their time at home. Before moving to the door to say goodbye, Robin spoke to him sotto voce. "I have a snuggery. Top of the stairs on the left." Certainly she wanted to talk to him;

[34]

apparently she didn't want anyone else to know about it. Drawing no attention to himself, he climbed two floors, went inside the room on the left, and shut the door.

What was this *snuggery?* A private study, a library, a place to think? A secure meeting place for intimate talk—for seduction? Half the width of the narrow house, shaped in the golden mean, the room was filled by a dictionary stand, a polished secretary, a love seat with a pretty pattern, and an armchair of complementary fabric angled beside a gas fireplace.

Two of the walls held built-in bookshelves. Since she was making him wait he was permitted to browse, though it felt a bit like going through her medicine cabinet. There were many books of literary fiction, whose fine condition suggested that she collected them—behind glass she had what looked to be first editions of Melville. The nonfiction was mostly professional. He smiled to see a copy of *Knight's Modern Seamanship,* a reference she mustn't have needed for a dozen years. Then again it might be something she read for pleasure. She had been an excellent seaman; after the nine-month deployment she had brought her destroyer home with a one-bell landing unassisted by tugs. He would never forget that day. Going up the brow to shake her hand, exhilarated by her smart approach, and finding her in a maternity uniform gravid with child.

The social noises dwindled below, and she was climbing the stairs. But another door was opened and shut. It was a further ten minutes before she came in. Her hair was down, and over her evening dress, over those splendid shoulders, she had loosely buttoned a Navy blue cardigan sweater—a change she editorialized with a goofy smile.

"So much better," she said, going to the cold fireplace and rubbing her hands together as if to warm them. Turning back, that perfect face slightly worn by years of responsibility, she added, "If some researcher ever proves that Spanx shortens your life, I'm a goner."

"Not that you need any help to look beautiful, Robin."

[35]

He wouldn't have thought the smile could brighten, but it did. "Aren't you kind! And may I say that I've never seen *you* looking so well. Prosperity becomes you, Brad. But that jacket can't be comfortable. Give it to me." In the shallow closet beside the fireplace were half a dozen sweaters like hers. She hung up his jacket and pulled off one, held it up for sizing and nodded.

The sweater bore the logo of the Naval Academy.

"Ex scientia tridens," he said, reading upside-down. "Through knowledge seapower."

"God, how I wish that were true," she exclaimed. "But here." She pulled the armchair so close that their knees nearly touched. Her dress, of green silk, followed the toned muscles of her legs to say that older women were desirable too. How urgently he wanted to place his hand on her thigh. They were only a few steps from her bedroom. Was this the reason she had asked him to stay behind? Could it lead to that? He buried the thought in a dungeon of his mind, where it pounded the walls to escape.

"It's been a hell of a time," she continued. "Destroyers collide with merchant ships in clear visibility. Submarines run aground from obsolete charts. A capital ship, four billion dollars to replace, is destroyed in a shipyard fire—with all the resources available to save it. China has a hundred more ships than we do, but every time I go to the Hill to ask for increases, their first question is why can't we take care of the Navy we've got.

"Last month I visited the training command. The usual dog-and-pony show, the admiral bragging about how much he was doing on an inadequate budget. Then I visited a class in the engineering school. Their top student was borescoping a turbine. She had the steps exactly right; the manual was lying open on the deck but she hardly needed it. The admiral beamed his approval. I asked her, 'And what do you do with your tools afterwards?'—a cookie if ever there was one. Blank look. I all but fed her the line: 'This kit has the tool shapes cut out of the foam so you'll know you've put them all back, yes?'

Nothing. 'So you'll know,' I pleaded with her, 'that you haven't left a tool in the engine that would destroy it on startup. Isn't that right?' She said, 'Oh, the chief takes care of all that.' There was a fire watch on *Bonhomme Richard,* Brad. And still we lost the whole freaking ship. Sometimes I wonder if anyone cares."

"I used to wonder that all the time."

"You and I are alike in this, aren't we. The difference between us and, apparently, the whole bloomin' Navy is that we try to do something about it. All my wonderful sailors and their leaders just seem to shrug and leave it to the chief to clean up."

"Believe me, it's the same in the civilian world."

"I *don't* believe it. I don't. And that's why you're here, old friend. Remember when Excellence was a virtue? You've managed to get an entire culture to rediscover it. I need you to do that for our naval service. For our country. For me."

"I'm sorry, say again?"

With a slow ripple of that lovely throat, she swallowed. Then she smiled. "I'm a little nervous here. You've always intimidated me, Commodore." He shook his head. "Yes you have. I'm trying to offer you a job. Assistant Secretary of the Navy for Quality Assurance."

She waited. His skin prickled and his chest hollowed out. It was both the offer and the offeror. She knew—had known for years—that he was attracted to her by something more than admiration for her gifts. In that dungeon of his mind were fifteen years of fantasies. It was hard to maintain a professional detachment when knee-to-knee with her and the sweater as though carelessly buttoned, allowing a suggestion of her breasts heavy in silk as she leaned toward him from that supple waist and entered his personal space, putting her hand on his knee. Her finely poured flesh looked as soft as the silk. It could hardly be a mistake to return her caress. He must look up. But those eyes, so lovely, so ready to feel pleasure! He wanted to say yes as a displacement from that other desire.

[37]

And: Assistant Secretary Hilty: a nineteen-gun salute!

"Full disclosure," she said. "The job doesn't exist yet. Congress has to authorize it, but they will. I had to work my tail off to get approval on our side. You know who the CNO is, Ed Juventude, my old XO and your great admirer. He's been resisting—partly 'not invented here,' partly to protect the uniformed leadership from civilian interference. This week, however, when I mentioned that I was planning to offer it to you, he said at once, 'No worries, then: if Commodore Hilty's the pick, I'll support it.'"

So, was yesterday's hearing an audition? Is that why Slate had delegated it to him? Were he and Robin working that closely together? Had he been in this room with her? Had they done more here than plot his removal from Chance-Stevens-Arrowsmith, from Slate's cabinet? And why remove him anyway?

Her enraptured face held no answers.

"But there *are* worries," he said. "I'm not qualified."

"Of course you are. You've proved that."

"The cases are different. In my present job I can fire the disobedient—or cause them to be fired. Even with Ed's support, the admirals would just stonewall me. Don't forget, I wasn't good enough to be one of them." When she started to protest, he saw another opening. "And there's the election in November. Trump is way ahead of Biden—I assume that's not news to you. Even if I were willing to serve at this late date, and even if I were confirmed tomorrow, there wouldn't be enough time to make a difference."

Since she too was a Biden appointee, the reminder was less than tactful.

"I expect to stay in this office for at least another term," she said quietly. "Either way." Such a thing would be unprecedented, but Trump was all about breaking china (and China). When he was president before, she had been commander of the Pacific Fleet. The Taiwan success would have shown him how talented she was.

That was certainly a plus, but most of all she was good looking!

One hundred and sixty flag officers in the Navy, and in any matter involving quality, which basically meant everything the Navy was and did, he could put his hands on it. And he needn't wait to be asked.

"It would be a tough sell on the home front," he said with a long face while his heart danced with joy.

She looked sympathetic. "I understand. If I had more courage and fewer scruples, I'd have arranged this with Mad behind your back. My feminine intuition says that she'll go for it. Slate tells me she's enjoying Chicago—a soft landing after Taipei—but knowing her I think she would embrace the lifestyle, the position, the importance of what we do. But you'll have to convince her, certainly."

"And what about Slate? His fingerprints are all over this. Have you seen him?"

"Not really. Well, occasionally."

"About me?"

"About you and some other things. Mostly you. This matters, Brad. Not to play the guilt card, but without you the project fails, the ships keep colliding."

"I doubt that. Anyway, I'll need to think about it."

His guarded attitude was true; also useful.

She chose to hear him more affirmatively.

"Do. Do think about it. With an open mind. You can be a change agent here. We'll name a ship after you. Or at least a building." She laughed, that girlish laugh, so charming in the sophisticated woman.

Far below, a car whisked down the rainy street. They con-tinued to sit, vis-à-vis, like travelers on a train waiting for a stop that had been announced but before the train began to slow. After a long silence, she said, "I suppose the ques-tion for both of us comes down to trust. Can I trust that you will commit yourself to this heart and soul? Can you trust that I'm not proposing to rip you and Maddy from your home only to maroon you after the election? All right, I'll go first. I do trust you. Way back when, when I knew that you wanted to fire me and end my career, still I trusted that you were an honorable man who was trying to discharge an unpleasant duty. Shall I prove it? Would it help you in this decision to know the truth about me and Petty Officer Paquette, my supposed lover?"

In other words, to know fifteen years after the most difficult decision of his life whether he might have been right all along?

The rain fell. She crossed her legs and hugged herself.

"No, I don't think so," he said. "Not now. In the one case I don't see how you could trust me to be silent, and I'd worry about consequences. In the other I'd still wonder if you had told me the truth, and we'd both worry. We should make this decision on its merits."

Was she relieved? She was: she came out of her defensive crouch. "All right, let that remain in the past. Someday when it doesn't matter anymore I'll tell you the story. As far as this job is concerned, we'll have to take it on faith. No problem: I belong to the faithful. Let me know."

That was all. It was late. She would go to bed alone, and he would go to bed with a different kind of fantasy, something plausible and right. Nineteen guns. Had he made four stars way back when, it would only have been seventeen.

He took off the sweater and reached for his coat. With a smile she pulled from her pocket his expensive tie and, left-handed, knotted it around his neck. There would never be more between them than this. She would never want him in that other way. At the moment he didn't care. He was alive. The ichor of the gods was coursing through his veins.

Cincinnatus Returns to the Farm

The next morning he received a text from Slate:

Go to BWI. The conqueror returns in glory.

Surprised, suspicious, he replied:

What's your plane doing at BWI?

Test flight.

The pilot, Roddy Denton, an Australian, whose uniform consisted of a white T-shirt, a leather flight jacket, a Bears ballcap, and a pair of naturally distressed jeans, met him at the ladder. Coming to something like attention, he rendered the approximate salute made famous by General MacArthur.

"Awaiting your reinspection, sir."

Last week Hilty and a small team from Quality Assurance had inspected the plane, both the aircraft itself and its operations and maintenance. Denton had joked throughout the inspection; then, according to scuttlebutt, had raised holy hell with his people.

Hilty asked, "How did you come to be here?"

"Proficiency flight." Denton gave him a slippery grin and a wink. No doubt there had been a boondoggle. As long as the problem wasn't quality, however, Hilty's friendship with the CEO required him to look the other way. None of his goals could have been achieved if the employees didn't trust him.

"So you've corrected all the discrepancies?"

"Every last one. This aircraft is perfect in all respects."

"The seat belts?"

The grin broadened: a private joke. The chief of quality assurance was thought to be fixated about seat belts, a peculiar obsession for which no doubt the Germans had a term. On their flights together Slate enjoyed watching him check them. Before last week's inspection he had the aircrew install one of the belts with an end twisted. Hilty had gone off about the carelessness until he saw the faces of the crew. This was his friend's sense of humor, from which no one was exempt. As an admiral, when a pudgy aide had talked a little too often about the diet he was on, Slate had trimmed a quarter of an inch from the man's web belt each day. *My diet has stopped working!* wailed the aide. Slate had him pull the belt through the loops of his trousers and hold it up. By then it would hardly fit a child.

"Yes sir, Commodore. Every seat."

"What about the flight log?"

"No gaps."

"Very good. Better let me see it."

After the takeoff it appeared on his phone, and he checked it at once. Yes, the gaps in the narrative—the aircraft began deicing but never completed it; the number of takeoffs didn't match the number of landings—these had been corrected. As he had often seen in the deck logs of ships, recordkeepers couldn't be bothered to read what their predecessors had written. Haste, carelessness, lack of attention to detail: he well understood Robin McGill's complaint about the service.

But here was something else, to irritate his suspicions. Taking the easy path, Denton had included the entire log, going back to the plane's acquisition from Gulfstream. In the past two months Slate had traveled alone to Washington seven times. That in itself stood out, for he himself couldn't remember so many. He looked deeper. According to the CEO's official schedule, he had made only two trips to Washington, both of them to assist Bill McIntyre with high-level lobbying. A little deeper, Starbuck. In the flight log was another cluster of trips from three years before, shortly after Robin McGill had been sworn into office as secretary. Solo trips.

Guilty or not guilty? The two documents were prima facie evidence of an intent to deceive. On the other hand, a guilty man would have been more careful to keep the deception from his old friend. On the other, other hand

the defendant might have *wanted* the old friend to discover the folly and save him from it. Wasn't that, ladies
and gentlemen of the jury, what old friends did?

During the rest of the trip he binged on fantasies. A critic
might call his life a rolling fantasy in which real moments
obtruded. Robin was joking when she spoke of their naming a ship after him, but it wasn't out of the question for
him to become a gray eminence in successive administra-
tions, a partner at a national security thinktank, a talking head on public broadcasting. When he died, *The New
York Times* might publish his obituary, having passed
over James S. Greene for the honor (though *he* would die
a far richer man—unless a third divorce ruined him).

It was dusk when the car dropped him off; light glim-
mered in the trees behind the house. Pausing on the
driveway he shook his head. The sight of the house, his
childhood home, no longer comforted him—perhaps, like
Cincinnatus returning to his farm, it caused that pang of
sadness that followed achievement.

In fact he had never gotten over the changes made by
the people who had bought the house from his father. He
remembered it as beautiful, as meant to be—gracefully
proportioned, distinctively sited, surrounded by a soft
welcoming lawn. No other child had been so blessed. The
new owners clapped on ugly additions, poured a lot of as-
phalt, dug the swimming pool, added a bathhouse, and
grossly overplanted the property until it felt like a clearing in an impenetrable forest. Impenetrable and confining. Full of threats.

Well, he had tried it. You can't go home again. It would
do well on the market, at least, if they moved to Washington. He unlocked the door and carried his bag inside.

"Just a minute," called an unfamiliar voice, and a figure hurried down the stairs. A girl, a young woman.

"Why Sarah!"

"Wrong generation, Pop."

[43]

It was his granddaughter—Lisa, her name was. When he reached for her she hugged him with both arms, giving him her shoulders from a half-step away.

"It's great to see you," he said, not quite confident enough to try her name. Sarah was his own daughter, Lisa's mother. Sarah Hilty-Nichols, M.D. Married to Phil Nichols, also M.D. Mother to a younger girl as well, a sweet girl—but her name eluded him. "You're so tall." He remembered that she was seventeen. "Where *is* your mother? And Nana: what's going on? I didn't know you were coming—not that I'm not glad you're here. How long are you staying? What's going on?" He was babbling.

"I *don't know* what's going on. Nothing good. Sarah told me to wait for you. She's with Nana at the hospital. Nana has a fever, a high one. When she left here she was delirious." Impatiently she shook her head. Her mother was famously calm in emergencies.

"It's all right, Lisa. Just tell me what you do know."

"Today is—what day is it?—Sunday. We've been here since Wednesday."

"I must have just missed you then."

"Nana might have been sick when we arrived. I guess so—Tuesday night, after a phone call, Sarah and Phil decided that she would go and I would go with her. Stupid: at first I thought it was one of her medical conferences: sometimes she takes Megan or me—"

"Megan!"

"When we got here Nana seemed to have a cold. Happy to see us, but she slept a lot. Then at breakfast this morning she threw up into Sarah's lap, like a cat throws up, no warning and then *le déluge.* Sarah just nodded *Okay, don't worry* and cleaned up the mess and put her to bed. But this afternoon her fever went up and the ambulance came."

"It must be COVID."

"Pop, I don't know. I don't know how bad it is except that she was mumbling about needing to cover the plum trees before you got home. The only thing I've heard is a text from Sarah reminding me to wait here for you. Like what else would I do?"

"We should go there now, don't you think? Which hospital did they take her to?"

But this drew a blank, prompting more headshaking. One of Lisa's mantras growing up had been *I'm such an idiot!* For that matter it had been Sarah's growing up as well. And his. "They just got in the ambulance and drove off. This is how people die, isn't it. They drive away and don't come back!"

"Why don't you text your mother?" It would distract the youngster to work on a problem.

No surprise, Madeleine had been taken to Evanston, to what in his childhood had been known as Evanston Hospital, and where he himself had been born. The place, greatly enlarged, like his home, was now a "healthcare systems delivery center," merely one asset in a corporate portfolio. At this point in the pandemic, it might be hoped that the COVID caseload would be light but the treatment protocol still familiar.

In the darkened car he used speech as the distraction.

"Your mother must have taken you out of school, Lisa."

"That's right. I have to make up my final exams."

"How's the year been going?" He was tempted to ask her about colleges, but she was anxious enough. She had always been at the top of her class, and her board scores were nearly perfect. Still, she worried. Like her mother. Like her grandfather.

"Another mile or so, Lisa."

"Actually, Pop, I prefer to be called Blake."

"I'm sorry?" They looked at each other just as the headlights of an oncoming car filled the windshield: in the sudden exposure he noticed that her hair was buzzed on one side beneath a thick overhanging sidelock, the way lesbians wore it. She was dressed in patched denim coveralls and a short-sleeve shirt tight around her biceps. A butch style. In lesbian relationships butches probably acted the role of the male.

"Blake."

"That's right."

"Why Blake?"

"*Lisa* felt too girly-girl, and someone else picked it, not me. Blake is better."

"Because it clusters toward the middle of the spectrum?"

"The middle of the spectrum?"

"More ambiguous. Neither female nor male."

"I suppose so, Pop."

"Have you, then...come out?" He asked not only to know the answer but also to know the right terms for asking. Were they talking about sexual preference or about gender? Something she was born with or youthful experimentation?

She said, "To get you to understand would require an awkward discussion—or two or three. If you need a label you could say I'm questioning. But your wife is ill. This isn't the time to go into my problems."

"Very good. Blake it is—Blake you are. We'll talk later, then. Maybe it won't be as awkward as you think. I'd like to make a small claim for myself: I'm openminded."

"That would be helpful," she replied neutrally.

As he got out of the car, he struggled for a medical term. Surely Madeleine wasn't really sick. What was that nerve that traveled through the chest and was often overstimulated? The vagus nerve. One time Slate had fainted giving a talk: *vasovagal syncope,* it was called. After a night in the hospital he was perfectly well. Madeleine had probably eaten something spicy; the nerve didn't like it. She would be fine. Or it was the other thing that they knew how to treat.

Sarah met them at the entrance. His heart quickened—as always in her presence he felt responsible. She gave him one shoulder to hug, but he took the other too and held her away to look at her. This was she and no one so beautiful. When she leaned in to examine her patients' eyes, they must see kindness itself. She would be forty-five in September; now the years were having an effect. She was thinner, her face was drawn, and what used to be tracings around her mouth and across her forehead had deepened.

"How are you, Sarah?"

"I'm fine. How are you?"

"Good. Things are good. Are you sleeping?"

"Not as we stand here."

"And Phil is good?" catching the humor too late.

"Very good."

"And Megan? Megan has a cat. She loves the cat."

"Oh yes. Nutmeg. Inseparable."

"And Blake was telling me about school."

Again the babbling. What he meant was *I want your life to be perfect, always happy.* But he was trying too hard.

She gave him her professional smile. "Let's catch up later. We should go see Mom now, and while we walk I'll tell you about her."

In other words: *Now that my bedside manner has put you at ease, let me tell you how I will pierce your eye.*

She managed this during the short trip to the ICU. His wife was stable, out of the ER, lucid and free of pain. The fever was under control. There was no immediate danger.

"She just fainted," he offered. "The vagus nerve."

"Not that. She's ill."

"All right. Is she on a respirator?"

"It isn't COVID either."

"What is it, then? Do we know?"

She looked at him. "We do. Mom has AML."

"Good God! Lou Gehrig's disease?" His heart went hollow. She was going to die, then.

"No, that's ALS. AML is acute myeloid leukemia."

All he heard was *leukemia.* "But that's treatable, yes? Gene editing or something like that? A cure or—what do you call it?—it can be arrested, put into, yes, remission."

"I'm not conversant with the latest research. There are new treatment options. She has an aggressive subtype of the disease, however, and I'm, well, I'm worried about her."

Worried was the doctors' euphemism for terminal.

"How long?" he asked. "How much time?"

"We're here," Sarah said. "She's just inside. We'll see her now, doing our best to be cheerful"—she looked at Blake—"and talk more later. She has an appointment on Tuesday with the senior staff oncologist, highly regarded. We'll know more then."

Madeleine's room in the ICU was small but private, with a curtain that could be drawn around the bed, presumably if the crash team was needed. The face on the pillow, partly elevated, looked small, and her body made hardly a lump under the sheet. She had come here from a full-sized house. After this her quarters might be on a gurney in the morgue, a wooden casket, an urn. Here was a vision of the end of life: successively smaller confinement, a person being reduced to a memory.

Her eyes followed them to the bed. He reached through the rails to take her hand.

"Welcome home," she rasped, speaking around the intubation tube, which turned all speech into sarcasm. "How was your trip?"

Just this effort caused her to look at the ceiling and catch her breath. After a moment she said to Blake, "Sorry I threw up on you."

"No, Nana, that was Sarah."

"Right. Sorry I threw up on you," she said to Sarah.

"I've had worse. You don't need to talk."

"How are you feeling?" he asked, something he had started to say before Sarah discouraged talking.

"Not so good. It hurts." The shadows in the different planes of her face looked like bruises. Her forehead and cheeks were flushed. Her eyes were restless, searching from one visitor to another as someone in pain keeps shifting positions to find relief. "They can't give me anything stronger after the drugs the ER gave me. They told me I can have more in two hours. I try not to watch the time on the monitor, but I can't help it."

All of them looked at the monitor, where the trace seemed to be keeping secrets about her future while the numbers spun the public version.

"Anything you need," he declared, which sounded false enough to kill her on the spot. He had no idea how to give her what she needed, from more comfortably elevating her head to purging her blood of cancer. Over his shoulder Blake began to cry. Far below, louder than the beep of the patient's pulse, the siren of an arriving ambulance spooled down into a silence imitative of death.

As they were leaving, Slate and Julia Greene came in, like the fog on silent cat feet but unlike the fog with his booming presence. Julia was carrying a bouquet of white and yellow jonquils from their garden in Kenilworth, while Slate produced a box of expensive chocolates and a pinch bottle of Scotch from the distillery near their home on the Isle of Arran. Several years before, during a visit there, Madeleine had gone into ecstasies over this Scotch, and from then on he always had some to offer her.

"Beautiful flowers, thank you," she rasped. "But they'll never...." Meaning the nurses and the rules.

Julia and Slate smiled at each other co-conspiratorially. Certainly they seemed easy together. But seven trips to Washington in two months?

Slate said, "They tell me you'll be in this lovely place tonight, but you're getting well so fast they'll move you to a regular ward tomorrow. All your belongings will be transferred in this bag"—he held up a Company flight bag. "I happen to have spoken to the head nurse on your new ward."

"But that would be a different shift," he said, needing to correct an error when so much was at stake (and, his friend would say, at all other times).

"It is," Slate said, returning his superior look. "The head nurse of the morning shift is Ms. Beverly Ward. I reached her ten minutes ago at her home in Skokie. Charming lady and pragmatic. Chocolates and whiskey, consumed in moderation, will have absolutely no harmful effects on your recovery—quite the contrary." He put both treats back in the bag and set it on a chair. To Sarah he added, "Your oath binds you to secrecy, doctor."

"But it won't keep my hands out of that bag."

"With our compliments. How is she? How are you?" he asked Madeleine.

For one thing, her pulse was ten beats a minute faster than before. Slate always had this effect on her, usually manifested in irritation and disapproval. Like her husband, she had seen him through two previous wives and numerous affairs; moreover she was devoted to Julia.

"There's some pain," she said, although she never liked to complain to him. She closed her eyes and turned her head away.

"I think that's our cue to leave," said Julia.

"We should all go," said Sarah.

In the passageway Sarah thanked them for coming. Her tone combined a proper deference to her parents' friends with her long-accustomed authority as a doctor. Slate hugged the two Nichols women and shook his friend's hand, giving him a raised eyebrow. Hilty stared back. No intelligence was exchanged between them.

Two

Songs of Death and Life

The Quality Assurance Department

At home, they sat until midnight, intermittently filling in minor items of personal news, but their main subjects, naturally enough, were Madeleine's diagnosis and whether and how and with what degree of alarm they should tell other family members.

The Hiltys' son, Adam, a sculptor, was in Taipei, installing a complicated project in the 228 Memorial Peace Park. (This no doubt had been awarded on merit, though Hilty suspected that his old friends in Taiwan may have influenced the judging.) Of course they must tell him. Because he might want to come home, which would be too soon, they would all be on the call for added moral weight. It was afternoon in Taipei, one day in the future. Using the speaker phone formalized everyone's participation. Adam was persuaded that his mother wanted him to keep working on his project, and and all of them assured him that they would report any developments.

Four hours later Hilty was at his desk in the library preparing for the workday. In the war against entropy he allowed no malingerers: his inbox was empty except for those tasks that required, as Churchill had, *Action This Day*. Whatever he couldn't answer at once he sent to his deputy, Dorothea Billups. When they had first begun to work together, overwhelmed by so many changes, she had tried to have a subordinate screen the messages, but back then no one in the office seemed to know his mind. Now that she understood him, she did the screening herself, almost by reflex, but when in doubt she still referred them to him, and like a good captain he never reprimanded her for calling him to the bridge.

"Are you going in?" Sarah asked at breakfast. Though open-ended, this might have implied an accusation.

[53]

"Just for the morning, after being out last week. You?"

"I have video conferences basically all day."

So, not an accusation. "Knowing your mom," he replied, "she'll have all the staff by her bed today."

"Especially since she's offering refreshments."

"Do you really think he called that nurse at home?"

She shrugged.

"Are chocolate and whiskey safe for her to have?"

"I wouldn't give them to her. But we'll know more tomorrow. Her oncologist is Dr. Kohl."

"I'll see her this afternoon. You and Blake can join me."

Blake. By the flattening of her lips Sarah wasn't happy with the name either. Of course the "someone else" who had named her Lisa, in that special joy of welcoming a child, were her parents.

"I'll see you then, then," she answered and shook her head at the solecism. As a child she might brood about an innocent mistake like that for the rest of the day.

He parked in his usual spot at the tower, relieved that there was no squatter to report, and took the express to the thirty-third floor, three from the top. When he had started there, the Quality Council had been hidden in the bowels of the building. He hadn't wanted to assert himself so soon—on the principle not to change sails in the first quarter of the watch—but Slate, sailor though he was, had thought differently: "Make 'em know that we're actually going to *assure* quality." Hence his revolutionary changes in the office. So that now, in place of a faceless council, he led a department with actual authority, which occupied an entire floor as close to the CEO as Company politics would allow.

In fact, his mission and the tower had a history together. From its founding in a hangar by Glenn Chance, an aviation pioneer, Chance-Stevens-Arrowsmith had had its headquarters in Dayton, Ohio; its center of gravity through the decades of spectacular growth, from World War II bombers to transcontinental commercial aircraft to missiles and munitions and spacecraft and ships. In earlier years CSA was known for two important things: a peerless quality of workmanship and, thanks to powerful unions, a high cost of labor. For the workers it was possible to make a nice living—to own a house and send their kids to college—on nothing more than a high school education; and besides the nice living they felt immense pride in the work they did.

During the Reagan era, however, with its greatly increased defense budgets, CSA's growth had both fueled and been served by a mania for profitability, as a result of which, with a speed that felt like a collapse, quality had been hollowed out and organized labor had become not a partner but a threat.

A succession of improvident CEOs, looking no further than the next quarter's returns, failed to reverse the trend. Labor was cut, muscle as well as fat. Every task on the production line was analyzed, quantified, automated if possible, and above all expedited. No one with any authority seemed to understand that serving your employees is essential to inspiring their work.

One ambitious CEO decided that if he moved the headquarters out of Dayton, the unions would learn their lesson. He did. They did. Land was purchased on the west bank of the Chicago River; union workers at the emblematic home lost their jobs, but many new workers, especially in the South, voted to organize; and from the first groundbreaking of the tower no labor contract was signed without a painful strike first. As CSA's products became more sophisticated and therefore more difficult to make, the poor quality practices burst into view. Airplanes crashed, sales declined, lawsuits proliferated.

Then Slate Greene was appointed, with his inherent toughness and authority, and the turnaround began.

ᗷ ᗷ ᗷ

Depending on their mood, Hilty sometimes contrived a theatrical appearance in the doorway of his deputy; the joking reprisal of a moment early in their relationship when, being late for a meeting with her, who was displeased with him anyway, on arrival he shouted *Don't pay the ransom, Mother: I escaped.*

Certainly the beginning of their relationship wasn't as easy as now. Her resistance to his reforms had been difficult to overcome, to the point that Slate had told him to get rid of her, offering to do the deed himself. As part of their *modus vivendi* since then, Dorothea and he sometimes acted as if she were indeed the mother, prudent but straightlaced, of a gifted but impulsive teenager.

"Welcome back," she replied. "How did it go?"

He dropped into the chair by her desk and stretched his legs out. "Pretty well, I think. There were two characters on the committee—one was the chair. In general lots of kind words. The powers that be said it went well. What's happening here?"

"Very quiet for a Monday. I don't know if you've looked at your mail since zero dark thirty this morning"—she paused, he shook his head—"but I have some answers for you."

"Yes, good, but I need to tell you something first."

"Oh?" She was watching him.

He stuck to the bare facts: Madeleine's dangerous fever, the frightening diagnosis, her wasted appearance, Sarah's opinion. What he didn't say was how guilty he felt to have been away, receiving plaudits, loving the ballet, being offered the job of a lifetime, while his wife had suffered. Nor that he had missed the signs of her illness to begin with.

Of the thoughts he omitted, most important to Dorothea, of course, would be the job offer.

"That's hard, Brad. I'm sorry. Both of you—all of you—have a hard time ahead. When my father was sick I thought knowing would be a relief, but it wasn't." Her father had died of lung cancer after a long decline; a few months later her mother had died of COVID, probably picked up in her husband's cancer ward.

"I appreciate it, thank you, Dorothea. If I may take advantage of our friendship to ask...well, it seems that maybe you had already heard."

She nodded. "Slate called me last night. He said to be extra nice to you today. I've told our senior people. By now probably everyone in the tower knows, the way news like that spreads. You'll get tired of the commiserations."

"Any chance Slate also called to put you on alert?"

"He did, but he didn't have to. You really need to take a leave of absence. As much as you put into your work, it wouldn't be fair to Maddy. Come back when she's well. The department will be fine. It's not like I haven't done this before."

She looked off, toward the place where she kept festering memories. Three times in the past, after a disaster or scandal, CSA went through a purge: the CEO, the chief of the department concerned, one or two victims of intramural malice, and the quality guy. Each time Dorothea had stepped up to be the acting chief and had done a creditable job; had even instituted her own program of reforms, no doubt on the assumption that she would be confirmed in the position. She never was. The new CEO always brought in an outsider, including Slate with him. Uncomplaining, she reverted. Perhaps her complaisant manner did her a disservice, suggesting that she was better suited to the role of a subordinate.

That was Dorothea, the quintessential team player. But so was the quietly stubborn and skilled infighter, expert in her subject and keeper of the corporate memory, who had resisted him at every turn. It was only after a real fight, throwing their gloves down on the ice with the fans looking on, that she and Hilty acknowledged to each other that they hated being consumed by their differences. Of course, she must yield then, loyally supporting his changes, however much she disagreed with them.

[57]

By temperament and experience the differences were hard baked. She was analytics, he was culture. In the past six years it had ever seemed ironic to him that he of all people, who took comfort in numbers, who loved nothing more than an integer, should advocate for the emotions. But CSA had become so data-driven that its leaders couldn't understand why numbers alone, together with an arbitrary coerciveness, must only make the problem worse. In their first conflicts he had tried to show Dorothea that this was exactly why the country had lost Vietnam. Unfortunately, Saigon had fallen the same year she was born, and she knew nothing about the war.

Still, she had given in more or less gracefully. Any further dissent she kept between them. Although she continued to work at strengthening and clarifying quality standards, she went to uncharacteristic lengths to explain them. She referred to the earlier time, whose disciple she had been, as "the days of your predecessors." If an initiative failed, she never recriminated.

For his part he allowed her to tease him for "his famous imagination" and "his bleeding heart." He looked past the obvious, that with all her gifts she lacked a measure of sympathy. Besides sparing her from the axe, he had done a great deal to befriend her. Madeleine and he had made pets of her nieces and nephews. He had helped her girlfriend advance in business. With some self-study he had opened his mind to at least the first three letters of the *LGBTQIA+* alphabet. It would not be wrong to say now, after so many years, that he and Dorothea esteemed each other and never agreed on anything. He trusted that she would do her best to further his ideas in his absence no matter how illogical she found them.

But that was the question: should there be an absence? And if so, should it be for the duration of his wife's illness or, Congress willing and the creek don't rise, forever?

Hippocrates Himself

Dr. Kohl glanced at some papers on his desk then leaned across to address the patient.

"So tell me how you're feeling."

As Madeleine described her symptoms, he wrote carefully on a legal pad that had a wad of pages folded under the top, presumably notes from earlier appointments. His notetaking was too slow to keep up with the answers; once or twice he asked the patient to repeat herself. In fact, he seemed awfully old to be working, let alone in medicine, least of all on the cutting edge of a rapidly changing specialty. He must have been in his seventies. His face was freckled with age spots. A tuft of white hair, growing upward from his crown, crested over a balding pate. His eyes, behind thick glasses, seemed immobile: to look at anything not in front of him, he turned his head. He was thin and wiry—the very frame to last a long time—but his hand trembled as he wrote, and he had to hold the legal pad steady. It wasn't the fashion for senior doctors to wear white coats, but Kohl did, a starched white coat over a light blue shirt with a blue and black polka-dotted bow tie. Besides the legal pad, however, he used a computer and seemed confident at it.

When Madeleine had finished, he nodded as if all the data, in his notes, on the computer, in his brain, formed a whole.

Then he said: "I don't know. This subtype of the disease is often a puzzle. The best practice is still chemotherapy. The dose is strong and will be a trial for you. I'd say we're looking at ten weeks of two sessions per week. You'll be more comfortable if we install a port in your chest, with a catheter to the jugular vein. Just below your collarbone, from here..." He pointed to his own bony collarbone then up to his wrinkled neck. "...to here. After a while you won't notice it. Every week we'll take your markers and adjust as needed."

Madeleine asked, "How bad?"

"You'll feel sicker than the disease would make you at this point. You'll spend a great deal of time resting. Your family will need to help you even with basic tasks that you've always done yourself, washing and toileting." He waved a freckled hand.

"What about my hair?"

"It will grow back, probably not as thick, possibly in a different color—I'm not quite sure what your real color is now." He ruined his attempt at humor with a ghoulish grin. "Your friends will compliment you on your wig."

"I can't wait."

"That's all to be said for now. We'll just have to see. You must realize that this is a pernicious disease. We will be hopeful but realistic. What else can I answer? Anyone?" He turned his head to either side of the patient. However crowded his schedule, he would make time for *this* visit until all concerned were satisfied.

"I have a question," Hilty said. In fact he had a technique for questioning experts like Kohl, working from the general to the specific, something he had learned in the Navy and that reliably discovered where, like a lode of ore, the expert's knowledge ran out.

"Please."

"I assume the chemo is maximally aggressive."

He hated the word *chemo*—the banality of it, the ignorance it represented. By now modern medicine should be way beyond the use of poisons. Chemo walked a wavy line between remission and legal murder. The wife of their vice chairman had tipped into a death spiral after an increase in the toxicity of her treatment.

"If the dose isn't efficacious," he said, "and since she can't tolerate a more aggressive regime, what's the prognosis then?"

"Medical school, eh?" Kohl's eyes gleamed.

"Near-term prognosis. This summer."

"Well sir, I never like to predict. The outcome varies. But if you press me for specifics, and in our own lexicon, I would say that the worst case—I emphasize this is the worst case—would be progressive asthenia to the point of sarcopenia and incapacity. Neuralgia unrelieved by analgesics. Inanition, anorexia. Spontaneous hemorrhage, swelling, and contusion of the dermis. Renal failure, progressive aphasia, dementia, syncope, and death."

There! the eyes said. *If you think you're so smart.*

Madeleine began to cry, which she tried to stifle only to suffer a coughing fit. He reached for her but she turned away.

Kohl left the desk and stood beside her, putting his freckled hands on her shoulders. A short man: on his feet he was hardly taller than his sitting patient.

"I wish I could be more encouraging," he said in a soft voice. "The truth is I just don't know. If you think it's too much I could refer you to hospice and palliative care. That's a rational choice. But I do think this course of treatment is worth the pain and suffering it will cause you. It's not out of the question that we may see even a dramatic improvement, even the remission your loving husband has asked about. There are other drugs to mitigate the worst symptoms of the medication. Healthful foods have been shown to support improved outcomes, so I will recommend that you consult one of our dieticians. Another reason to hope: your own attitude will make a difference in how you tolerate the treatment and may even play a role in your recovery."

"Thank you, doctor," Madeleine said. "At least I know."

But she knew it conceptually still, not as a reality. Nor did she know how helpful he himself would be. It was a false promise when spouses said *We'll see this through together.* Nonsense! Only the dying person would see it through. But he would care for her—would bring ease and comfort and joy into whatever remained of her life.

He would be a strength to her. Her last days, if these were her last, would be the closest of their marriage.

Sarah had been silent until now. "What about menin inhibitors?" she asked.

Kohl reacted as if a bug had brushed his cheek. He shook his head to rid himself of it then rubbed the spot where he might have been bitten. Returning to his desk, he replied, "Unfortunately, not indicated for this subtype of AML," he replied. "Not approved by the CDC and not authorized by the FDA."

"But."

Sarah must know that there was a way.

"It would cost your family a small fortune, with uncertain results. In any event I cannot support it."

"Why not?" he asked, though he had no idea what they were talking about.

If he were feeling defensive, Kohl remained dignified. Having called him a loving husband, he wouldn't take him to task again for his presumption to speak like a doctor. "I cannot reconcile it with good practice to prescribe an unauthorized and experimental treatment with such uncertain promise. Patients do ask for this kind of thing. A miracle cure for cancer! As if all cancers were the same or, in this case, as if all AML is the same. I'm afraid it would only raise false hope. I'm sorry, but I have to go by the data."

When this didn't seem to convince, he added, "Where is your practice, doctor?"

"Mass General in Boston," Sarah replied.

"You have an advanced cancer center. Not long ago I heard a paper by your director—I don't remember, a Slavic name."

"Hillary Mentov. She's a friend."

"You might talk to her, then. She might have a different opinion. Perhaps she could request a waiver from the Feds. In that case she would certainly want to examine your mother and supervise her treatment. I'm afraid I'm not persuaded of the efficacy"—he smiled at Hilty—"to try it myself."

"Tell me about this inhibitor," he said. They were sitting on a bench at the entrance to the medical center while a valet brought up their car. The people waiting in front of them, dealing with their own problems, formed a kind of privacy curtain, and the heavy summer air seemed to encourage sharing, a cultural trope except in his family.

"A menin inhibitor. The drug is called Revumenib. I don't know much about it. Menin is a protein that causes certain genes to be activated that, if corrupt, cause AML, including Mom's subtype. The idea is to turn off the genes and prevent the infection from spreading. In theory her immune system could then clean it up."

"In other words she'd be cured."

"*In theory.* Small-scale tests have been positive. Really positive. But its efficacy on a larger scale is unknown, as are the potential side effects. That's why it hasn't been approved yet."

"But approval could be expedited, yes? He mentioned that. Look what they did with the COVID vaccine."

"I think the FDA has already fast-tracked it, but I don't know, and I didn't want to challenge Dr. Kohl. I'll see what Hillary says when I get back to Boston."

Madeleine asked, "Should I go ahead with the chemo?"

"You should. I'm sorry. These things take time. Maybe the whole summer. I'll have to convince Hillary to convince someone at the CDC to convince someone at the FDA to designate you for the fast track. In the last resort we could look to foreign sources, although that would mean traveling there or we'd be breaking U.S. law. And more expense."

"I don't care about the expense," he declared.

At this Sarah smiled affectionately, which provided some compensation for the awful visit. She did love him.

"Meanwhile, Mom, you shouldn't wait. The chemo will be rough, and all the rest of it, but it might prevent another attack like Sunday's."

"Can you stay?" he asked. "Just for the start?"

"I have to get back. Multiple wildfires." She shook her head. "You don't want to know. I'm flying out this afternoon. I'll speak to Hillary tomorrow."

"But Blake is going to stay," said his wife.

Brood XIII

When he returned from the airport, Madeleine was sitting in the den, in his larger chair, holding a tumbler of Slate's fabulous Scotch. He sat in the wifely chair and smiled at her; the smile meant to ridicule the foolishness of conventions. After the consultation with Kohl he was an enemy of conventions.

"Any problems?" she asked.

"She cut it close but thought she'd make it."

"Sometimes all of life is last-minute."

"I asked her about Blake. I don't know if you saw it, but they seemed tense."

"Mm-hmm."

"She told me it was little things and big things. Things they could fix and others that only time could fix. It's Blake's age. It's her temperament—a dig at her own temperament and mine. According to Blake, it's Sarah's parenting style but not Phil's, who lets her do whatever she wants. She did say how glad she is that Blake will be here for the summer. As I pulled up to the curb, she said that maybe Blake will show me what life looks like through the eyes of a seventeen-year-old who is questioning."

"That sounds like a full report."

"Except for the redacted part."

"Sarah has a lot on her plate."

Surprised, he glanced at her. This was more empathy than most people would show who had received her news today. "How are you feeling?" he asked.

"I've been better."

She let him take her hand, which lay on her thigh, small and unresisting. When they had had their romance, out of which Sarah had sprung, her small hands and feet had delighted him. He himself with his long fingers could palm a basketball. Early on they laughed as they put their hands together to compare them. The

[65]

backs of hers were plump over the knuckles: it always felt good to stroke them, but he learned not to overdo it, for as some cats will, when she reached her limit she would scratch.

"How long have you known?" he asked at breath level.

"I knew something was wrong. When I walked into that restaurant table in Bucharest, the bruise never healed."

"That was back in January."

"It was. It happened again when my foot slipped off the bike pedal."

"A month ago." They had been riding along the lake, and she had fallen.

She drew up her pant leg to show him. Her calf looked like the inside of an overripe banana. "That's when my primary ordered blood tests."

"I wish you had told me."

But this found her limit. "So what?"

"You wouldn't have been alone with it."

"But I am alone, if we're being honest." She drank again.

"That will change."

She snorted.

The lesson from Robin: to invite sharing, share.

"Actually, I have a secret too." He described his weekend.

"Did you accept?" She withdrew her hand.

"The job doesn't exist yet."

"And someone else will fill it when Trump wins. She'll be out office too, praise the Lord." She had never liked Robin since the affair of Robin's pregnancy. Then too, she had always suspected her husband's feelings toward her.

"It doesn't matter now," he said.

"It does if the stars align—for you."

"I'm going to take myself out of the running."

"I can get through this alone, Bradford."

"But you don't have to."

"Oh, you're coming with me, are you?"

"You said a moment ago that we've always been honest with each other."

[66]

"Sometimes we've been honest with each other."
"Do you really want to go through this alone?"
"Yes." But two long pulls of Scotch later: "No."

The next day they implanted the port and on Thursday, while it was still healing, started the chemo. From then on time was measured by the semi-weekly visits to the oncology service and the recovery afterwards, and the reality of the summer was evident in the early decline of the patient's condition. As Kohl had predicted, the chemo, not yet the cancer, made her sick while the cancer marshaled its forces. On Sundays, her one good day of the week, she had enough energy for visitors. The other days she moved from one resting place to another, getting no rest, and called for Hilty or Blake to help with her basic needs. This she received in silence, doing her part automatically, thinking about something else or about nothing at all.

One early challenge was to find, in this overbuilt house, a room to serve as a sick room. They talked about a stair lift, easily enough installed, but she would soon be too weak to use it. The first three nights he carried her up to her room honeymoon style, but on the fourth night his back was sore, so he carried her as a fireman would, and the indignity of this caused her to cry as she never did on the toilet.

First thing the next morning, Slate and Julia arrived with a team of contractors, who put a hospital bed in a corner of the great room, enclosing it with tasteful dividers, and made over the kitchen bathroom with grab bars, a taller toilet, and a shower stall with a seat. The rain from the eight-inch shower head felt like the tropics—all of them wanted to try it. Shortly afterwards a dietician arrived with Yannick, the Greenes' chef, and bags and bags of food.

"How...?" he asked. Slate tilted his head at Julia, who tilted hers at Blake, who looked modestly pleased with herself. As he learned later, she had identified the need, asked the Greenes for the resources, and drawn up the plans. How many seventeen-year-olds had such aplomb? Certainly she was a capable, responsible girl, whatever her mother thought.

Slate said, "Let's show our superior leadership and get the hell out of the way."

"Good thinking."

They walked out to the pool. Slate, who looked like a catalogue model in his plaid shorts, with beads of shower rain in his hair, took off his sandals and dangled his feet in the water. Hilty, in long pants and repelled by the floating cicada necropolis, sat at right angles to him.

"Maddy looks like hell. She looked better in the ICU."

"Well," he said, "the news."

"What is the news?"

"Not good. She's going to have a rough bout of chemo and still her chances aren't good."

"What about Revumenib?"

"Promising but caught up in the Federal bureaucracy."

"Makes you almost want to vote for Trump," Slate said.

"That would kill her, forget the cancer."

"We have people who know how to cut red tape."

In their bubble, time had come to a stop. All around them the cicadas were singing their paean to reproduction. Their parents and older siblings had already died for love, unburied as they fell.

"I'll have our gardeners come by and cover your pear trees," Slate said, "and sweep up a bit."

"I'm grateful. And for everything. For today."

"So you had a good trip?" Slate glanced at him.

"I did. Lots of praise for CSA. Did I tell you I saw Robin? She invited me to dinner on Saturday, along with some muckety-mucks, as your wife likes to call them. Then we had a longish talk."

"Oh? What's *her* news?"

"Why do I think you already know it?"

Slate laughed and kicked the water, sending a ripple under the carpet of dead cicadas. "Tell me anyway."

"She wants me to be Assistant Secretary of the Navy for Quality Assurance. A new position."

He nodded, either because he did know or because the idea appealed to him. Even retired sailors cared about the service.

"You'd be perfect for it. The Navy would never be the same. Actually, I'd sleep better at night."

"However the election goes. Biden, of course—she might be promoted. And Trump seemed to like her when she had the Pacific Fleet. She sounded confident, anyway."

"Always. But for now you can only think about Maddy."

"That's right."

"Though you are loyal—and capable enough—to believe you can take care of her and keep working for me."

"I don't know. While Blake is here—"

"You do know. We both of us know. If the worst happens, you'll need to feel that you did your best. I'm going to take the decision out of your hands, Brad. I'm putting you on a paid leave of absence. Dorothea will stand in for you—God knows she's qualified. When the time is right you'll rejoin us…unless you become a muckety-muck for Robin."

"Have you seen Robin?"—as if he had just thought of it.

"Once or twice. We pitched her, you'll remember, on the corvette deal."

"Yes, that's right, isn't it"—hoping that his even tone of voice might be interpreted as exposing a falsehood.

"There's something deliciously disgusting," Slate said, "about these animals. It's like watching bug pornography. You know, I could get you a supply of that medicine."

"Slate Greene the drug dealer. Thank you, but that's not really my ethos, is it."

"With you there's not much difference between ethos and self-love. We could fly you guys to Sweden. You could check in tomorrow morning, in fact. She could start getting well tomorrow afternoon."

"She's not ready to abandon the doc with the bow tie."

"Kohl. I've checked on him. We'll have to bring her around. Don't make me kidnap her, Brad. This is one of those cases when the latest inventions really do mean progress. When money and influence are a good thing. If anyone in the world deserves to recover from this, it's your wife."

Money and influence and privilege and power.

"Let's wait and see," he said. "It's still early. Sarah is working the problem from her end. She has a friend at the hospital who's apparently a national authority on cancers."

"Sarah might pull it off, but I'd be surprised if she did, meaning no disrespect. What's between her and Blake anyway?"

Ellifiknow," he replied, an old sailors' joke: What do you get when you cross an elephant with a rhinoceros?

He could have done both jobs. In any event he now felt unemployed. With all the resources and conveniences of modern life, caring for his wife was not like working for CSA—or serving in the Navy, either: night and day watching over a candleflame cupped in his hands against an uncertain breeze. He was idle more than he wished; out of loyalty to the suffering patient he did little but wait for her calls.

Unfortunately, these became more frequent and plaintive. The chemo was doing all the harm expected but none of the good hoped for. Her markers, her stem cells, were out of control, and now in addition to the side effects of the treatment she was as fragile as a royal child begotten by too much inbreeding. Her hair, once so glorious, came out by the brushful. She had trouble paying attention, and anything more abstract than her present needs, whatever required planning, was too much for her. Her weight declined toward one hundred. When in bed she lay flat on her back and stared at the ceiling. He wanted to gather her in his arms and crush her into health. Each day had become a nightmare, the kind where the body seems to be suspended in viscous dreamwater and the horror is seen in silence.

Slate kept after him about the Revumenib. Trying to be stronger and wiser than he, he resisted, but after Madeleine's worst days he usually called Sarah for a progress report. She wasn't getting anywhere. Her friend Hillary Mentov had taken her on a deep dive into the cellular biology of APL, the dangerous subtype of AML. Sarah could barely follow her. The takeaway was that Kohl wasn't being old-fashioned: the research was truly sketchy, so that prescribing a menin inhibitor here might be a fatal act. *First do no harm* was still the dictum. Then again Mentov admitted that she was wary of interfering in another doctor's case. Then again, for reasons unexplained, Sarah's own position in the hospital made her reluctant to assert herself, even for her mother.

May became June. Madeleine continued to weaken, alternately querulous and silent, lost in her thoughts. Her response to any new thing was apathetic. The three of them sat through Biden's disastrous debate with Trump. Blake threw her hands in the air. Madeleine, with no energy for gestures, said, barely moving her lips, "Why should I care?"

The cicadas made the summer worse, if that was possible. They looked like small red-eyed aliens come to take over the Earth. There were so many of them the children must have been born pregnant, like babies in the tabloids. Their song was unrelenting: *Sex, sex, death, death.* It struck randomly from the background of consciousness as tinnitus does, and when present it made him think of murder-suicide, like that Thurber short story.

A Presidential Nomination

Among other complaints, Madeleine had tired of her diet, about which they no longer heard from the dietician or from Julia or Yannick the Chef either. Since in theory the healthy foods might assist her recovery, he made excuses. For the first time she complained about *him.* Escalation might bring worse, perhaps a running account of all the ills of their marriage, which would be difficult for either of them to get over, so he drove to Hubbard Woods to pick up a family treat: Vienna Beef hotdogs and coffee milkshakes from the Telltale Diner.

The July sun was beating down on the car, and the car was an oven when he returned with his purchases.

The phone rang. It was from Robin McGill.

He turned the engine off and opened the windows.

"Is now a good time?" she asked.

"Of course. It's always good to hear your voice."

"How is Mad?"

"No change, unfortunately."

"I'm sorry to hear it. Would you do better with another doctor—even in another country?"

He lifted the hotdogs onto the dashboard to keep them warm and put the sweating milkshakes into the shade of the passenger footwell. During these awkward exertions he managed to reply, "Yes, Slate suggested that. There's a new drug out there, not approved for Madeleine's condition, however. At this point we're relying on Dr. Kohl."

"Please give her my fondest hopes. Would flowers be appropriate?"

"Very kind. I think she'd be touched." Probably she'd throw them in the trash.

"I don't suppose you can guess why I'm calling," Robin said. Since these were essentially the same words spoken by the king to Winston Churchill when asking him to form a government, he had his answer ready.

[73]

"Ma'am, I simply couldn't imagine why."

"I have owed you a call for weeks."

"I was sure you hadn't forgotten me."

"This whole place has been in a tizzy. We're not supposed to care about politics—"

"The Hatch Act!"

"Yes, and what is more powerful, custom. Anyway, between world events and the campaign, I've been alternately giving hugs and waging war. Have you ever tried to secure a floating dock in an open roadstead?"

"Not since I built the mulberries at Normandy."

"Oh, that was you?"

"The one that survived. The one that washed away was built by the Brits."

She laughed. "You know it's a crime to lie to a Federal official."

"I always tell truth to power—sometimes anyway." *Sometimes we've been honest with each other,* his wife had said.

"I'll take it and rely on you to know when. Congress has finally acted. The ASN job is authorized, and the president would like to make a nomination at once." She paused. "On my strong recommendation he would like to nominate you, dear friend."

"Holy shit."

"I know: holy shit!"

"But the timing."

"Yes. However, I think we might just finesse that. Realistically, no routine business will be done until after the election. I don't like that word: it's not routine to you and certainly not to me, but there it is. Our idea is to nominate you ASAP in a White House ceremony, get the benefit of the favorable press that that will receive, and dig in for confirmation in late November."

"No matter who's elected."

"I know I said that. The situation now, after the debate, is anyone's guess. If the president drops out I can't promise anything. Still, my feminine intuition likes our chances. You're not in a position to decide right now anyway. We all hope, following Mad's full recovery, that you'll be free to go through the confirmation process and actually take office in November or December."

"Leaving that hope out there," he said, "I do have a job already."

"You do. I've spoken to Slate about it. Actually, since we're always sometimes going to tell each other the truth, I should add that I raised the subject with him last spring—nothing definite, mostly did he think you might enjoy a new challenge."

"Hence his decision to have me testify."

"Well—yes."

"Followed by your invitation to dinner and talk."

"That's right."

The bag containing the milkshakes was soaking wet. The temperature in the car must be a hundred and twenty.

"I did enjoy our talk," he conceded.

"As did I. I was sure of you before then, but doubly sure after we met. I really think it's a great fit—for you, for me, for the country."

"Even if you're not in office."

"That's the rub. No one knows."

"What do you think Biden will do?"

"Truly no one knows. The debate was so unfortunate, he's done such a good job. I'm guessing he'll bail. It shouldn't matter to us. Your appointment as assistant secretary is the right thing no matter who the president is. Will you come out here and be nominated?"

"When?"

"Next week. Travel on Monday, brief on Tuesday, ceremony in the Rose Garden on Wednesday."

"Which happens to coincide with the Republican convention."

"It does. That was a no-brainer. You're very popular. The president hopes that some of that will rub off and steal some thunder from the MAGA love-in."

"I think that's optimistic. No one really knows me."

"Biden's best people are asking for you."

It was bad, then: the campaign was grasping at straws.

"I'll have to talk to Madeleine," he said. "My worst fear is that she'll think I'm lining things up for after...."

"You haven't told her?"

"I have told her, and she said I should do it. But that was before the disease got the upper hand. Before the suffering she's going through. When dying was just an idea."

"I understand. Let me know as soon as you can."

"I will."

Well, the call was worth the food: the dogs were congealed and the ice cream had melted. He threw everything away and started over. When he brought the treats home Madeleine, weak as she was, reached for them like a greedy child.

While she ate was no time to talk to her. Nor did he find a better time in the following days. On Saturday Trump was nearly assassinated in Pennsylvania, and on Sunday a manager from the Biden campaign told him not to come to Washington, the ceremony had been postponed.

Understanding His Granddaughter

The entomologists had it wrong. About this time there was a recurrence of cicadas: the babies of the pregnant babies had emerged from the ground to conceive. You could open a cicada and find four generations nesting inside like Russian dolls. Within the forest surrounding the house was the constant singing of death and life.

Some days it seemed that when the song ended, so would his beloved wife, all her healthy cells crowded out by tiny cicadas. The downward path seemed evident from her apathy, her grim-faced reveries, and her complaining, which began as a trickle through a crack and ended in a dam-burst. Kohl's prognosis at the first consultation had failed to include the breakdown in courage. This he found, warrior that he was, the most painful of all.

It was obvious that the twentieth century chemicals weren't working, yet Kohl refused to risk—what: his traditions? his household gods?—on the technology of the twenty-first. Hilty lost his temper with him. During a consultation the two men stood shouting at each other as Blake looked on appalled and Madeleine struggled to keep her eyes open. At home, after he put her to bed, he needed live company instead of the nemesis in his mind. Blake too needed a distraction and perhaps some perspective. He put the car keys in her hand.

At the street she turned right though left was shorter, because she liked the houses better on that side. When he stifled his protest she glanced at him amused. It was good to see even this much levity. The summer hadn't been easy for her either. She had made no friends here. The many hours alone in her room, silent and thoughtful, were not the usual life of a teenager.

"And for what?" he asked.

"For what what, Pop?"

"What do you think about Harris?" he recovered. "Pelosi endorsed her this morning. I expect Whitmer, Shapiro, and the other potential candidates will give it up now."

"I don't know her. And there's not much time."

"That says it." She preened a little at this. "Whatever happens, Biden has done the most selfless deed by a president in my long lifetime." Assuming that one overlooked the selfishness of holding out for a second term.

"Not so long, Pop. You still have your teeth. Where are we going?"

"Lakeside. We're running out of healthy snacks."

She drove to Winnetka, a trip she knew well by now, and parked behind the grocery store. He remembered when Lakeside Foods had been the A&P. The head butcher, a man named Archie, had bought it from the chain and immortalized it. His mother shopped there, often taking him to be her bright eyes. She gave her family meat every night—if she didn't, his father would say something at the table. Even the dog was fed Archie's meat; a better cut, as Hilty's rebellious sister liked to point out, than the black people of Cabrini Green could afford. If his sister were a young woman today, she might buzz her hair and change her name as Blake had done. It was the times. All the old ways were under attack. Archie, of course, was long dead, killed by his meat.

Having assumed the role of the mother, Blake took over the shopping cart and read to him the items on the list, which he was quick to find, her own bright eyes.

"So," he said, bringing her a sweet-smelling cantaloupe and six gleaming ears of yellow-white corn, partly shucked to reveal their bona fides. "So: Awkward Conversation Number One."

She smiled into the card, understanding what he meant. "Why not?"

"First, teach me the alphabet."

"That's easy. *LGBTQIA+*. There's also *2S*, meaning *two-spirit*. But that's Native American, I can't go there."

"I know *LGBT.* I don't know whether *Q* is supposed to stand for *queer,* which seems redundant, or *questioning,* as you said you were."

"It can be either. It depends on who's speaking."

"But if you already know who's speaking, why would you need to label it?"

"You need to label it for the phobic majority. The person concerned can then adopt the meaning for theirself."

Themselves, he thought. If you must misuse pronouns. But anyone so disrespectful of a basic part of speech wouldn't care whether the case was correct. He moved on.

"All right. What about *I* and *A* and the plus?"

"I is for *intersex, A* for *asexual, aromantic,* or *agender.* The plus is for all of the above. It works on the same principle: put it out there and let each person adopt it."

She was pleased with herself, a moment of happiness in a dismal summer: he should leave it at that.

"I have no idea what you just said."

"What I just said about what?"

"What what? Which what?"

"Which what did you mean?"

"Who's on first," he said.

"On first? On first base? You mean kissing? What has that got to do with it?"

A shopper walked by, interested to hear *kissing.*

He said, "This reminds me of baseball statistics. *WARC+.* If you don't speak the language you can't belong." And who would want to?

"A box of whole wheat penne," she said. "A large can of diced tomatoes—get the expensive Italian ones—a bag of quinoa, and a bag of lentils." She scrutinized each item as he brought it back. Her assumption of superiority was becoming hard to bear, but they might be on the verge of a breakthrough.

"May I quibble?" he asked.

"Of course." She tilted her head to listen.

"Actually, it's more fundamental than a quibble. I see a logical error in the taxonomy."

"Meaning?"

"What I see—and what, to be honest, I struggle with—is that the *LGB* and maybe the *Q* and the plus, depending on the person, as you say—these speak to sexual preference. And that's good, that's accepted, at least now by most of us. Anyway, it's codified. It says that it doesn't matter whom you love or how you love, which is just right. After all, the manner of sexual congress is a triviality compared to our loving one another. There's no such thing, for example, as recreational love, while for certain young people recreational sex—"

"I don't suppose seniors ever use Tinder."

"Point taken. But that's about *sexuality*. The remaining letters are about *gender*. They're not the same thing."

"They're not. But they have the same enemies."

"Anyone who cares about justice, about freedom, would support a person's choices of whom and how to love. But gender is something else, a fundamental element of identity. Those other letters call on society to throw out gender—throw out the painfully acquired, understood, and long-accepted conviction that gender is binary."

"Understood by people who to this day cannot stop killing each other. Shouldn't we hope for something better?"

"Again, you're speaking of different things. We can hope that humanity becomes less violent and learns to save itself in the face of existential challenges. One of the tools for that is knowledge, scientific enquiry. If gender isn't binary, science will have to start all over again."

"Maybe it already has. Maybe it's a spectrum. Maybe my generation is more enlightened than yours."

"Now you're just being argumentative."

"Appropriately so when we're having an argument."

Perhaps both of them had left the realm of fair debate. Best for them would be to agree to a future Awkward Conversation, when passions had cooled.

"At any moment," he said in a lower, slower voice, "the *Q* people may not be sure of their gender, and the *T* people may be transitioning from one gender to the other."

"Not *may:* it's happening: it's real!"

"Granted. But that's my point: from one to the other. Just because they don't feel like their biological gender doesn't give them the right to say that gender can't be distinguished. Rejecting the settled conviction of billions of our ancestors, people equally smart and, frankly, more thoughtful. Just to suit themselves and just now, in this difficult era. Speaking not only for their own particular situation but for the vast majority in the world who think differently...and if they're successful, committing humankind to this notion for generations to come. Such arrogance, Blake! Growing up is supposed to teach us that we don't know everything and the world doesn't revolve around us. Through some sleight of hand, our culture—not just your generation, but certainly many young people—seem to have forgotten that. It's a direct line from the tyranny of political correctness to the reactive tyranny of Trump. Where's the critical reasoning in all this?"

He was sweaty from the effort. For a moment he was afraid to look at her. This felt like an earlier version of himself, channeling many resentments into one, frustrated by his inability to address them.

She stopped the cart and consulted her list, or pretended to. "That's not worthy of you, Pop," she said finally. "My life is hard enough without your microaggressions."

"My what?"

"You're judging me."

"I disagree. I'm not. I never have."

In that moment she belonged to him, finally, and he loved her more than ever before.

Her eyes were shining. "Since I'm just a young person who thinks the world revolves around her, I don't know much, but I know three people who don't judge: my father, my sister, and her cat. Nana judges: she condemns herself because she's sick and everyone else because they're not. Your friend Slate judges: judges the world and exploits its weaknesses. His wife judges him and is afraid and says nothing. I'll give you the benefit of the doubt, since you claim to be different, but you'll have to prove it to me as we go."

And Sarah? But Blake offered no opinion on the most important person in her life, judgmental from birth.

They returned home. The TV came on in the enclosure. Blake finished unpacking and went up to her room. When he checked on his wife she muted the TV but still kept her eyes on it.

"Her life is hard enough: what do you think she means?"

A real judge, or an actor, was delivering a verdict to a chagrined couple, condemning each.

The lecture of the judge behind the bench was vocalized by the sarcasm of the speaker in the bed, as if the actor were lip-synching.

"Put that keen mind of yours to the question. Do what you do best: write something. You'll figure it out."

Despite the tone in which it was delivered, the advice wasn't bad. At times like this he thought best on paper. More than once or twice he had made an improvement in CSA's quality operations by starting with a blank sheet and syllogizing his way to a conclusion. He went to the library.

At the end of an hour he had eight hundred words of text, half a dozen bullet points, and one conclusion. Leaving the document on the screen, he walked upstairs and knocked on Blake's door. When she didn't answer he went inside.

She was lying on the carpet in her gym clothes—red trunks and matching shirt, both featuring the emblem of a one-eyed buccaneer with a *W* on his tricorne. A rolled-up towel was under her neck, and two small hand weights were at her sides. She pulled out her earbuds, which

[82]

made a tinny sound with a beat until she silenced her phone.

Beads of sweat stood on her brow: she had exerted herself, a private recourse. This had been his room growing up. Now, thickly carpeted, it was all but soundproof. When he had lived here, his mother used to know what he was up to by the creak of the floorboards.

"Good for you," he said.

"I'm getting fat," she replied in a conversational voice, as if there had been no unpleasantness.

Her calling attention to her body was convenient.

"When's your baby due?" he asked.

She scoffed, turned her head away, turned back. The mask she presented tried to congratulate the sleuth, as a master criminal might. Underneath she looked relieved and afraid.

"Second week of January. How did you know?"

"It made sense. Are you well?"

"Yes."

"Are you getting care?"

"Yes."

"Do you want to talk about it?"

She allowed that she did. With little prompting she told him all. At her age there was no such thing as oversharing.

She'd had one sonogram and was due for another. She wasn't ready to know the baby's biological gender, nor did she want to see its face. She was sixteen weeks' pregnant, late for the first meaningful decision. But this was proving too hard for her—she couldn't bear to think it. Her mother? Her mother was leaving it up to her, but she wanted her to end the pregnancy. Her father too, probably. What doctor wouldn't see an abortion as simply an outcome? Both of them were concerned that she would drop out of school and end up as a cashier at Walmart. Could that happen? She would be grateful for any insight.

"All the retailers are switching to self-checkout," he said.

[83]

"Thank you. Customer service, then."

"I think you need a degree for that. Where does the father fit into this?"

"They don't."

"They?"

That was another story. The father—this was TOP SE-
CRET EYES ONLY BURN BEFORE READING—the father
was her friend Hannah Brigand, formerly Peter.

"Is he—are they—questioning too? How…?"

It was hard to ask this without sounding judgmental,
but she was already ahead of him. "It's so stupid," she
exclaimed. "Stupid, stupid, stupid. How does a questioning person get pregnant?"

"Well…."

"Kids' stuff. We were acting out the opposite genders.
To see what it was like. A 'scientific test,' we called it. I
was supposed to be the male. We had—a toy. We got carried away. I'm an idiot."

"A human mistake," he said, "made by two people."

"No one knows it's them," she continued. "And no one
must ever know. Not my parents, not my sister, not her
cat. Not Hannah, of course. It's so humiliating. If I just
think about it I get sweaty. I'm trusting you, Pop."

"You can trust me, Blake. I have actually safeguarded
TOP SECRET EYES ONLY BURN BEFORE READING myself.
But you know that everyone will figure it out."

"As long as no one asks me about it. I'll kill myself."

He shot to his feet, a quaver in his voice.

"No, you will not. Will not. Are we agreed?"

"Yes, sorry, I was being theatrical."

"And you won't ever threaten that again."

"All right. Yes. I don't want to kill myself"

"And whatever happens, you'll finish high school and
go to college."

"Do you know," she asked, "how many single mothers
there are at, for example, Wellesley College? Me neither,
but I took an informal survey of the campus. None. Zero.

[84]

No strollers, no baby carriers. No nursing mothers with a textbook in their laps. You can't worry about a nicety like your education when a helpless being depends on you for its survival."

"Their survival."

"Very good, make a joke about the worst thing that has ever happened to me." But a burden had been shared, and her face was brighter. For the moment they were pals. It was possible that he could help her.

"So you knew," he offered to Madeleine the next morning, when her morale was usually highest.

"That's why they came out here. I was only the excuse. Sarah was afraid of making the decision for her. If she decides on the abortion she'll go home for it. Though it's getting late."

"Or she could decide to raise the child."

"That's her problem. I won't live to see it."

"None of that talk, please."

Yet he had always believed talk, as if talk were reality: talk of suicide, talk of an early death from an aggressive cancer. Anything in life could happen.

A Break of Sorts

"I won't live to see it." Perhaps the words meant acceptance, but she said them in some form every day, and besides the horror they struck in him, he was, if he was being honest, tired of hearing them. She wouldn't live to see her grandchild. What difference did it make who won the election? He would keep this house that she hated, and before long he would find someone thrilled to live in it—what about that sexy programmer in his office? To which he replied that deathbed matchmaking was clichéd.

He steeled himself to greater patience, but the horror stayed with him. Her decline now belonged not to the chemo but to the disease. She wasn't up to visitors; she didn't read the books he brought to her, even those she had requested; and he was appalled by the vulgar TV she watched, all day and much of the night, as if giving herself a foretaste of hell.

He was tired as well of dealing with Kohl, demanding, imploring him for the lifesaving medicine. On his wife's behalf he was tempted to accept Slate's offer to fly her to Sweden for treatment.

But even that was a problem. In their long friendship neither man asked favors of the other. If an offer wasn't accepted on the spot, vanity tabled it. What was needed was the right setting, a question, likely enough, how Maddy was doing, and upon the doleful reply, a cocked eyebrow: *I could have solved this for you long ago.*

Just as he was imagining such a scene, Slate, ever prescient, invited him to golf.

"You need a break from caregiving," he said, "and I'm struggling to run a major multinational corporation without your caustic advice. Sunday afternoon. We'll tee off after the adorable mixed foursomes."

"You and I?"

"Well, here am *I,* inviting *you.*"

[87]

"I meant, just a twosome?"

"Just a twosome. As fast as you play, we'll probably go around in an hour and a half. If you need help getting your liberty card punched, put me on to Maddy."

Despite its tone, this was not farfetched. He expected her reaction to be something like *I wonder if you'll come back and find me dead.* When he went to see her she was watching two women mud-wrestling, and she kept watching as he brought up the golf game. A moment passed, a nearly naked woman splashed with ochrous mud was thrown on her back, and Madeleine turned to him.

"But of course you need some time away," she said in a voice he once had heard when they were lovers. "You've devoted your whole life to me." Although she meant his recent life, still it was nice to hear. He ironed some golf clothes and brought up his clubs from the basement.

"You're sure?" he asked on Sunday.

"Go!" she replied. But the voice was not as nice as before. What if her last words to him were impatient?

Slate and he were members of the Glenarden Club, the oldest in the state. During the last Gilded Age the president of the Chicago and North Western Railway used to stop his train there, saying "I'm going out to golf," thus giving a name to the adjacent township. As CEO and a retired four-star admiral, Slate was an attractive candidate to be a member, but in an ironic turnabout it was Hilty who proposed him, for he had been a member growing up and had, despite years of acerbic remarks from his wife, kept paying his dues.

Some of his best memories were here. Once, as a string bean with a picture swing, he had scored a hole-in-one, at which his father, so formal, so distant, had leapt about with the caddies, and Frank Underhill, his father's friend, had driven a cart all over the course rounding up members to drink for free on Hilty's kid. Whatever Slate's own motives might be today, he himself felt powerful, influential, for both their sakes. He could say anything to him.

Only they weren't alone. When he arrived at the first tee, Howard Barr, CSA's vice chairman, and Julia Greene were there. "What a nice group," Slate said, forgetting his promise.

And the remark had an edge. Something was bothering him, and as usual when unhappy he played the tyrant. Throwing down a tee for partners, he claimed no decision though the tee pointed at Howard and threw it twice more until it pointed at Hilty. In the match he was determined to win and even to humiliate his opponents. He conceded no putts. After each hole he announced the score. His manner to Julia was so imperious that one of the caddies murmured to his mate, "No nookie for him tonight."

"Come here," he said to Hilty on the eleventh tee, which looked uphill to a bilevel green set among conversing spruce trees; beyond was the halfway house, where his father had often shared beer with his underage son. "Come here, you are needed," Slate said, leading him a few yards into the woods and stopping behind a gnarly oak, out of sight of Howard and Julia. "Right here."

"What?"

Slate turned his back toward him and dropped his golf pants. "Give me a tuck, will you?"

"A *tuck?*"

"You haven't forgotten, have you?"

"What on earth for?"

Slate laughed.

The answer was soon apparent: the girl at the halfway house was marvelously pretty. There seemed to be nothing between them—nothing to further his suspicions—except an older man's desire to impress a young woman. Still, the flirting was noticed. Feeling this, with excessive gallantry Slate served his wife first.

They went on. Slate's manner was intolerable. The intimacy of the tuck, a reciprocal courtesy of shipmates (and a pleasant reminder of the days when old salts used to plait each other's pigtails) failed to lead to a question about Maddy. On the eighteenth green Slate snatched his winnings from Howard's hand. Julia offered her payment, neatly folded, with a sad smile. When he shook his head, Slate insisted, "Take the money, Brad. The good guys won, didn't we?"

The news of the day was that Ukraine, after more than two years of defending its homeland, had invaded Russia, catching the aggressor by surprise. Whatever the invasion meant for the combatants, here was a business opportunity. Slate and Howard, having followed developments throughout the back nine, left the club to orchestrate a plan. In this they had apparently no need of a department head on a leave of absence, no matter how successful and influential he had been and no matter his thirty-plus years of outstanding military service.

Above the eighteenth green was a kidney-shaped terrace with a low brick wall, a rose garden, and a few tables and chairs. Julia and he, left to their own devices, stopped here to have a drink and watch other golfers finish. It was a beautiful day in mid-August, warm enough not to need a sweater even as they cooled off. The mild sun was still high above the horizon, and the usually humid sky was clear.

Julia stretched her arms as if luxuriating in pleasure.

The contrarian in him must be heard: "That was a little grim. I apologize."

She looked up in surprise. "But I enjoyed it! Such a beautiful day. And the golf! Your golf! I have to say I couldn't follow some of your drives, they disappeared in the distance. I was really hoping you would shoot your age. Bad luck coming in."

"I was a little distracted, I think."

"This news from Ukraine."

"Actually, Slate was in a mood, and he put me off."

"I didn't notice."

"I thought so anyway."

"Blast! I'm afraid he must have hurt your feelings."
Confident herself, she turned her sympathy outward.

"I might have been part of their planning," he said. "I know our products better than they do, and I've been following the war more closely. Of course we're old friends, lifetime friends, there's no doubting that, but I've often felt recently that I'm in his way."

"He values your opinion, Brad. I hear that all the time."

"Plus, I was hoping to talk to him about this new treatment. I wanted to take him up on his offer to fly us to Sweden."

"You think it will help?"

"I think without it it's hopeless."

Her face was still, except for the movement of her eyes; she was searching for words of comfort to give him. Apparently there were none: "I've been afraid it was coming to this."

"You can't cure cancer by slashing and burning. Her doctor is an eminent man but small-minded."

"And what Maddy needs is a great doctor. I wish I were one. But there's no reason why you couldn't take her to Sweden yourself, Brad. You don't need Slate for that."

True: how timid he'd become: timid, whiny, feckless, the mimic of his dying wife.

A threesome of juniors approached the green, two overweight boys and a string bean like the seventeen-year-old Hilty who had made the hole-in-one. But the heavy boys had outdriven him.

"Something needs to happen," he said, which probably sounded like more timidity, whining, and fecklessness.

"And that's you. I have every confidence."

This would be the time to unbosom himself of those other problems, both of them related and, in the extreme, affecting her.

The string bean, farthest from the pin, hit something like a six-iron. He too had a picture swing, as fluid and regular and inevitable as a millrace. The ball started low and pulled itself upward, ever higher, soaringly high—and long, fading toward them. Toward their own table, in fact, an object of beauty turned into a menace. Toward Julia, who was waiting for him to speak, who didn't see it.

He leapt up and cut in front of her. The abruptness provoked a cry of resentment. He didn't care, he would save her—a golf ball could kill. He put up his hand as the outfielders did making their one-handed catches. The ball stung his palm in one of those blows where the initial pain and its successor travel up the nervous system together; hit him and kept going and made him eat it.

He was lying on the grass surrounded by solicitous people in loud clothing and with his mouth full of blood. He sat up and reconciled the disparate advice by sipping a gin-and-tonic until he couldn't taste the blood any longer. The ball lay by his side; he tossed it onto the green, where it rolled near the cup. Then he resumed his seat across from Julia, loudly declaring himself well even as he tested with his tongue the moorings of his teeth.

The boy dropped the ball to play it from the terrace.

"Play it where I threw it," he said, speaking with the authority of age and injury. "The rule is called a rub of the green."

"Are you all right sir?" the boy had the decency to ask.

On the other hand, Julia's smile was ten percent concern for his well-being and ninety percent disapproval. "Really, Brad, that was a little foolish, don't you think?"

"It was going to hit you, Julia."

"Maybe so. But I've always thought that it's never as serious when you're hit by surprise. Fear contracts the muscles, opposes the impact with a harder surface."

"Very good. Next time I'll remember that."

She nodded. "You have a lot—"

Don't say *on your plate,* he thought.

"A lot going on. Taking care of Maddy must complicate everything else."

"Among which Blake is pregnant," he said, selling her secret in order to buy more friendship from this person.

"I know. Maddy told us."

"When?"

"Oh, a while ago. Has she decided what to do?"

There was no point in pursuing who knew first; and this felt like justice for his own indiscretion. He said, "She's at nineteen weeks tomorrow, so the first decision has basically been made. I'm glad of that, although I don't think Sarah and Phil are. She goes back to Boston soon, and back to school, so they'll all have to deal with the remaining decisions."

"Being in school won't be easy: she's begun to show."

"She has. And—not that it's all about me—my own situation is part of what's going on."

There was recognition here too. Of course Slate would have told her about the job offer, an ideal cover for his meetings with Robin.

"That should be clearer after the election, *n'est-ce pas?*"

"If Harris wins, as I think she will, I'll have to decide."

"It could be great for you."

"Are you guys so eager to be rid of us, Julia?"

But it was one of her foibles that when moved to speak up, which happened so rarely, she had no sense of humor. "Don't be silly, Brad. It's been a delight. But think how you felt when we first met back in Norfolk, when you were so unhappy about the flag list. This would be redemption—par excellence.

"Yet it might be nice to coast for a while."

"You never will. You can't bear to be idle. More than anyone I know, you need to set the world aright."

"O cursed spite."

"O cursed spite." She lowered her voice. "Not to mention what none of us like to talk about. All this good news with the company can't go on forever. Sooner or later another airplane will crash, the share price will fall, economic conditions will turn against us, people will discover other ways to travel, there will need to be cutbacks"—she rolled her hand: and so forth and so on.

"Does Slate agree with that?"

"He does. Strictly *entre nous,* he's trying to prepare for a downturn. It's not that you're in his way, but he thinks you might be happier out of it. He believes he needs to cut overhead—by a lot," she finished in a whisper.

He didn't know what to say, and he didn't want to sound melodramatic by telling her that. The disclosure was so important that the right response seemed to be silence. Had she been assigned to tell him? This might explain why Slate, sensitive as he was, had been acting out on the course.

Cries of joy carried downhill from the swimming pool. He listened. After such news they sounded at first like cries of alarm. A near miss with a golf ball and a disclosure of trouble at the company might be followed by a swimmer on the bottom. He could be there in seconds. In the Navy he had always dreamed of rescuing one of his sailors from the sea.

"Really, I can't think of anything now but Madeleine," he said finally.

She looked at him closely, trying to read his mind, which he kept screened from her. They finished their drinks, and she left him, and he sat a little longer sucking his rich salty blood.

The Fast Track

The golf ball had sought him on a Sunday. On Thursday of the following week, Blake packed her suitcase for the flight back to Boston. She would certainly have the child; but what then? Now that he had been read into the secret (however belatedly), Sarah and he had talked about it. He had tried his inductive method, but she had refused to see the logical conclusion—indeed, though so capable she hadn't made sense. Maybe she was up to her neck in alligators, and so forth and so on.

He reported the conversation to his wife, who said, "No one in that family is going to work for Walmart."

She begrudged the effort to say even this. She was very weak. Sometimes when he came into the enclosure he imagined he'd find her dead. The markers, the markers: but apart from the science of it, anyone could see that she was failing. And whatever Kübler-Ross would have, she was terrified and resentful.

She especially resented those who might save her life who were failing to do so. Oddly enough, this didn't include her own oncologist.

"What about the menin inhibitor?" she asked Sarah.

Sarah, defenseless against her mother's criticism, even in better times, began to make excuses for the approval process, all of which were true.

She cut her short.

"If your brother wants to see me before I die, now's the time. You don't need to be here unless you have approval for the drug. I don't need your bedside manner."

And to him: "I'm going to die. You'd better get ready."

"Don't say that. Sarah is breaking down doors."

"Bullshit."

"Adam can get the drug in Taipei."

"Illegally. For all we know it might be arsenic."

"I'll fly you to Sweden, then."

"I'd be dead before the International Date Line."

"Actually, that's in the Pacific."

"Greenwich, then, or wherever. Bradford, it's not going to work. We don't have much time, and the children are no help. Do what you do."

"We've had a happy life together," he said at once, having prepared for this moment. "I'm sorry for any pain I've caused you. Please forgive me, just as I forgive you for any pain on my side. Thank you for all these years. I love you."

"Not that, you ninny. I meant do what you do best: rattle some cages."

The doorbell rang. Beyond the screen an older man waited. A small man, thin and dapper, with a blue fedora hat, a seersucker jacket, and a bowtie. It was Dr. Kohl, making a house call.

With, he feared, a desperate greeting Hilty opened the door, and the doctor came inside. Other than asking for the patient he said nothing, as if his presence here were explanation enough. Before the door hissed shut a trio of late-season aliens flitted past him onto the tile. Blake, coming downstairs to see what this was, stamped on them mercilessly, that tender heart, to prevent their plaguing her Nana.

Kohl carried a country doctor's bag, well worn and probably resurrected from storage. Hilty brought him to the enclosure, giving Madeleine a warning first, then retreated with Blake to the den, where they spoke in whispers.

They were a long time together, then Kohl raised his voice: "Could you come here, please, Mr. Hilty?"

He was standing beside the bedside table. On it were a sheaf of papers and his yellow legal pad. Madeleine was sitting up holding her knees, independent of support.

"As you know," Kohl said, "despite the treatments, her markers remain stubbornly high."

"More than twenty percent blasts among leukocytes."

"Ah yes: more medical school. Unfortunately, none of the combinations we've tried so far—chemo, arsenic trioxide, all-trans retinoic acid—have turned the situation around. The data suggest a low chance of survival, and there is no question now that extraordinary measures are indicated."

"My daughter, Sarah," he began, but Kohl silenced him. He had an announcement to make about which he seemed more than a little pleased.

"I have obtained a Fast Track certificate from the FDA for a course of treatment of Revumenib."

"You haven't! You have! Truly?"

"I'll administer the first pill now. Beginning tomorrow morning you will give her one pill twice a day, always at the same time. I'll want to continue to see her every week or if there is any change in her condition. I assume you find this agreeable."

Which translated as *Feel free to admit your ignorance.*

His chest filled with something—relief? laughter?

Kohl continued: "The side effects should be minimal and easily tolerated. These include—Oh, dear girl!"—for Blake was kissing his hand.

"How?" he asked. "How did you manage it? We've been moving heaven and earth to get approval."

Kohl palmed his snappy blue fedora over his freckled head. "I followed the science," he replied.

The doctor was about to leave, trailing astonished gratitude, when the doorbell rang again. It was Slate and Julia, wearing that same look of self-satisfaction. Kohl, seeing that they too had something to announce, in which his own interests might be concerned, took off his hat and returned with them to the patient's bedside.

"Pack your bags, young lady," Slate said. "Bring your prettiest clothes."

"Where am I going?" Madeleine asked.

"Tomorrow morning you and I and your admirable husband, who arranged it all, will take my plane to a very nice clinic outside Stockholm where all the tiny cicadas in your blood will soon be expunged."

"That would be nice, sir, but I don't think I'm up to it."

"She is not," Kohl said, speaking in a voice from an era when doctors' orders had the force of law.

Slate looked thoughtful. "All right, that's a glitch, but not insurmountable. The Swedes are reluctant to release the medication unless the patient is present, but I imagine they can be persuaded. They want to join NATO, after all. No doubt Roddy Denton has a secret compartment on the airplane for bringing in contraband."

"What medication?" Kohl demanded.

"Revumenib, doctor. We understand that the sources of supply here have been a problem."

Kohl, as in Churchill's parable of the bear and the man, blew first, and the insult went back down Slate's throat: "That is false, sir. I have prescribed that medication for my patient and administered the first pill to her not fifteen minutes ago." The anger drained from his face, leaving the thrill of victory.

But Slate was so swift in reply they might have been singing a duet. "Excellent news, doctor: all that red tape cut away. Maddy, you're going to be cured!"

"A premature conclusion," Kohl said, holding up his hand, but clearly he thought so too and in that moment his victory was complete.

Possibly he hadn't known who Slate was, for in the general talk that followed some reference was made to Chance-Stevens-Arrowsmith, and suddenly he became deferential. Slate noticed it—sent Hilty a comical glance—but continued to be gracious, while Julia seemed happy and relieved. Madeleine would live. Their fortunate lives would go on.

But how? Assuming her early recovery, should he return to his job at the company, where apparently he was a moral impediment to his friend's plans, or should he take his chances on this election and the high appointment that would get him out of the way?

In reply to a line of small talk from Julia, Kohl was explaining that he did fish and that this summer he had, after years of disappointment—northern pike, small-mouth bass, the occasional laker—finally caught a musky. "A record for the lake, I may claim modestly. My late wife and I used to own a cabin there. I hadn't been back for some time. The odds reset, you know. So I never expected that on my first day back, practically on my first cast, I should have such a fight and such a fish in my net."

"Your wife died," Julia said with her ready sympathy.

"Yes—cancer. The irony of it."

"I'm sorry"—a feeling that traveled among them.

"What lake?" Hilty asked, to change the tone.

"Do you wish to break my record, sir?"

"No sir. I used to spend summers in the North Woods."

"Lake Noquebay. Near Green Bay."

"We have the shipyard at Marinette," Slate said.

"That's right, that's yours, isn't it."

"Sarah's here," Blake said almost without inflection.

There she was, standing inside the enclosure door, looking just like herself as famous people do. In their surprise they greeted her casually as if she had come from another room; only Julia thought to embrace her.

"Good news," she said to her mother. "Hillary Mentov has got the FDA to fast-track your case. As you asked, I've brought Revumenib."

The announcement was also an offering; she wanted her mother's approval. The reaction of the group, exclamations and laughter, was not what she had expected. "What's going on?" she asked.

"Dr. Kohl gave me my first dose just before you came in."

Madeleine was pleased with herself. But it would take a superior person to accept the redundant gift with kind thanks and no thought of the delay in its bestowal.

"You're kidding!"

She opened her mouth and stuck out her tongue as if the pill might still be there.

"We had a specific waiver, naming you and all the conditions," Sarah said. "The treatment plan was six pages long."

"Does it look like this, doctor?" Kohl asked, pulling the sheaf of papers from his country bag.

"They would never have granted the same waiver twice."

"Apparently they did. You know bureaucracies." Now his victory meant even more. But he was missing the mother-daughter dynamic.

Puzzled, hurt, obliged to look happy, Sarah said, "And I thought I was saving your life."

"It doesn't matter who," said Blake.

"What are the conditions of the waiver?" Kohl asked.

"That the case be transferred to our Cancer Center and supervised by Richard Alexander, senior oncologist, and the medication administered by competent practitioners."

"So your mother would have to be in Boston," Slate said.

"That's right. That's why I'm here."

"Maddy, you might want to think about that. You and Brad could go with Sarah and Blake and—what?—stay with them until you're cured."

"We do have room," Sarah explained, speaking slowly as people did when the subject was hypothetical. "And of course either Phil or I would be competent practitioners. But we said in the plan, to anticipate any concerns, that you and Dad would have lodgings near the hospital, and I've already rented an apartment in Beacon Hill that does this sort of thing."

"That seems like a lot of trouble and expense for two pills a day," Kohl said. "My plan is simple and already in effect."

[100]

"But it might be just the change you want," Slate said. "Don't a patient's surroundings contribute to her recovery?"

"You seem to want her to leave my care, sir."

"Not at all, sir. My wife and I want what's best for her. This isn't our bailiwick."

"Let's not get ahead of ourselves," Kohl said. "Despite this breakthrough her condition is guarded. I couldn't possibly agree to release her without an air medevac, to include an attending physician and a triage nurse."

"Yes, doctor, I've arranged it," Sarah replied.

"Indeed? I have trouble imagining such resources."

"What does Nana want?" Blake asked.

As Nana was considering what she wanted, a red-eyed alien dropped onto her pillow. She started. Without a lost moment, Slate cupped his hands around the insect and carried it to the back door to toss it into the future.

"Well, that seems to be a sign," Julia said.

So the tables were turned. Sarah was smiling in the same way that Kohl had smiled not long before, and Kohl looked like someone determined to be professional. But the humiliation! To have stuck to his opinion for so long, despite all the opposition; then, properly following the science, to have come to a radical solution, so varied from the practice of a lifetime, only to be upstaged by a younger generation...if such a thing had happened to Hilty, he would wish to be eaten by cicadas.

"I know Richard Alexander from several conferences," Kohl said, dapper dignity intact. "You'll be in good hands, Mrs. Hilty." But earlier he had called her Madeleine.

"And you'll go too, Brad," Slate prompted.

"Oh yes, of course. This is a great relief. Thank you all."

Understanding His Wife

Yes of course I'm going with her, he had told them. Had told Slate, who seemed the most interested. In fact, he changed his mind about going a dozen times that night, so that he hardly slept. The current tumbled him every which way, as chaotic as a riptide.

First of all, family: Most important, Madeleine. Blake's pregnancy and future. Sarah's career. Her marriage, amid hints of tension about Blake (see second item).

Then his dearest friends: Whatever Slate was up to. Whether his narcissism would lead him into such an infamous act as depriving his workers of a decent wage. Whether, in the fever of such wickedness, he would crush the hopes of his loyal, loving wife by leaving her for someone decidedly her inferior.

And himself: Whither goest, Hilty? Whether Boston wasn't too far away for him to be of service to his friends. The putative appointment in Washington that would redeem his bitter failure to become a flag officer. His attachment to this house in Chicago, purchased while in his own fever, that of new wealth, and for all his wishing a failure of memory or perhaps imagination. And finally the larger, deceptively simple question: What to do with this last productive period of his life, his one life?

At three o'clock, giving up sleep, he got dressed. The house was silent, foretelling its state with everyone gone. Sarah's door was shut, like her personality, and Blake's was open, like hers. He edged down the back stairs and tiptoed through the kitchen so as not to awaken his wife.

The basement, the one thing unenlarged, was most like the old house for memories. The principal space was a TV and game room, where his sister, as she proudly confessed to him, had lost her virginity; its vinyl floor would have been ideal for indoor hockey except for the thousand stick marks which he'd had to scrub away with steel wool. In a storage room his unhandy father had built for him a bi-level train set complete with trestles and tunnels and a roundhouse: every New Year's Day, while his parents were recovering from the night before, the town repelled a surprise attack by Communist troops. In a closet under the stairs he and Rob Bullock, briefly his best friend, had proved that glycerol and potassium permanganate do indeed combust spontaneously. In the laundry room his mother, despite her own unhappiness, had heartened him against his fear of nuclear war.

Outside, he had work to do. The pool would have to be swept clear of cicada bodies, drained, and covered for the winter. The pear trees would have to be unnetted. The scant bit of lawn left from the landscaping would have to be mowed through September and many of the plantings cut back. The water in the bathhouse would have to be shut off and the pipes drained against freezing and the door sealed against winter vermin. The more you had, the more you worried.

But these were just excuses for putting off the greater decision. He didn't want any of this except her recovery. He could accept changes forced upon him by circumstances, but he didn't want, as the saying went, to be the change he wished to see. No doubt it was a universal feeling: he wanted the status quo minus its problems.

"You're not going, are you."

His wife was speaking to him across the clotted water.

He turned. She was standing by the shallow end of the pool, supporting herself against the ladder rail; dressed in her bathrobe, which he had recently wondered if she would ever wear again. In the glare of the security lights she looked like a cadaver.

"You feel better!"

"Don't kid yourself. Kohl said it might take months." As if to show this, she dropped onto a lounge chair, nearly capsizing it. He rushed to her side, stabilized the cheap thing, and sat beside her.

[104]

A breath of wind came out of the woods, soft against his cheeks but acrid with the smell of dead leaves.

"You're not going," she repeated. "On the medevac."

"Not tomorrow," he agreed.

"Today. Tomorrow is here. I'm going to live."

"And that's all I want. All I *have* wanted since you became ill. But you're in good hands, and I need to winterize the house and tie up some loose ends before I can leave this place behind."

"Spill. It's not the house. We can hire someone."

"Shall I tell you?"

"Didn't I just ask you to?"

So he gave her the executive summary of his problems, including his most private thoughts about himself. It felt good to share this with her, a first step away from caring roommates and back toward marriage.

He looked at her.

"Got it," she said. "The Bradford Hilty Entropy List. Off the top of my head, I'd say thank you for taking care of me; don't worry about Blake; something is going on with Sarah at work; she and Phil will figure out their marriage just as we did; I've never trusted Slate in any ethical question; Julia undoubtedly knows more of the truth than her pride will let her acknowledge; you can't help them anyway; I don't know what you should do about the job—if you have a choice, which I doubt—but even if you get it you'll still be bitter about the flag list; I hate this house but so what; and the best thing you could do with your remaining life is to throw away all your lists and start enjoying it."

"Impressive," he said as she caught her breath. "I'll take that under advisement."

After a moment: "So is this a separation?" she asked.

"No way." But it felt like one, or it might lead to one.

"If you say it's just a time-out I'll throw up on your penny loafers."

"I certainly won't say that, then."

[105]

"A long deployment?"

"More like a short training exercise. Do you remember what I said when I thought it was the end?"

"Yes. You were sorry for treating me so badly."

"And ditto. But the important part: I love you."

"Then stop calling me Madeleine, which sounds horribly formal. You've been calling me that since Taiwan. Call me Mad, as you used to." She chortled. "That's it, I must be Mad."

Three

Genetic Engineering

Labor Week

Mad reported that the medevac had gone smoothly but that she had decided not to live in the apartment rented for them in Beacon Hill, since for the time being there wouldn't be a "them." Instead, the Nichols family made her welcome in their home in Wellesley, near the college. She took the medicine twice a day from Sarah or Phil, eminently well qualified as they were to administer it. There wasn't a miracle cure—she didn't leap out of bed one morning and run five miles—but she stopped getting worse.

At his end he brought in people to lay up the Northriver house for a long absence or a sale.

Labor Day came. Slate and a senior sales team were in China pitching the new aircraft. Everyone else was off, of course. The Cubs were hosting the Pirates at Wrigley: hoping to see certain people there, he called Anna Hart, Slate's assistant, and got a ticket.

By then the Cubs were all but out of the race, which was too bad. First the hitting, now the pitching. Each loss poured the bucket of *All right, now they really are out of it* upon the embers of hope. It wasn't settled mathematically yet, but everyone knew, and there was no joy in Wrigleyville as the seats emptied.

Except for him: if not joy at least serendipity: among the staff taking advantage of the free tickets was Anna Hart herself, high on his list.

They were not exactly friends, though they shared Slate as a friend. Anna presented to all her coworkers the same attractive, interested, and helpful manner beyond which was a wall. Never married herself, she was raising a ten-year-old grandson: that much was public knowledge. How hard her life must have been, being on-call essentially 24/7 not only to Slate but to anyone who wanted to speak to Slate or get on his schedule or simply know what he thought about a multiplicity of questions, he could only imagine.

What united them, if not as friends then as kindred spirits, was that each was a perfectionist who never left a task unfinished. When he was one of those late-evening callers, she always seemed gratified.

"What time is the pitch?" he asked, meaning work not baseball.

Anna and he were sitting in the company bleachers with Drake, her grandson. The seats around them were filled—staffers here for baseball not work. Unfortunately, the Cubs were losing, the embers of hope already doused, and Drake was fidgety, wanting to go home. So far Anna had asked about Mad and told him some desultory news from the tower.

"Eight o'clock our time," she said. "Ricky Mountjoy is giving it." Ricky, the COO of Commercial Airplanes, was widely considered the company's best salesman. "Also Franklin Townes"—the CEO of Airplanes—"Nancy Beeman of Legal. Oh, and your friend Dorothea, to put a face on our commitment to quality."

"Who's on their side?"

"Li Qiang."

"That's something." Li Qiang was the premier of China and Xi Jinping's right-hand man.

"That's Slate."

"So, looking good...?"

"Fingers crossed."

A cold draught blew in from the lake. Anna pulled down the visor of her Cubs ballcap. Drake whined.

He said, "The Politburo is seven old men with granite faces and jet-black hair. I'm a little surprised that Slate included a woman in the pitch."

"We gamed it, for sure. Li has a reputation for supporting women, although now he and Xi want to turn them into baby machines. But Dorothea is so solid, so impressive in her way, and then the quality angle...."

[110]

He laughed. "I never got to China when I had her job."

"Oh, you still have her job, Brad. We can't wait to get you back, and that includes Dorothea." But out of what confidences between her and Slate had the Navy job been mentioned? Was it possible, even, that she had been on the plan from the beginning?

"Grandma, puh-lease," whined Drake.

"In just a minute, Ducky."

"Ducks and Drake," he said, without effect.

"Certainly," she agreed.

"Can I ask you something?"—orienteering with no topo and a suspect compass.

"Oh sure."

"About Slate. I'm a little concerned that he seems...I don't know quite how to put it."

"Preoccupied," she offered. "Determined."

"All right. I was going to say fixated, though that doesn't sound right. Maybe impatient." Or maybe manic.

"In that sense I would say forehanded. With everything else going on—by the way, I don't think we're going to be able to bring those astronauts home—with all the demands on his time, he has to look five or even ten years ahead for us. Of course he's pleased about the share price. But more than anything he wants to position us for the long term."

"That must be it," he said. "I was worried that it might be something—more personal."

"You would know about that better than I would," she replied. "You've been his friend for so long."

All the mansions in Kenilworth, where Slate and Julia lived (in addition to their other residences: London, the Isle of Arran, the French Riviera, and Bangkok), overlooked the lake from a bluff. Viewed from the public road, they made a seemingly endless perspective of uncrowded wealth, something that had both impressed and disturbed him as a boy whenever he had come this way. Impressed him, obviously. But disturbed him too because they seemed to require him to do something with his life that he would not be capable of doing.

Even with the owner away the place was busy and sounded like it. Gardeners were deadheading roses before the frost. Leaf blowers were clearing the lawn from under the avenue of London plane trees. Vans from a plumber and a security consultant were parked in front of the row of garages.

As he pulled up, Frank Mastrangelo, the butler, came out to beat the dust from a Turkish carpet; very little dust. He had seen Julia out back. Laying down the beater, he opened the door so Hilty could exercise the privileges of a family friend to cut through the house.

What a glorious day! The sun, a steady breeze from the west, the brilliant lawn that had no idea of the coming winter—in such environs he was all-powerful. Not only did he belong to such wealth, he felt a trifle condescending toward it. There was no danger that might befall this family from which he would be unable to save them.

Julia wasn't in sight, but an inspiration produced by the moment caused him to look over the edge of the bluff. There she was, sitting on her private beach, just beyond the brown scalloped edge of wetted sand, engrossed in a book. He went down to her (watching his feet on the slippery steps) and sat beside her without a word. She looked over, smiled, and put the book down.

"Good?" he asked.

"The new biography of Baryshnikov. Not *very* good—or good for a different sort of interest, I suppose. Too much about the defection—spy stuff—and not enough about his dancing. I'd like to know, beyond the athleticism, what made him such an interesting artist."

"Maybe the writer lost his cars keys in the dark and had to look for them where the light was."

"I wish he'd parked under a different streetlight, then."

[112]

The beach was secluded between a promontory to the north, down which rocks occasionally fell, and a seasonal dock to the south, where a sailboat and a motorboat were moored. The grey-green waves endlessly reached for a greater purchase on the shore. Out beyond the sandbar, the surface was greener still and in the distance grey-blue, with a few pretty sails to be seen. All in all, the setting was ideal for his purposes, even to an escape route up the stairs. Only: speak!

Before he could, she asked, "What do you say to a sail?"

"With all my heart."

The boat was a Rhodes 19, broad-beamed and stable, right for the conditions but a lot to handle unless you knew her. Which indeed Julia did. In no time she had them underway, mooring lines coiled, fenders stowed, jib and mains'l drawing well, and sheets precisely belayed. On the other hand, candor was hostage to the confining cockpit and his inability to walk on water.

Close-hauled, the boat nosed its way over the bar and cleared the shore. She came about with hardly a burble and headed north, the tiller pinched behind her knee.

"Well done, ma'am! You're a sailor."

"Thank you, sir. When we were stationed in Hawaii I took lessons and actually raced a little. Slate needed a distraction, and I wanted it with me. I just love it."

"I've never seen you at the helm before."

"The Rhodes isn't much of a boat for entertaining. If the money keeps pouring in, Slate talks about a sailing yacht. Jeff Bezos has one with three masts, but of course we aren't in that league."

"It's been a nice run—but sobering."

"Really, it's obscene. We have so much money now we couldn't spend it if we lived to be a hundred. That's true: we did the math: it doesn't run out. I'm embarrassed to think of the houses, the country club memberships, the dedicated plane...and now a sailing yacht?"

Halved by any divorce, he thought. He said, "If you'll be the master I'll be your bosun."

"It just pours in. Any more and we'll be forced into a new bracket."

"Tax bracket?"

"Security bracket. We'll need a secret service detail. Ready about. Helm's alee." She yanked the jib sheet clear of its cam as the boat's head crossed the waves, the two sails luffing in protest. Smooth and spare, she shifted knees, switched hands, and sheeted home while he ducked under the boom to the new high side. When he turned to look, the boat was steady on course and the sails drawing well again with no loss of wake.

She smiled at him. He saw a way in.

"I've been thinking about our talk at the club. You told me he's planning to cut overhead. Breaking the unions would be an obvious next step once he starts down that path. As far as my own position is concerned—"

"I didn't say anything about breaking the unions. We support the right to organize."

"Yes, certainly. But I do feel a change in the wind."

She turned her cheek to make a joke of his metaphor. It seemed that she felt a serious conversation coming and deplored it, as a Victorian maiden might deplore an offer from an unwanted suitor. But the drawing room was seven feet by five and neither of them could walk on water.

"Brad, at the club both of us thought we were going to lose Maddy. Of course there's been a change in the wind."

"I'm sorry, this is something else. Something I've worried about even before she got sick."

"Yes, you felt that Slate wanted you out of the way. I assure you it's not true."

"Only I have a little problem with the facts."

"Please, no facts." She laughed. "I don't want to hear any facts. Haven't we learned from this election that they don't matter?"

"Julia, I'm worried about Slate and Robin."

A larger sailboat with a young man at the helm was coming up from the south on a close approach; close but safe if he held his course. At the last minute he tacked across Julia's bow. With a curse she fell off...but too far: the Rhodes jibed itself—the rattle of the boom in its gooseneck sounded like disaster—as they ducked to save themselves the boom swung viciously over their heads— and its unspent force rolled the hull until water poured over the gunwale. Just in time she regained the tiller.

The lubberly skipper was a bare-chested Adonis, and his friend was another. The friend said to them, "Sorry," as if two parties were waiting at a restaurant and the headwaiter had taken them out of turn. Hilty called an admonition, "Starboard over port," at which both men waved.

Julia sheeted in with murder in her heart. Her lips were thin and white, and the tan had drained from her face. "Don't you dare bring that ugly suggestion to me. That *I'm just sayin'* poisonous thing."

"But I'm not just saying."

"You of all people know our history: I went through hell before with Slate, and I will never do that again."

She was so upset—so upset with him—that he took the coward's way out. "He's devoted to you. I'm sure there's nothing to it."

"Robin is his friend, I accept that. They had feelings for each other a long time ago—a lifetime ago. He was lost. I accept it all. But he changed. He did change, and I helped him. I myself, lil' ol' me." She struck her breast.

"Since that awful time, I have no reason to believe that he has ever betrayed my trust. Against these so-called 'facts' of yours I will happily put our many years together, the countless secrets we have shared, even the way we have picked each other up after fighting. That's trust. And if, for whatever reasons, mounted on your high horse, you disagree, then you, you Brad, are the real threat to me, not some figment of your overheated imagination."

"Julia, I—"

"Look to your own marriage, friend, and stay away from mine."

After that, of course, no apology would do. They parted almost without speaking, conscious, no doubt both of them, that only time and distance would move them past this moment. And yet, as badly as he felt, he also felt that in difficult circumstances he had performed a duty.

His phone buzzed and the cheerful bell tinkled. A text from Robin. Rather, a series of texts. People who hadn't gathered their thoughts needed a running start, learning what they thought after they wrote it.

Good morning.
I'm thumbing this with my hands under the table.
The most useless God-awful briefing.
By comparison Trump is a master of logic.
No big deal: only fifty billion at stake.
I wanted to let you know it's looking good.
The VP is surging and at just the right time.
Reviewing the troops here we exchanged that BFF look.
When I'm reappointed I'll make sure of you.
Don't call realtor yet but talk to Mad about location.
Georgetown? Also, Southeast has been cleaned up.
Dear Mad.
Dear You.
Good God, I have to say something now.

Although officially on leave and expected to return (see Slate Greene for details), he had disciplined himself not to interfere in the running of the office. Occasionally he sent Dorothea a message of encouragement. Until today he had not spoken to her.

A voice other than hers said hello.

"Tabby?" he asked.

"Yes? Are you calling for Dot?—for Dorothea Billups?"

"I am. It's Brad." As surely the phone had told her.

"Oh, Brad. Yes. Yes, she's here. But she only got home from a long trip—from China—an hour ago."

Sounds in the background suggested a scene—Alexa would know it. The bedroom with the shades drawn. The lovingly-constructed village of scented candles. Perhaps a printed balloon. Then the familiar but unwelcome ring-tone. The *sorry I have to take this.* The phone snatched from the recipient's hand in a vain attempt to sustain the mood.

"Here she is, Brad."

"This is a bad time," he said. "I'm sorry."

"How did you know I'd be here?"

"I thought wheels down was hours ago."

"That's odd."

"It's not urgent. I'll call back later."

"Well, you've got me now."

But she was so guarded in her report of the China trip that he forbore from asking her how Slate was or if he had spoken of him.

By Friday the house was laid up, and he could leave any time. Not to mention that he had promised Mad that the separation would be brief. Not to mention that if every-thing stayed on track, after November their home might be in Washington.

On the other hand, househunting in Washington now would look presumptuous. He might not be confirmed un-til well after Harris's inauguration—the pecking order was cabinet secretaries and agency heads, their deputies, and finally assistants like him. By then Baby Nichols would be born: where would Mad—a healthy Mad—want to be then? He suspected her of having the grandmother gene: how ironic if she treated him like a Navy wife. *I'm sorry to decline the honor, Madam President, but I am needed for babysitting.* The question, then, wasn't what to do with the house: it was what to do with himself.

[117]

A question that might not be answered for months.

Though his BMI was precisely normal, it was true that when stressed or bored he turned to food. On that Friday he went—perhaps for the last time—to the Telltale Diner in Hubbard Woods, where he ordered two Vienna Beef hotdogs, a side of fries, and a large coffee milkshake.

So much food was before him that even after he had made an inroads there wasn't that sad realization that the treat was dwindling.

As he eyed the second dog, which seductively showed its grill marks, like cleavage, there was Slate, sitting across from him.

The occupation of eating was a sedative.

"Why, hello! Welcome back. How did the pitch go?"

Slate smiled. "Never better. A major contract."

"Well done, sir. If not for the SEC I'd sell my shares."

"But you can, you know. It isn't insider trading if you're not an insider."

Dignity and self-respect called for him to carry on with his lunch, despite the interruption. "You trying to tell me something, Slate?" he asked between mouthfuls.

"I am. I came here expressly to tell you. You're fired, Brad. Actually, you were fired before we got to China. Dorothea has performed extremely well, she deserves the promotion, and it wouldn't have impressed the Chinese if quality assurance had been represented by an acting. I promoted her on the plane going over but asked her not to tell you. I wanted to spare your feelings, fool that I was, which is why she was so evasive on the phone last night. And why Anna wouldn't tell you anything on Monday. All your sleuthing around."

He reached across for Hilty's dog and stuffed half of it into his mouth with a gratified look. After a vigorous chew he continued:

"Actually you were fired as soon as you doubted me. Your so-called investigation has troubled six sources that I know of—the secretary of the navy, from whom we hope to win a major new contract; my personal pilot; my personal assistant; my chief of quality assurance; my own wife, despite the terrible hurt your 'facts' have caused her; and—oh, yes!—myself, your old friend. That's six, correct? I'm sure you were counting."

He sat back. He was too canny to choke on food.

"Let me sum up, just so we're clear. I am not having an affair with Robin McGill. Those feelings ended years ago. In fact I have never been interested in other women since a sad time in my past when, fool that I was, I trusted you with my secrets. We live and learn, Brad. Everything isn't baked in. Your own life should have taught you that. Whatever 'facts' you think you've uncovered...are false. Not that it matters: I repeat: you're fired, and I doubt if our paths will cross again. Someday I might feel pain about that, but right now my only feeling is a nearly overpowering desire to reach across this table and squeeze the life out of you."

He started to get up, a tall, handsome, distinguished man, powerful and cruel, bound to leave his mark on the world. If he squeezed the life out of a few enemies along the way, no one would care.

He held up his hand. "A moment please, Slate. Just a moment more. Of course that's your call. Someday, in turn, I will thank you for the wonderful opportunity you've given me, this chance to make such a difference. However, your personal schedule states that you went to Washington only twice last spring. The flight log, provided by your pilot in the course of my official duties, says seven times. I didn't go looking for misbehavior. Given your history and the coincidence of who lives there, anyone would be suspicious of the discrepancy."

Slate smiled again, cruel and self-satisfied.

"That's correct: seven is the right number. Anna suppressed it from the schedule at my direction. Bill McIntyre—*your* friend, I might add—is suffering from untreatable prostate cancer. He'll be dead before the next season of cherry blossoms. Among other visits I sat on the Mall with him to feel the lovely pink blossoms on our faces. Goodbye, Brad. Don't be you anymore—it's exhausting for the rest of us."

The next day he flew to Boston.

Houseguest

For most of their working lives Sarah and Phil had lived in an apartment on the back side of Beacon Hill, a place that looked both west to the river and south to the hospital. It was nice for them whenever they could walk together to their clinics, ophthalmology and hand surgery. Happy families are alike, he thought; and not just happy but nearly perfect, imperishable, doing everything right.

But recently it had seemed that Sarah was unhappy. Her work no longer excited her—though she was determined to excel at it—and more and more she complained about the healthcare system: the automation, the politics, the defensiveness; lawyers and petty bureaucrats. She had warned her mother, using the language of youth, that now she would make her bag and get out. Perhaps the malaise was understandable after so many years of striving for excellence.

But there were hints too of tension in their marriage. Raising children did that, of course: the temperamental differences of two strong people. She was the disciplinarian, Phil the diplomat. But money too had become an issue, for having decided to make her bag, Sarah started to watch the markets, and two years ago she had moved her family out of Beacon Hill to Wellesley, to a grand sprawling modern house whose paper value, as she liked to boast, was rising, always rising, but whose mortgage only both their incomes could afford. In this decision it seemed that she had stiff-armed her husband just as he in buying his childhood home had stiff-armed his wife, and the result was the same: though less apt to complain than Mad, Phil didn't like his home.

And now Blake. From the airport he drove straight to Wellesley.

🃏🃏🃏

He had to call at the gate, and they were all on the gravel to meet him. Mad, standing unassisted, reached up to his broad shoulders in the old way of holding herself against him. Although nothing had been said about his staying Phil took his bags and disappeared into the house. But Sarah looked askance as if they were giving shelter to a homeless man.

The youngster: "I'm Megan, Pop, and this is Nutmeg."

Blake: "Of course he knows that, you dork."

She took his arm—he belonged to her. "Fancy a tour?"

"I'd love a tour. Lay on, Macduffy."

"It's Macduff," Megan said, delighted by his mistake.

"Shakespeare didn't know," he said over his shoulder, "that Macbeth and Macduff were BFFs."

The house: The five bedrooms and seven baths; the basement theater with its stadium seating; the sentient washer and dryer in the laundry room; the kitchen that would do for a restaurant; and the living spaces, modern and convenient but too many of them, lacking that one homey place where the family would pile together, arms and legs woven. Still, Sarah had worked hard to make the house beautiful (and increase its value). When they ran into her he praised it extravagantly.

Apparently it felt different if you were seventeen and your life was in crisis. Taking him outside, Blake began a running critique, beginning with the family's croquet pitch. "The world's most boring sport," she said. When he reached into the storage box to heft a mallet and came away with a paint splinter, she added, "Sorry. Megan and her friends leave them out in the rain. Irresponsible as fuck."

"As fuck. What does that mean exactly?"

"That I'm vulgar as well as stupid?"

"Sorry. I thought it might mean something specific. And you have a hammock!" he exclaimed.

"You're on a roll, Pop. That's where the deed occurred."

"The deed? The deed! Good Lord, in a hammock?"

"At midnight on April first. Some April Fool's joke."

"I can't imagine the physics of the problem."

"There's no accounting for youthful hormones."

"Have you decided anything?"

"Not yet. I'm trying the old trick: make a decision and then do the other thing if it doesn't feel right."

"Yes, I often did that in battle."

She smiled. "If I apply to colleges in the area, I could live here. My peeps could help me with childcare. How solipsistic is that?"

"Solipsistic. A good word if not a good idea."

"You know Gen Z: ever entitled."

"Who are your peeps?"

"Immediate family, as available. You and Nana, now that you're here. You're here, yes?"

"And Hannah?"

"Them? Poof! They've made it to the other side of the spectrum, except psychologically. No mothering instinct. Every time I see them they look away from my bump. You are absolutely sworn to secrecy, right?"

"Absolutely," he promised. "I hope you aren't too worried, Blake. Someday I'll give you my lecture on entropy."

"You've already done me that honor. We were sweeping cicadas from the driveway."

"So then you know that my mission in life is to keep things from falling apart."

"Including me?" She made a comical pout. "Am I job one? Or is Nana more important right now?"

"Good old Gen Z," he replied.

After Blake it was Megan's turn. In her room she showed off Nutmeg the Cat. This consisted of taking him in her arms, wrapping him around her neck, and turning him upside down to prove how "malleable" he was; then giving him to Pop, in whose uncertain hold he purred and purred. Since he weighed twenty-five pounds and felt and smelled wonderful, holding him excluded all other sensations. Not until he gave Nutmeg back was his power of thought restored.

"And you love your new home?" he asked.

"Not new, Pop. It was built in 2016."

"Oh, then it's ancient. I meant new for you."

"We moved in two years ago!" But between taking him literally, which was her nature, and understanding his intended meaning out of kindness, kindness won: "I was just a teeny bit scared"—she held Nutmeg's forepaws an inch apart to show how scared—"because I didn't know anyone. But I'm pretty good with people, as you may have noticed." Nutmeg emphasized this by nodding his head up and down. "And my besties Taylor and Katie are in my homeroom—you'll meet them tonight, they're coming for dinner." She was truly excited by the prospect of being with her friends, of giving them her energy. There must have been a time, as a child himself, as a shipmate, when he too would have been that excited. But then he had always been an elderly child and a duty-bound shipmate (and a well-intended though occasionally mistaken friend).

"So now it's perfect."

"Perfect!" Although she knew he was teasing her, she joined in his smile.

The house hid all its people until they appeared at the table. Placed between the two besties, he got them talking about themselves with Megan chiming in. Taylor had a head start on the other two with her curves and her air of knowing what lay ahead of them and welcoming it. Already she was something to look at, therefore vulnerable as Blake had been but without, it seemed, Blake's intelligence. Katie was as innocent as Megan. Tonight the three friends were silly together and spoke in tongues.

Phil, an amateur chef, provided the main dish—grilled fillet of cod coated with chipotle sauce and dredged in a paprika-cornmeal mixture—while Sarah had ordered the rest of the meal as takeout.

Knife and fork poised, a half-smile on his lips, Phil was waiting for his father-in-law's reaction. His soft face and wispy hair gave him the appearance of a regular guy, nothing like the man with a dozen years of higher education who could restore mangled hands to everyday use.

"Delicious, Phil. Well done."

"Blake says I'm competing with Chef Yannick."

"I think it's just what he would like." And this was true, though Yannick might slip in a suggestion of how to keep the skin of the fish from sticking to the grill.

"Who's Yannick?" asked Megan. Katie wanted to know too but thought it might be rude for a guest to ask. Taylor sat with a smile on her lovely face, having learned already that information would come to her unbidden.

"An old friend of mine is lucky enough to have his own chef," he explained.

"An old friend from the Navy," Phil said. "An admiral."

"Now CEO of a Top 100 company," said Sarah.

"And you're friends," exulted Megan, happy with hers.

"Well, yes. I've been working for him in Chicago, but once upon a time, long ago in the Navy, he worked for me. In our ship, a destroyer. I was his lieutenant. He was just 'George'—the junior ensign. I put him on report once."

"What's that?" asked Phil. Sarah too was interested, having never heard this story, since he had never told it before (whatever Slate might think of his loyalty) except once to his wife, during a shared condemnation of service infidelity.

She remembered it. Beyond that he couldn't tell what she was thinking. Despite his careful phrasing she knew that he no longer worked for Slate; she didn't know why. They were due for a candid talk.

"We had gone to Portland, Oregon for the annual Rose Festival. It was fun piloting on the Willamette River—that's what I liked. The Festival was a big deal there, an international event. It included a parade with a queen and her court, beautiful girls from countries all over the world. The queen sat on a float in her lacy white gown with her ladies around her and the floor covered with rose pedals."

"What about Slate?" asked Sarah.

"I'm coming to him. After the parade we opened the ship to the public. There was a steady stream of people, and the crew were at various stations to explain the equipment—the wheel, the signal lamps, the engines."

"And Slate?"

"This was before 9/11, and there wasn't great security, but we did have a quick-response team standing by, and Slate was in charge of them. They were supposed to be paying attention to the visitors. Looking out for potential troublemakers. I was the duty officer, responsible to the captain for the safety of the ship in his absence. I might even have to get the ship underway without him."

"And *Slate?*" all of them asked.

"I was making my rounds through the ship. I stopped by the wardroom, the officers' mess, for a cup of coffee, and there he was, on the couch, feeling up the queen of the Rose Festival."

Almost everyone enjoyed this story. Mad remembered and smiled. The young girls were plainly thrilled. Sarah, however, doctor that she was, who liked the risqué as much as her mother did, felt obliged to disapprove of a man taking advantage of a vulnerable woman.

Blake asked, "How did he explain it?"

"I mean, they were all tangled up, her gown was half off her shoulders, he had his back to me. Her eyes told him that something was wrong. He stopped kissing her, twisted himself around, and said, as formal as you please, "Haruko, may I present Lieutenant B.R. Hilty, third in command? Brad, this is Haruko Imanaga, from the float."

[126]

"He was feeling her *up!*" cried Megan.

"In her *gown,*" said Katie.

"Was she stacked?" Phil asked, which prompted more shouting and one dissenting voice: "What can that possibly matter?"

"How would Phil know?" he put in. "He works on *hands.*"

The hilarity overflowed the table.

Phil helped Mad to her feet, and she leaned against Sarah as the two women walked off for her evening dose. Katie collared Megan and Taylor to clear the table and do the dishes. He went to his room—Sarah's study had a sofa-bed—and changed out of his travel clothes. A car came up the gravel driveway; adult women had a moment together, and then hilarity went out the door. He walked down the hall and knocked at the guest room.

"Come in, Bradford."

The curtains were drawn, the TV, muted, provided the only light, and he was a moment finding her among the shadows. She switched on a reading lamp near her head—her hair covered her scalp like a bathing cap, for she had taken off her wig. Her eyes were sunken and large: if the medicine were saving her life, it wasn't obvious. No doubt the dinner had tired her.

"Am I disturbing you?"

"One person to talk to is a blessing. Six is agony. Do you know how addicted I've become to that stupid TV? I can't bear to listen, but the image is company."

Which preempted him from asking her to turn it off.

"Have you ever noticed that everyone has an opinion?"

"I had noticed that," he said.

"I can't bear to hear them. I want unanimity. When Dr. Kohl and Sarah and Slate were all fighting about what to do with me, it was too much to think about: I would rather have croaked."

"Thank God you didn't Are you glad you came here, then? Are you feeling any better?"

"That's too many questions." This, from the woman who in their talk by the swimming pool had repeated back to him his Entropy List exactly in order. "If we're going to have a chat," she said, "put on some other lights and I'll turn off the TV."

She seemed to have settled in the room. He had been under the impression that she was only visiting until he could join her, when they would move into the apartment Sarah had rented for them on Beacon Hill. Her usual photos stood on the vanity, but a large one taken at the Grand Canyon, a favorite, which had hung on a wall in Chicago, had been hung up here. A golden family. Sarah would have been fourteen and Adam seven. In their hiking clothes, surrounded by the ancient rock, they hardly looked as if they belonged to the Navy...except for Adam's ballcap from the *Fletcher* and his own preoccupied smile that chafed to be at the next duty station.

"What happened with you and Slate?" she asked.

"The end of my leave of absence. The end of my employment at CSA. Possibly the end of my friendship, with both Slate and Julia."

No apparent shock. "What's the severance package?"

"It wasn't discussed. I assume, angry as he was, he'll take care of me."

"Why angry?"

He told her about his suspicions, apparently founded upon false evidence.

"I don't know," she said. "Character is destiny."

"What do you mean?"

"He's capable of it, as is Robin. With you out of the picture, there would be no one to fight him. Julia's angry with you because you uncovered what she's always suspected herself. Eventually, Slate might forgive you, but she never will."

"He's also going to break the unions."

"Now you're talking about actual harm."

She was pleased with herself for this didacticism.

"Actual harm?"

"What are a few lives—exceptionally privileged lives at that—compared to tens of thousands?—employees, investors, customers. He's going to do to CSA what Welch did to GE. By the time he dies, he'll have only a worthless lifestyle and a fourth wife who despises him."

"And the memory of a friendship. It seems a shame after thirty-nine years. Telling that story at dinner about the Rose Festival, I could hardly believe I was talking about an ex-friend."

"I always thought it was a one-way friendship."

"And now you don't care."

She was still, too tired to gesture. Like a talking head, only her lips moved.

"All those months after the diagnosis, Bradford? Feeling so bad? Feeling that I really must be dying because I was so weak and hurt so much? At some point I just gave up on the world. Do you know what that means? It wasn't acceptance or resignation either: Yes, I stopped caring. You, Adam, Sarah, this family, all of it. Certainly Slate and Julia and the evil Robin McGill. I adopted the attitude I'll have when I'm dead: *Thank God it's over!* Now, apparently—Sarah's friend Dr. Mentov says it's a certainty—I'm going to live for a while longer, maybe a normal lifespan. It's frightening. It is. I've got to start caring again. I understand duty—wife, mother, grandmother; friend if I still have any. It's not the same as caring. How do I get that back? What is important enough to care about? When I do die, what will I have cared enough to be pleased that I did. On the other hand, what will I have cared enough to regret?"

"I think it will come back," he said. "Unless the rest of your life is a misery. But gradually, maybe imperceptibly, until one day something really moves you. Maybe something I do," he added with a smile.

"And who knows what that will be?"

"Apparently it will *not* be as chief of quality assurance at a major multinational aerospace firm. That simplifies the choices. Either the Navy or bust."

"My money's on bust. While I finish treatment, you're going to stay at the Beacon Hill place?"

"With you?"

Here was a gesture: she wiggled her little person, from shoulders to feet. "Not yet, please. We'd probably be fine together, as much as we irritate each other. But despite what I said a moment ago, it would be too much silence. I need some normal life around me, after all. I'm better here for a while. Maybe I can help these people. The cat will keep me company."

Which belied all that came before it. What she really wanted was to be alone. It would have been nice if she had said something warmer than *fine together.* But as Megan had done with him, he gave her the kindness of accepting her intended meaning. She needed to be re-called to life: As a sign of acceptance he kissed her cheek.

"You know," he said by way of parting for the night, "firing me and breaking up the friendship were bad, but what was worse was that he made me feel like a bumbler, a clown, some combination of Don Quixote and Inspector Clouseau. I mean, am I not a competent person? Have I not made a difference in the world? Have I not done all the things I've prided myself on?"

"You have, very competent. Other than a tendency to fall in love. But none of it matters," she replied.

The Ghosts of the Fifty-fourth Massachusetts

On Monday, after a weekend of feeling superfluous, he moved into the apartment on Joy Street, in Beacon Hill. As a short-term residence it met expectations. All the powders and liquids were properly stocked; an artificial agent responded to his questions. The only thing lacking was the patient for whom it had been rented.

He was one day getting settled and another wrapping up his life in Chicago. About the house he contacted three realtors and asked for bids. About his late employment he learned that his office belongings would be boxed up and shipped to him. The chief of HR explained his severance package down to the fine print; as expected, Slate had been generous. His company email account had been closed, but he was given the option, which he accepted, of attaching to it an innocuous auto reply that provided his contact information, so far as there was any.

Two days: by Wednesday he was bored. The election wasn't for eight weeks. Mad's treatment might last through the end of the year. Adam's project in Taipei would keep him away at least that long. Blake wasn't due until the second week of January. His Entropy List was paused, all except for that item that asked what he would do with the rest of his life.

Boston, the home of legendary heroes, was a real place in his imagining. The American Revolution had started here; and the Emancipation. Many historic sites were still to be seen. USS *Constitution*—"Old Ironsides"—was still in commission, still rigged and armed as if HMS *Guerriere* were still waiting for her just outside the harbor. Sometimes she got underway as far as Fort Independence, mooring again on her opposite side so the worms and sea creatures had to start over. If only he had commanded her, or any of the big frigates of the era, he could retire on the glory.

[131]

Glory: none shone brighter than The Glory Regiment. On this thought he went for a walk.

At the north side of Boston Common, across from the State House, stood *The Shaw Memorial,* flanked by still-living elm trees that remembered its unveiling in 1897. He never came to Boston without paying a visit, and now he could see it every day if he wished. His own refuge from boredom and low spirits, from apathy: these young Black soldiers, resolute of face, marching toward the unknown. To break the chains binding both Black and White; to prove their own manhood, for many of them at the cost of losing it.

As subjects of the sculptor's supreme art, these soldiers were living characters. As ghosts they were insuperable, indefatigable, incapable of losing hope. Colonel Shaw on his horse, certainly; and in the ranks William Carney, thanks to whom, in the doomed assault on Fort Wagner, "Old Glory never touched the ground"; Stephen Swails, the first Black officer in the regiment; Lewis Douglass, son of the great Frederick; and G.G. Cezar who led the charge at Olustee shouting, "Three Cheers for Massachusetts and seven dollars a month!"—perhaps the first cynical battle cry in history, the Blacks having been denied the same pay as Whites for risking just as much.

"Any food, marse?" From behind the monolith a Black soldier in Union blue approached him. Wearing a forage cap with a brass bugle and *54* on the crown. Holding, properly grounded, the Enfield 1853 rifle-musket or something like it, with a carving knife duct-taped to the barrel. Across his shoulder was a cartridge box and on his back the standard knapsack. His blue coat had three gold chevrons on the sleeves, apparently glossed with paint. About five foot five, he looked emaciated.

"Perfect!" Hilty said. "You've stepped out of history."

"Doan know nuttin' 'bout no hist'ry. Been marchin' summat terrible. Ise powerful hongry. No stoppin' to eat since yestidy, allus marchin' 'n' fightin', 'n' we'se attackin'

Wagner this evenin'. Aincha got even some liddle biddy morsel of bacon?"

"What's your name, Sergeant?"

The soldier came more or less to attention. His blackened shoes had once played basketball. "William H. Carney, C Company," he said in a different voice, crisply articulated. "Born into slavery. Escaped through the Underground Railway. Enlisted to serve my country—my country as well as yours, sir. At Fort Wagner, though badly wounded and many comrades fallen around me, I didn't let Old Glory touch the bloody sand. On behalf of a grateful nation, the President of the United States gave me this."

He drew apart the lapels of his coat. Underneath was a gold medal on a blue ribbon hanging around his neck: the Congressional Medal of Honor. Probably the pendant wouldn't bear too close a look. The tiny stars had been splotched onto the ribbon with acrylic paint.

"I know you, Sergeant Carney."

"Then you know my sad ending. The medal came thirty-seven years after the deed. Hero that I was, I struggled to feed my family. In 1908, as a lowly elevator boy, I fell to my death when the cable parted."

"A tragedy. Can I find you among these soldiers?"

"No sir, all the soldiers were too old to pose for Saint-Gaudens. He hired boys off the street—two bits apiece."

"Oh. I just thought—"

"Does make you think, doesn't it. Here: it's all in this book." Laying the musket and knapsack on the ground, he proffered a few pages stapled together for a binding, reproduced as the toner was running out.

"Thank you. I'll treasure it."

"And a map, if you want to walk in their footsteps."

"That would be great."

"And DVDs of *Glory,* the movie about us. Morgan Freeman plays me."

"So he did"—a kindly falsehood, since Carney's role was unscripted. "This has been a wonderful experience," he said. "I've taught Civil War history myself. No matter what the revisionists claimed, it was all about slavery, wasn't it. Slavery sanctioned by racism. You've brought those days alive. Now, tell me: what's your real name?"

A mistake: the soldier returned to character.

The moment was suspended between them.

"Here," he said. "To support your research." And gave him one hundred dollars.

"You should write about me," the man called to him as he crossed Beacon Street.

"So what was he?" Sarah asked. "Homeless?"

"I wouldn't think so. He was well-spoken."

"A walking sandwich board for some museum?"

He shrugged. Since that encounter he had avoided the *Shaw*. "More of a busker, probably," he said. "I don't know where he got his kit. Some of it was authentic."

She looked thoughtful, then her thoughts moved on: she had enough mysteries in her life.

They were having lunch in the hospital cafeteria, the only time she could give him. Even so, a hurried lunch: she was wearing scrubs after a surgery that, it seemed, had displeased her, and with another to perform in an hour. While they ate, her phone kept *ting*-ing and she kept looking down to read the little tiles; so frequent and invariable a habit it became irresistible: glancing up, she shielded the phone with her other hand. As a child, at *Scrabble,* she would hide her letters in just this way. Sometimes he would sneak a look and suggest words to tease her.

"Are you settling in all right?" she asked, having apparently forgotten that this question at the beginning of the meal had led to Sergeant Carney.

"It's been three weeks. All lights are bright lights. My inbox and my call log have never been so quiet. As you know, since you arranged it for Mom, there's maid service at the apartment. I have so little to do I'm finding myself cleaning up after the maid."

"I'll take the average of your life and mine."

"Deal. Mom is looking better."

"The treatment is working," she said while reading a text. "Markers are down." She looked at him, back in the moment, actually thinking about her answer as a physician must. "Still, there are risks. The long-term research is incomplete—that's why we had such resistance to enrolling her. COVID, a URI, pneumonia, almost any infection could be serious."

"And what do you think of her morale?"

"Seems all right." She smiled briefly to cover her evasiveness. It would be typical of the triangular relationship if Mad had shared with both of them her lack of interest in the world, but each, thinking that they alone held the secret, didn't speak of it with the other. "No doubt it will pick up," she added, "when she's really cured."

"And is there such a thing? Could it come back?"

"Hillary says there is."

"She's been a good friend to you."

"As far as she can be." At that moment her phone sounded an imperative *ting,* which forbade further talk until she had thumbed an answer.

He leaned back and stretched. Around him was the hospital tableau: knots of healthcare workers in the scrubs of their service, along with families and patients at the mercy of the others' care.

She looked at him with her jaws clenched, a sunburst of lines around her lips.

"What is it, love?" But he never called her that.

"One of those short, dry messages that leave so much unsaid. My surgeries, some of them, haven't been meeting benchmarks for standards of care. Not that any patient hasn't done well. Still, metrics. The chief of our service has assigned me a coach—that text told me his name. He's a dickhead. But if my performance doesn't improve, I may be suspended from certain kinds of procedures—the interesting ones. I'll be the bitch in the expensive suit who tells the patients they might lose their sight but my colleague, the dickhead, will save it through his brilliant technique."

She looked off. She hated confessing to him any failure or even problem in her life.

"That sounds like just a pause." It was on the tip of his tongue to say that baseball players in a slump often benefitted from being taken out of the lineup for a few games; to gain some perspective.

"It would be more than a pause, but thank you. When they bench you in eye surgery, it's a long road back. Long and humiliating."

"I don't worry. You're a star."

She smiled, sad and fond. "Always the cheerleader."

They fell silent. The time left was dwindling to the moment when she would rise and remind him of her surgery and he would regret all the things unsaid.

She slid the phone into her purse. "Dad, the one reason I wanted this lunch—besides seeing you, of course—was to ask what you thought about Blake."

"I can't be sure, but from the look of her I'd say she's going to have a girl. She's carrying high."

"Very good. It can't be an old wives' tale if my father believes it. A girl, then."

"I'm not sure she'll allow it to be assigned a gender."

She laughed, a single bark. "You can't say such things."

"I can't. I wish—and I'm crossing a Rubicon of political correctness here—I wish she were Lisa again. When I talk to her, I always have to translate *Lisa* into *Blake*. There's a time-lag, as if we were speaking through a bad internet connection. What's worse is I think she knows."

"Try dealing with the subject as a mother and a biologist. But that's for another time. What I wonder is what you think she should do after the baby is born."

Which meant that she wanted him to support her own position. Blake must give up the child. Her life would be ruined otherwise. Especially now, single motherhood was an impossible burden, and it was only going to get harder. She needed a superior education, she needed to do high-level work, and she needed to make money. She listened to him, they had bonded. Whatever he thought personally, he must convince her to give up the child.

She finished with a winning smile, as if confident that he agreed. They had always been a team.

"What does Phil think?" he asked. If this had been an open discussion of the case, he would have replied that self-reliance was even more important than education.

"He thinks he's Oprah Winfrey," Sarah replied.

In Maslov's hierarchy of questions about the rest of his life, one question felt as fundamental as breathing itself: he must become the assistant secretary of the navy for quality assurance.

To that end he was now worried about the election. He sat in his apartment and devoured the political coverage. Its contradictions didn't help. Harris's charismatic smile made the voters want to see her as not Biden, but behind the glamour her ideas were as old and feeble as he was. She would not let the country go backward (she said), but her vision of forward wouldn't reduce the cost of eggs. Four years in the White House Sit Room might have trained her to be president, but hadn't this included the botched withdrawal from Afghanistan? Like Biden, she loved Israel to a fault, only the fault included thirty thousand Palestinian dead.

On the other side, madness, but people weren't listening. Trump was a convicted felon; he disrespected, objectified, harassed, assaulted, and bought off women; he was promising essentially to overthrow the government, to avenge the last election against basically all Americans: nobody cared except those cheering him on. According to the polls—and they couldn't be wrong about him again—it was a distinct possibility that the electorate would be brought to believe that he was what he said was, a mythical figure, a demigod, the image of himself on *The Apprentice;* and all his enemies, all the women who didn't score at least a seven on the scale of Trump, everyone in the way, and losers everywhere would be fired.

The only one he could share his fears with was Mad, who was still beyond fear, who didn't care about anything.

He returned to his rambling.

The sun mellowed, the sky softened, and autumn fever gave him courage. He revisited the *Shaw.* Under one of the shedding elm trees Sergeant Carney had set up a table with his kit and his products for sale. He was beguiling a family of tourists, who bought the stapled pamphlet, the much-folded map, and the DVD of *Glory,* refusing the change.

While he waited he read the inscriptions on the monolith. One of them said:

> The Black rank and file volunteered when disaster clouded the Union Cause. Served without pay for eighteen months till given that of white troops. Faced threatened enslavement if captured. Were brave in action. Patient under heavy and dangerous labors. And cheerful amid hardships and privations.

How splendid! How he wanted to be cheerful amid hardships and privations!

"Any hardtack, marse?" The soldier was leaning over the balustrade to solicit him.

"Sergeant Carney, do you remember me?"

It seemed so. But he looked at him warily, as if he might want his hundred dollars back. "Yes sir?"

He came around to the front of the memorial. "What have you been up to?"

"Just soldiering. It's been wet." Had it? "One day last week I crawled into my *tente d'abri*—my dog tent. People thought I was homeless. Actually, that was a good day for receivables."

"But you're not homeless."

"I'm not. I live in Southey with my wife and child."

A promising fact. Without some other employment a part-time Civil War reenactor couldn't make a living.

"I want to talk to you about this knowledge you have. I've been thinking I could use your help."

Carney looked at him slightly askance. He might be interested, but he must know first whether helping this white man would be safe; safe and dignified.

"I have a project in mind. I need a research assistant. The work would be indoors, not very exciting but steady. We'd search references—books, magazines, newspapers— and if they seemed right for my project we'd make copies of them. I'm an historian—at least I used to be—and I want to write a book about the Fifty-fourth. Do you know Captain Emilio?"

Of course he did. In his kit he had Emilio's book, which he produced now. On its deckle edge was stamped *Boston Public Library*.

"I want to write from the perspective of the survivors when this memorial was dedicated, thirty-two years later."

Carney waited for more. He might go either way.

"Those men fought—volunteered to fight—for justice, and when the survivors returned for the unveiling here, it must have seemed to many of them that the country had retreated from its promises: the end of Reconstruction, Jim Crow, the KKK, the lynchings. Separate and unequal, cruelly so. It's happening today too, isn't it. This election is about that, though my book won't be finished by then. Retreating on promises. You yourself, I imagine, are living with the results. I want my readers to see the parallels."

"And would I find your other books in the library?"

"I'm not published. Well, a few papers, no books. I taught high school history in Virginia for six years. Before that I served in the Navy. I was a senior officer, of equal rank with Shaw. I can organize material, and I can write—write to make a reader feel my meaning—but it would be a big job and take a long time if I had to do it myself. Would you like to help me—say, three days a week? On the other days you could come here or do any other work you have."

"For how long?"

"I can guarantee you at least two months. If you'll meet me tomorrow morning at the library"—a public place in case Carney still worried that this might be a trap—"I'll bring a contract for us to sign. The job pays five hundred dollars a week until the end of November—no, that would leave you high and dry before Christmas—let's say until the end of the year. Even if I'm called away, you'll continue with the research. After that we'll assess."

"What do I wear?"

"Whatever you like. Not your uniform unless you want to. I should ask"—he should have asked already—"if you are comfortable in a library setting."

"Do you mean, am I literate?"

"I guess I do." Do you know what you read? he added to himself. Do you think?

"I guess we'll find out, then. By the way, my name is William Carney, same as the soldier."

"No kidding!"

"No kidding. Emilio's book is why I do this."

Of course he could read. As it turned out, this William Carney was better educated than one would think. And he was reliable, he wasn't lazy, he had an eye for the telling detail—he would have been an outstanding research assistant...except that he was indiscriminate. He couldn't make up his mind what was useful so he copied everything. An optimist would say that he was taking his

[140]

responsibilities seriously. He was more than casually interested in the subject. He wanted to set the world straight about the electric fences he himself had faced. His employer might write the words, but he would give them moral sanction. Only he, of the two, had that standing. So on the one hand he overwhelmed Hilty with material for notes; on the other each note must meet his standards. As a result the work progressed by inches.

With better teamwork it would have gone faster. Hilty was sometimes away from their carrel in the library, and when he returned he might find a boxful of material to digest. All well and good: he could sift through this while Carney himself was away. But at this next appearance Carney would review the siftings with a powerful memory of the originals, and an entire session might be wasted as they argued the merits of decisions already made.

It was possible, however, that they were making progress of another kind. Sometimes the arguments were heated, but every argument ended with an understanding and occasionally with a joke. He tried not to throw his weight around. It was possible that a friendship was being formed. Once or twice he proposed a meal, but Carney always made an excuse, never reciprocating. Possibly he had secrets to keep. Sometimes it seemed that the default position of the two races was distrust, distance, the unconfessed racism that might be costing Harris so much. Whatever was going on, he wanted this man's respect. He had never had to work for such a thing before.

The Croquet Match

With the precision that marked him as an eminent hand surgeon, Phil drove his blue ball through the wicket, earning another turn. He and Hilty were a team, blue and black; Sarah and Mad, red and yellow, were their opponents. The match had begun with lighthearted trash talk, but by now Sarah and Phil had gotten on each other's nerves, the taunts were a little cruel, and the outcome had become more important than it should have been.

Phil used his continuation turn to roquet Sarah's ball, at which her face wore a hard smile of acknowledgment. Like Chamberlain at Munich, he tried peace at any price: his croquet stroke, hardly more than a tap, left her with a reasonable line to the next wicket.

She, unappeased, measured the shot with care, and Mad showed where to aim with her foot. Sarah's mallet swung like a pendulum, and the red ball rolled toward the wicket, followed the side-slope expertly—and stopped, nearly through.

"Point!" Mad cried, applauding with one hand and the mallet head.

"I don't think so," Phil said. "Only partway through."

"Close enough?" Hilty asked.

Phil turned on him. "Whose side are you on, partner? It needs to be one hundred percent through the wicket. You of all people should uphold the rules."

"So *now* the rules matter?" Sarah asked. At the beginning of the match, Phil had scoffed when she brought out the deadness board. Sarah and Phil played in a Wellesley league, which kept track of deadness and required white attire; they were wearing white today.

"Your rules always matter, dearest," he replied with elaborate gallantry. "The rest of us labor in ignorance. Brad, a firm shot through the wicket and into the red ball would stop all this nagging."

"Do my best," he said, not knowing whether he should do his best or not. The ball had its own ideas: it hit a twig he'd neglected to remove and jumped onto another line, rolling past the wicket rather than through it.

"No way! You're tanking to appease your daughter."

"But what a daughter!" he exclaimed.

The errant shot reordered the pattern of play into a chase. Phil led, then Sarah, then Mad, and finally himself. Each turn was skilled, generally getting through the wickets in the minimum number of strokes, but no player was able to roquet the ball in front of him. In fact the game went flat: Megan, who sat just beyond the court, stopped cheering for both sides and devoted her attention to twisting Nutmeg into pretzel shapes. After the hilarity of that first dinner she had been her usual happy self but with occasional faraway moments. Her BFFs had left her: Taylor for a more mature group of girls who went to parties and had boyfriends, and Katie, whose parents were Trump supporters, after a fight about the election.

"Where's Blake?" he asked. "Why isn't she rooting for the Blue and Black?"

"In their room reading organic chemistry," Sarah said. "They'll be ahead of their classmates next year."

"Sorry, I meant *they*"—but at their lunch in the hospital, Blake had been *she.*

Phil put his hands on his hips, so that the mallet jutted down at an angle, like a dislocated leg. *"She* is just fine," he said. "Both the word and the person. And she hasn't made up her mind about next year, despite frequent attempts at parental pressure."

"Gap years are delusional," Sarah replied. "They need to continue their education."

"She'll be nursing a baby."

"They're going to give birth. After that no one knows."

Mad sat next to Megan and stroked the cat. Only Nutmeg looked on.

"She says she wants to raise it," Phil replied. "If so, we've agreed to support her decision. Her first priority will be the

[144]

child. If she has to take a gap year—or two or three—in terms of her long life it won't make any difference."

"Except that they'll fall behind."

"And what good has being ahead done you? Megan, you are not to get pregnant until I say so."

Megan agreed by way of Nutmeg.

"It's your shot," Phil said to end the discussion.

Sarah walked to her ball, set her feet, and made a perfect swing. Along the only line possible, the ball traveled a re-markable distance through the next wicket, changed course slightly after clipping one wire, and smacked into Phil's. "You've got to be shitting me," Phil said amid the general praise. As a follow-through Sarah strode to the two balls, put Phil's in front of her own, which she trapped under her angled foot, swung the mallet mightily a second time, and sent his ball out of bounds, whizzing past Megan, who had to lunge into Mad to avoid it, and over a rise and down the thicketed bank toward the creek that fed Wellesley lake.

An emotional anticlimax: the ball had disappeared, stop-ping play, and the four adults couldn't find it. Megan took this opportunity to carry Nutmeg into the house. Sarah and Phil followed her, perhaps to score further points off each other in private. Phil called over his shoulder, "Leave it. We need another set anyway." But Hilty and Mad had too often looked for their children's toys to aban-don the habit now. First they searched the creek bank, sweeping their mallets through the growth, hoping for an answering *clunk*. Then they followed the creek through unlikely places while he poked at the shallows.

"Are you well enough for all this effort?" he asked.

"I'm supposed to be. Actually, I'm better."

"Three cheers for genetic engineering. Maybe your genes think you're twenty-five now."

"God forbid."

"But that was a happy time, don't you think? Married with a child—a child like her. I was doing well on the old *Fletcher*. Washington after that."

She smiled.

"Blake knows her own mind," he said.

"If Sarah will let her."

"Personally, I think she ought to keep the child and go to college—no gap years."

"I do too."

How good this felt.

"They'll make it work somehow," he said.

"They meaning the family or they meaning Blake?"

"The family."

"She'll be nursing a baby"—mocking Phil. "She can study while she nurses. And these days colleges are super flexible."

"I agree. So you have no problem calling her *she.*"

"Pronouns really piss me off," she said.

"Me too!"

"Of course she's *she.* Just as Hannah Brigand is *he.* Yes, she told me about Hannah. I know you know."

"I was sworn to secrecy."

"He—the one with the sperm. How else did they get into this predicament? I'm sorry but biology counts."

They were well down toward the lake now, so that with each thrust into the water the mallet, unresisted, nearly slipped from his hand. The ball could never have carried this far. They turned back.

"Does Hannah know?" he asked.

"He must. How many girls has he slept with?"

"Even if he does, it's not likely he's told his parents."

"Not likely."

"It needs to be out in the open."

"I'll leave that to you. Put it on your Entropy List."

"I don't know. That list is getting awfully full."

"What's number one?"

"You, of course. Feeling well. Caring again."

"I was sure telling you that was a mistake."

"Not a mistake. Over the years I've learned—sometimes to my cost—that life isn't much without feelings."

"A nice bit of wisdom except that it doesn't take into account PTSD, adult children of alcoholic parents, and unexpectedly surviving terminal illnesses."

"Me, me, and you."

"Correct."

He slashed through some rushes to delay responding. "Here's a thought, Mad: you might set aside the question of whether *you* care about life and simply focus on living for others."

"As if I haven't done enough of that already."

"You have. And I've gotten the benefit of it more than anyone. But I don't mean me. I mean other people you can help."

"Like the people I'm living with now."

"Maybe. If you think you can help them. But it could be anyone. It just might be your way back in."

"My way back in?"

"Into caring. Rather than feeling you're already dead."

"I'd like to help Sarah," she admitted. "If she'd let me."

"What does Sarah need?"

"Balance. She's with a coach now, someone she doesn't like. But she says he's helped her—they have metrics for everything, just like your baseball. He evaluates her next month. If she passes she can return to performing some of the more difficult surgeries, and there would be a plan for the others."

"And if not?"

"Continued probation—whatever they call it—or if it's really negative they put her on the bench."

"Might not that be better for her stress level?"

She grunted. "You know Sarah: she'd never get over it. If she doesn't retire as chief of medicine her whole life will have been a failure."

"And is Phil helping or hurting with all this?"

"Hurting, no doubt about it. Everything comes so easily to him. Everything except sympathy. When you poke below the surface—speaking of which, is that the ball?" It wasn't, it was a rock. "When you poke below that good-old-boy manner...well, I wish he were more sympathetic. I wish he'd take her in his arms and tell her how exceptional she is. How great. Great by anyone's standards but hers. And that's—"

"That's the problem," they finished in union.

"Aha!" For just then he found the ball. Heedless of the consequences, in truth seeking her approval for even this small act of daring, he waded into the creek and pulled it out. His shoes filled with water, his socks wicked it up to his calves, and when he had the dripping ball in his hand he found that his shirtsleeve was dripping too. The feeling was uncomfortably cold and deeply satisfying. She led him to the house, for the recumbent sun wouldn't warm him. After sliding open the glass door and taking a step inside, she turned to take his clothes, which she wrung out over the patio. In his briefs and T-shirt—white for croquet!—he followed her inside.

Sarah met them, holding her phone. "It's Slate. He needs to talk to you. Says it's urgent." She looked at him frankly: his termination from CSA following a rupture with his best friend had made its way into the family scuttlebutt.

"Can I call him after I've changed my clothes?"

"He says now. He doesn't care if you're naked."

They were all at general quarters. In the basement theater Sarah passed the phone to Phil, who hooked it up to the giant screen. The image divided. On the left was Slate, in shirtsleeves, waiting expectantly in his office. On the right talking heads reported a developing story.

As Phil adjusted the lighting, Blake trained a camera, and there he himself was, a postage stamp in the corner of Slate's frame: this was not to be just a phone call but a video conference.

Before speaking Slate looked him up and down with that half-suppressed, half-projected smile of amusement. Receiving this Hilty resisted the temptation to cover his groin. Whatever else he had on his mind, Slate's sense of the ridiculous was always at work. Another characteristic of greatness; he himself, when he spoke to a purpose, was insensible, his audience a blur.

The smile disappeared, and the lips began to move. Whatever this was, it was important enough to reach out to his former friend after *I doubt if our paths will cross again.* That scene was fresh. How do you follow it?

"Phil, has he been briefed? Very well, I'll wait. I can see he's in the middle of something. Brad, raise your hand when you're ready to talk." He turned to someone off camera—Anna, perhaps—received a leather folder, and began to peruse its contents, or appeared to.

The news anchor was interviewing a series of experts across the split. The gist of the story was clear at once: shortly after 6 p.m. local time, El Al Flight 72, traveling from Munich to Tel Aviv, had disappeared from radar a few miles west of the city of La Spezia, Italy, apparently into the Ligurian Sea. The aircraft, a popular export built by CSA, had once had a troubled safety record, but its problems had seemed to be fixed in recent years after a major overhaul of both the aircraft's design and CSA's management team. La Spezia was home to Italy's largest naval base. Already choppers had located a debris field. There were no apparent survivors.

A video clip that played repeatedly in the background showed what looked like the piece of a wing, light grey against the beryl green surface, floating to and fro in the waves. Evidently a strong mistral was blowing through the Alps, causing high seas—challenging conditions for recovery.

He raised his hand. When Slate didn't notice, or didn't appear to, he said, "All right, I've got the picture."

Slate set the folder aside. He looked confident, indeed weirdly confident, as he did when announcing a dividend to the shareholders. "I'm sending a team there to help with the investigation and protect our interests. Some folks from Commercial Airplanes. Melissa Trent Richards"—Melissa, chief of Corporate Communications, possessed such gravitas that she was usually referred to by her full name. "And you as my personal representative. If you agree."

Whichever part of his brain it was that signaled caution was trying to get his attention. So were his wife and daughter with all they knew about his friend. So was the sting of *I doubt if our paths will cross again,* unaddressed, which felt as raw as this news.

"Of course I'll go," he replied, even as he saw Phil nodding his encouragement.

Of course he would; Slate had assumed as much. "My plane will stop at Logan to pick you up. At—when is it, Anna?—at nine p.m. your time. Does that work for you?"

"It does." He would need to make a stop in Beacon Hill. "But tell me"—he glanced at Mad and Sarah—"what's my position?"

A thoughtful pause, certainly disingenuous, for Slate would have spoken already to HR and Dorothea Billups.

"Better for you to go as contractor. An expert in the subject area. Name your price."

But this wasn't about money.

"Can we take this offline?" he asked.

Slate reached toward the camera, and the left side of the screen went blank. He picked up Sarah's phone and switched off Bluetooth. The edge of the phone hurt his ear.

"What's the buzz?" he asked. "Was it us?"

"You know what?" Slate said. "I wouldn't be surprised if it was terrorism. El Al? Flight 72?—the year of the Munich Olympics? What in hell were the Israelis thinking to give a flight that number and then to operate it on that route, from Germany to Israel, a country at war on three fronts? How many terrorist groups, known and unknown, would love to bring down that plane?"

"But their planes have antimissile defenses."

"Sometimes the obvious answer *is* the answer. A bomb, slipped through German security. Not that whatever the cause, this isn't a terrible thing, of course."

"Are you in trouble, then?"

"Who knows? It's all imagery anyway."

"But we're going to look at this honestly and report what we find, correct? Without regard to our image."

"I'm asking you to do this, after an admittedly unfortunate passage between us, because I trust you to do the right thing. Will that do, Commodore?"

Meaning: *Will that do for a promise?*

And: *Will that do for an apology, which I never give?*

In the darkened theater his face was warm. He was blushing for something that hadn't happened yet. Slate had picked him because he trusted him to go along.

"What do you think?" he asked, hanging up the call.

Mad snorted. "A little late to be asking that, don't you think? *Whatever you say, master."*

"What else could I tell him? *No, I don't care how many lives have been lost, you hurt my feelings?"*

"You did the right thing," Phil said. "You'll keep the turkeys honest."

Sarah looked as if she wasn't so sure.

Four

El Al Flight 72

An Impartial Investigation

On the plane he was warmly welcomed by Roddy Denton and Melissa Trent Richards. The others, led by Ricky Mountjoy, though civil enough, appeared to be wary of him, Slate's friend after all. He never knew what to say to Ricky, a former test pilot with a ballsy attitude. Then again, if the accident proved to be CSA's fault, Ricky would be looking at the wrong end of the sword. Typical of the breed, he pretended not to care.

After an overnight flight, whose occasional turbulence reminded them of the doomed jetliner, Roddy landed them at Pisa, the closest airport, and several cars took them to La Spezia. He rode with Melissa Trent Richards, who gossiped about life in the tower as if he still worked there. Slate was in final negotiations with the Chinese for the biggest contract in their history, which apparently they wanted to sign before, as they thought, Trump took office. Bill McIntyre was dead—she sympathized with him that he hadn't been told. Dorothea Billups was doing well in quality assurance, having waited all her life for this chance.

The cars in front of them turned off at Lerici, the resort town; his and Melissa's car continued to the naval base. By the end of that first day, while Ricky and his team were resting on the beach, he and she had become conspicuous in the headquarters of the recovery effort. This was in one of two giant domes raised for the purpose. The Italians, sensitive to their responsibility and perhaps to the opportunity, had moved their warships from the Molo Grande, which dominated the inner harbor of the base. Beneath a hanging American flag Hilty and Melissa set up their cubicle and looked around for ways to be useful. The sight of the two of them, senior people in business clothes, carrying tables and chairs across the plastic floor

[155]

could not help but make a good impression, whatever the investigation proved.

The headquarters was truly international—from the first he felt proud to be a part of it. Naval officers, crash investigators, figures from intelligence and law enforcement, the news media, politicians...not to mention the teams of workers who dove on the site, craned up pieces of the wreckage, barged them to the port, and assembled them in the center of the dome into the three-dimensional puzzle of the aircraft, whose outlines were already taking shape.

In the second dome coroners identified the remains, and morticians prepared them for return to their families. Hilty and Melissa spent time there as well. Including the crew, the victims numbered two hundred and three from eight countries, among them eleven children. Their last moments must have been unimaginably horrible: the shock, confusion, pain, and dislocation, feeling their lives leave them, reaching for empty space. Perhaps there was false hope; perhaps they were bitterly undeceived.

"Maybe it was sudden," he said.

"Better that way," she said. "Better a bomb onboard."

That first evening Melissa walked with him as far as the Corso Cavour. She had taken a hotel room near the train station, farther north, while he was staying in a piazza close to the base. When he pressed the button of the intercom, a voice called something cheerful in Italian, the door was buzzed open, and he took the lift to the fourth floor, where a woman almost his own age and a young girl were waiting to check him in.

The woman was named Vittoria. She lived in an apartment on the fifth floor, the top floor of the building, with her granddaughter, Romola, age twelve. Vittoria spoke English but not well, and Romola, then and later, interpreted for her in a clear voice with a natural inflection.

Still on Boston time, he wasn't ready to go to bed yet, which was good because Vittoria and Romola gave him the fullest possible introduction to the apartment. They bade him log into the wifi to be sure the credentials worked. They showed him how the steel shutters were raised and lowered and how, when lowered, they blocked the sounds of the street. To use the stove he must turn on the gas main; besides cooking, it brewed coffee in a clever device called a Moka Pot, one cup at a time of pure espresso, the grounds for which Vittoria had furnished from a favorite bar. When he praised the coffee, they excused themselves and a few minutes later returned, smiling, with a decorated plate of Canestrelli, delicate lemon shortbread cookies powdered with sugar and shaped like a flower.

Vittoria made sounds like a confection, and Romola said, "She baked this for you in the afternoon. The kitchen was hot, but she didn't mind it."

"So kind!" he enthused, and both of them were pleased. Romola was in love with the world. Her grandmother was the child grown up, soft and giving, with hopeful eyes.

From this happy start his stay at the apartment could not have been more pleasant—it was just a shame that the reason for it was so sad. Whenever he came home, after eight or ten hours of reconstructing the horrors of the accident, one or both of them were waiting with a treat. He enjoyed Pan di Spagna, a cake from Genoa; Pandolce, a sweetbread with candied fruits and nuts, ineffably spiced, also from Genoa; and Meringhi Genovese, pastry swirls filled with cream.

"All so nice," he said. "I wish I were *in* Genoa."

As received the wish became a command. "She said she will take you to Genoa on a visit."

"Oh, no—too much kindness"

"Ma noi siamo Genovese," Vittoria said, and apparently that settled the matter. Since he was unlikely to have any time for sightseeing after the investigation, he simply thanked them and accepted the gifts. Besides the treats they showed him the hole in the wall on the Via del Prione from which the coffee grounds had come; a place

that served the best coffee he had tasted outside of Turkey. They shopped with him at the farmers' market on the Piazza Cavour and at the fish market at the marina where he was handed chunks of fish that just an hour before had been swimming. When they learned about his background, they took him to the naval museum, which featured the models of extremely beautiful ships and also weapons of the Second World War, many of them used with the highest courage and ingenuity against his own country. Perhaps because of this, with their delicacy of manners they didn't go in with him.

He and Melissa worked long hours with ever more sober forebodings. (Not Ricky: after a symbolic appearance at the dome, he flew back to Chicago.) Almost daily other causes of the accident were ruled out. As the aircraft shell took form and it became clear that there had been no bomb or missile, the security people left, and the investigation narrowed its scope to equipment failure and pilot error. Telemetry received by El Al had reported a sudden loss of cabin pressure. On the port side of the aircraft a panel was missing at one of the emergency doors.

After a delay caused by the weather at the crash site, the voice and data recorders were found. The cabin pressure alarm confirmed the telemetry. With the loss of pressure the plane had pitched up and inverted. The cockpit voices, eerily businesslike, revealed frustrated attempts to restore controlled flight: evidently the master computer had failed to respond as the pilots had been trained to expect. Multiple commands; for each one a negative. *The aircraft belongs to God now,* the captain said in Hebrew. Then came incoherent sounds suggestive of the world ending. Then silence.

"I need air," said Melissa.

So did he. They walked from the dome, through the naval base, and out the main gate to the public garden, but there the statue of Garibaldi, victorious, dominant, seemed to inhibit free speech, so they continued down through the marina to a bench overlooking the gulf. Like Sandburg's *Grass,* the hard blue surface hid what was underneath.

"Pitched up and inverted," she said. "Can you imagine what that must have been like in the cabin?"

"The senselessness of it. The feeling in the dome just now was *Who's responsible for this?*"

"That's becoming all too clear, isn't it."

Behind fashionably oversized glasses, her small eyes burned. High-minded as she was, she had competed all her life. *"The aircraft belongs to God now:* social media will be a lynch mob. I need to do a presser."

"With a statement from Slate?"

"Too soon. We don't know for sure, and we don't know how or why. But we need to be proactive. Legal will want to craft something to cover our six."

"I suppose so."

"And that's part of the problem, Brad. If this goes the way I think it's going to, Slate will be under tremendous pressure to obfuscate it. I won't be a party to that. I won't lie to save someone's job."

"Nor I. He'll need to accept responsibility."

"And I worry about that. There's something off with him. Maybe it's the China deal. He's obsessed with the share price. He's going after the unions. He's got some sort of personal entanglement. I know he's your friend, but I need to say it."

I know he's your friend—the classic disclaimer. She was right—she was saying all the things he believed himself—but along with everything else now, and with all its difficulties, life was calling him to stand by Slate. Friends did lie for each other. Even killed for each other. Crossed continents and climbed mountains and weathered storms for each other. Gave away personal fortunes as if they were nothing. And introverts like him, who hated to ask for favors, pulled one lever after another to achieve that last glancing influence that would save a friend.

[159]

Then again, friends didn't let friends drive drunk. Friends showed up at interventions.

"I don't know. He did fire me, Melissa."

"He did, I'm sorry. More prickishness. I framed that as creative differences. But this is something else again."

"So how can I help?"

"Find the facts. Then persuade him not to make up some bogus story that the press will tear to pieces."

An airplane flew high above them; an immeasurably small and remote event, like a silver penpoint drawing a line on the other side of a glass. How difficult to think that the source was a ninety-ton aircraft carrying hundreds of people with thousands of years of existence. Too high, too fast, too cold, too thin. Humans were never meant to fly.

He touched her hand. "Something I learned as a ship's captain, Melissa: when in doubt go to the scene and judge for yourself. That's North Charleston now. I'll need help from a couple of people at the office—quietly. Can you arrange that for me?"

Error Code

North Charleston was the site of the plant where the El Al model had been built. He arrived there on Monday the twenty-first, ten days after the accident. By then, as predicted, *The aircraft belongs to God* had gone viral.

The plant had a guesthouse, a red-brick Georgian with five second-floor windows across the front. No one had changed the door code. Inside, bless Melissa, were the two people he needed to help him discover how and why Flight 72 had crashed. One had been on vacation anyway; the other had called in with a fictitious family emergency. They worked in different offices on the quality assurance floor: it would require a highly suspicious manager to link the two absences.

Mike Wojciechowski had been Hilty's expert on airframes. After a dozen years in Dayton, he had transferred to North Charleston to build the El Al model, where, fearlessly outspoken, he was on the path to termination when Hilty brought him to Chicago. He was the personification of the changes in culture that the company needed. Slate supported him, Hilty counseled him to a softer approach, and as so often happens after a bad beginning, soon the factory leadership couldn't imagine building airplanes without him.

After the pleasant reunion Mike and he walked to the plant. Emily Loomis, his control systems person, tanned from Aruba, stayed at the house to troubleshoot the master computer code.

At the plant, though no longer one of them, he was welcomed—indeed, hailed. After so many years he had come to admire the character of these Southerners: that wire core within the soft braid of plantation hospitality; their gentle, slightly formal way of speaking unwelcome words; their love of design for its own sake; their oneness with nature, mostly to do with guns and fishing rods. He had learned to talk to them without posing, confident that forthrightness and honesty and tact (and discretion) would always be valued. Now, of course, he wanted to discover the truth about Flight 72. But another truth was present here too: he was biased to hope that the fault lay elsewhere.

His friends had similar feelings, but in reverse: loyal to their co-workers, with that first proof of loyalty called *omerta,* yet demoralized by grief and guilt. They watched the funerals as if they were happening in their own community. A young woman from Tel Aviv, who had lost the man flying home to marry her, said, "After the Seventh of October I didn't think it was possible to feel greater pain. Perhaps this is God's plan to unite Arabs and Jews through suffering." In the plant no one had found such hope. During that day and the next, workers lined up to confess both actual failings and improbabilities.

While he himself drank coffee in the corner offices, Mike on the assembly lines kept drilling down for nuggets of fact. By the end of the first day he had a poke of deviations from procedure that might have caused the emergency door to unseal. Tomorrow, once he had checked a few things, he would write up his findings. Half the mystery was basically solved.

Returning to the guesthouse for dinner, they found Emily stuck on the other half. In the living room she sat in front of three computer screens after a long session with the subcontractor who had written the control system code. She and the sub had run eighteen simulations using every conceivable response by the air crew to the sudden change in cabin pressure and aircraft attitude. In every case, including no response at all, the crew should have righted the plane. Both pilots were extremely well trained —among the best in the world. As reservists in the Israeli Air Force, flying F-16s, they had logged thousands of hours of flight time, including combat. Their experience, their training, even their voices on the cockpit recorder argued convincingly that they had remained calm and followed correct procedure. This wasn't pilot error.

Emily, a hard charger, knew and loved computers in the same way that the Greatest Generation had known and loved cars; but she never lost sight of the fact that the human brain is the most complex and capable object in the universe. For her the Turing Test was based on a false choice. He told her to keep at it, running the simulation as many ways as she and the sub could think of, including the pathologically unreasonable. Then he went up to his bedroom to learn how safe he was in his own simulation.

It was after midnight in La Spezia, but while Emily had been explaining pilot work flow, Melissa Trent Richards had texted him, wanting to talk.

"No, I'm in New York," she said. "Waiting for the flight to Chicago. I did the presser, which of course turned into a feeding frenzy. I'm going home to ensure our response is coherent. And accurate. What have you discovered?"

"Nothing for release yet." To this she responded with a sound originating in the throat like someone hocking up spit, so he quickly explained the mounting evidence that the missing piece from the port emergency door had been jury-rigged. "Even so, the computer should have righted the plane. We're running simulations with the sub to understand why it didn't."

"Who's the sub?" She was taking notes. He gave her the name and address, the number of years in business, and the other aircraft models whose control systems they had engineered. "And the exact nomenclature of the door molding? Technical terms help build credibility."

"I hope to give you concrete facts tomorrow," he said. "In both areas. Then I'd better return to La Spezia since that's my remit. Does Slate know I'm here?"

"Probably. Dorothea knows, for sure. She left me a stinker of a message this afternoon: didn't understand why I had sent two of her employees to North Charleston without asking her first, and what were they doing there, and why so much secrecy."

"I hope you blamed me."

She chuckled. "I haven't replied to her yet. Too busy."

"I'll take care of it. Have you spoken to Slate?"

"Twice, to hammer out an interim position. The terrible tragedy, the loss of life. Now is the time for mourning the victims. We are investigating the accident with all possible urgency, but in keeping with our values we will get it right not do it fast. When we know the answers, we will report them with total transparency."

"How's he holding up?"

"Not well. He kept wanting to emphasize that no cause could be ruled out, including pilot error, murder-suicide, and terrorism. It's what I told you, Brad: he's digging his grave with his teeth, and I'll not participate in a coverup. Someone needs to get his attention."

Some dear friend, no doubt.

Because Emily and the sub were still tracing code, Mike and he went for takeout. On an impulse, two men trying to please the lady of the house, they set the table with linen and silver, transferred the food to china, and poured the wine into a carafe.

"Well, this is nice," she said, coming in from the living room. She started to report on progress, but he stopped her with that adage from the Navy: no shop talk until coffee. To give other talk an impetus he described La Spezia: the excellence of its harbor, which didn't interest them, the glut of billionaires' yachts, which did; the food—oh the food!—the tomatoes, the olives, the basil, the handmade pasta. The comity, if that wasn't too grand a word, between people and resources. But more than this the devotion to living and celebrating life, with all things in their natural proportion.

"Here in the U.S.," he said, "we *pursue* culture. The Italians surround themselves with it, they breathe it in. You should see the stonework, the colors of the buildings, the tile! First they make beauty, only then money. Their language is more beautiful than precise—maybe that's why they speak with their hands so much." He laughed. "And maybe why they sing so well."

Emily was moved.

Mike said, "Maybe you want to live there, then."

"Not qualified. My world is more precise than beautiful."

"So are you coming back to us?"

She wanted to know this too. Now that they had gone out on a limb for him, would he be around to protect them? Not long before then, Dorothea had fired the most ardent disciple of the Hilty Method.

"Sure, it's possible," he began. Then, "No, forgive me, I was carried away by the moment, I told you what you wanted to hear. Transparency, right? Slate and I had a disagreement. Unrelated to work, but I probably won't be coming back. This is just a favor I felt I owed him."

"Don't worry, *you're* safe," Mike said to Emily, who had made a noise. "You and Greene both. You're below the line of fire and he's above it."

"I agree with the first part," he said. "Just keep doing your best. We don't shoot the messenger."

Mike scoffed. "We don't shoot anyone with good hair. Greene could say, 'Oops, we only installed one engine,' and everyone would say, 'Oh, so honest—and isn't he handsome!'"

"That's a bit cynical, Mike." Particularly since the guy with the good hair saved your job.

"Watch and see," Wojciechowski said.

"Coffee?" asked Emily. "Since we're talking shop."

ᗺᗺᗺ

After dinner he called Dorothea, but as before the call was picked up by Tabby Smith, Dorothea's wife, who was polite but cold. He flashed to a fantasy of what it must be like for two such cold women to make love. Tabby said that Dorothea was unavailable; perhaps she could call him back? So he sent her an email taking responsibility for Mike and Emily, reporting the progress of the investigation, and promising to remind all concerned that when the aircraft was lost, she had been chief of quality assurance for only one month, he for six years before her, instituting policies with which she had often disagreed.

Degrees of Transparency

At five o'clock in the morning—but after twice crossing six time zones his body had no idea what time it was—Emily banged on his door. "We found it!" she shouted. "Found it!" Throwing on his clothes, then untucking his shirt to match the hour, he let her in. She looked as if she might dance. At work her persona was cool, precise, expert, and wise beyond her years. At the Christmas party, licensed to be herself, she had been girlish, giddy, impulsive, and, frankly, immodest. If she had been worried about losing her job, now she was exultant to have solved the great mystery, a feat worthy of Turing.

"Well done!" he croaked, trying to match her high spirits. "What was it?"

"The crew responded to the emergency by being creative, and the software wasn't prepared for that."

"Why, what did they do?"

She waved the question away. "Too technical to explain. Basically, but this isn't it exactly, they pretended they were in their F-16s."

"But they followed procedure?"

"Oh yes. Creatively followed it."

"So would you call this a bug? Is there a fix?"

The joke in IT circles was *It's not a bug, it's a feature.* But if an inability to process creative airmanship was a feature, then the company—that is, Slate—might argue that pilot error, if not the cause, was an aggravating factor. Which, given the faulty door molding, would be a travesty. But Trump had taught everyone to double down on a lie, and now he could see that his best friend, who despite failings had never been a liar, would be tempted to follow suit. It seemed that leaders everywhere were making up their own reality. Maybe the public expected it.

If he himself didn't act, his own honor would be at risk. Act he must: like Melissa he would not be part of a coverup.

[167]

"Is there a fix?"

She had waited until his attention returned.

"Don't know yet. Some sort of *Else* condition might work, if a default response wouldn't cause more problems than it solved. They'll have to test every conceivable case, assuming that we keep them as the sub. It could be months."

"From this, can we rule out pilot error?"

"Actually," she went on, eyes gleaming, "AI could solve the problem. But you'd need a dedicated neural network on the ground with a constant two-way data link. The plane would no longer be autonomous." She too returned from her reverie. "Very expensive and years from now."

"So, no pilot error?"

"Not unless creative thinking is an error."

"He wants you to confirm that it's all our fault," said Mike, appearing out of the shadows.

"I don't know. Is it?"

"Yes!" Mike and he said in unison.

"All right, then. You've convinced me."

"*Whose* fault is it?" he asked.

"Ours, for sure," she replied. "And ours to fix."

"Very good."

Addressing them both in the dusk of the room, he said: "The story's on fire, no surprise there. We talked about this at dinner. Before we went to bed I spoke to Melissa Trent Richards. We need to help her craft an admission of responsibility that all the departments can unite behind—with Legal that won't be easy." He didn't add that with Slate it might prove impossible. "I'm leaving North Charleston in the morning. You two finish up and write your reports. Make them substantive but not too long. Then, Emily, you fly back to Aruba and, Mike, please tell your uncle I hope he's feeling better." This drew a smile from them. "And both of you feel proud of yourselves: you've done good, hard, honest work, a credit to Chance-Stevens-Arrowsmith, and you have nothing to fear from what's coming. I still have some clout in the tower, and I'll make sure you are safe."

Famous last words, his wife would say.

Twenty-four hours later he was sitting in a rental car in Georgetown, outside Robin McGill's Victorian townhouse. The streetlights shining through the rain on the windshield filled the car with spots. The house was dark. In front of him was Robin's security detail, one agent on watch (more or less) while the other slept. When he had pulled up behind their car at five o'clock in the morning, it had behooved him to introduce himself. He needed to see Secretary McGill on an urgent matter. No, he hadn't made an appointment—the matter had just come up. When the house showed signs of life he would phone her—he had her number, see?—and then share the phone with them so she could tell them it was all right. By chance one of the agents remembered him from the night of the job offer; perhaps they had heard the rumors about his appointment.

If he did say so himself, a piece of clever detective work had brought him here. After giving Mike and Emily their instructions, he had changed his clothes and driven to the Charlston airport, uncertain of where to go from there. Roddy Denton, Slate's pilot, was the cleverness. He called him, not directly but through that app which only the feckless needed to use. The map showed him—or at least his phone—in one of the buildings on the Washington Mall.

A minute later Roddy called him.

"Ah, mate. Thank you so much. You found my phone. How stupid of me not to look in my pocket! Scared the tourists around me half to death—they thought it must be some emergency alert—but what do they count, eh?"

"Where are you?"

"National Gallery of Art. Wonderful place. You?"

"Charleston. I'm coming your way."

"Excellent! Ordinarily I'd be delighted to drop down and pick you up, but we're on four-hour standby with *El Jefe*. Plane's at BWI being serviced. I saw a chance to get in touch with my feminine side."

"And where is Slate now, Roddy?"

"He didn't confide that particular piece of intelligence before he drove off. Anything I told you would just be a guess."

But his tone of voice knew.

"Are you heading back to Chicago?"

"I expect we are. I've a flight plan ready, just in case."

"Maybe I can do you a favor," he said. "Here's a head's-up. I haven't confirmed it with him yet, but I feel reasonably sure that you'll be flying to Pisa tonight. He's going to make an appearance at the La Spezia site. I don't know who else will be coming."

"Thanks, mate. Pisa again. I'll be ready."

"Mind you, I could be wrong."

"If I see any flying pigs I'll let you know."

When he got to Washington, Occam's Razor sent him to the hotel, at the Tidal Basin, where CSA had an account. Like the door code in North Charleston, the front desk agent welcomed him back. No, Admiral Greene wasn't staying just now: the penthouse was available if he wanted it. Thank you, he replied, his usual room would be great. He checked in, had a meal, and went to bed early, setting his alarm for zero dark thirty. He didn't sleep much.

Bill McIntyre's house in Bethesda would have been the other place to check, but poor Bill—his own friend too—had died almost before he knew he was sick; and before he could bring him any comfort. As he sat in the car, the ghosts of people to whom he might have meant more in his life walked silently by. They included—well, who didn't they include? Family, friends, shipmates, loves and lost loves. Playmates going back to Diane Ward, who lived next door to them in Northriver, whose diagnosis of brain cancer at the age of sixteen had been more than her father could bear, so that after the improbably successful surgery she must attend the grievous funeral—from all of this Hilty's parents had sheltered him, and he had carried on the privilege, the privilege of not knowing. He didn't know today whether Diane was alive or dead. Think of the Italians, *making* their lives. Why, he was just passing through!

Lights were on in the house—perhaps in that upper room. It was six. Twilight was diluting the street light. A caller could disturb her now. Propriety had stood the midwatch and gone to bed, relieved by the rough and tumble of governing.

Robin pretended to be surprised as people did when, beyond escape, they were found out. He said the right words, needing only a few of them, and the security detail heard her reply that she would be down in a minute.

Dressed for work, she led him into the dining room and sat at the table with her back to the open door, pointing to the seat opposite. A coffee service had been laid out, finely-boned china decorated with the secretary's blue flag: she poured for each of them and waited for him to speak. The dark brown coffee trembled under the light as he lifted his cup. Steam rose—it was too hot—Starbucks had been sued by a scalded customer—and he had to work the sip around to keep from making a fool of himself.

Familiar footsteps of a particular vigor descended the stairs, and Slate came into the room.

Robin offered her cheek as he bent over, and her eyes flickered with affection in return for the kiss. He poured coffee for himself and sat beside her, facing his friend.

"Good morning, Brad."

He was cordial, relaxed, well balanced, complacent.

"Good morning, Slate. We've identified the causes of the accident as you tasked me to do, and I've brought reports from two of my former employees—by the way I poached them from Dorothea on my own authority."

He handed the reports across. Mike's was a page and a half, Emily's almost three, even after some editing by him. Slate leaned against Robin so they could read

[171]

together. Her eyes moved faster down the page, and she looked at Hilty while she waited for Slate to finish.

"So," Slate said. "The Number Two Emergency Door Delta Corner Seal and Fairing"—he named the part with his usual ridicule of complexity—"and the control system logic."

"That's right. There's no doubt about either."

"I'll tell Dorothea *I* sent you Mike and Emily."

"Thank you."

Slate reread a passage in Emily's report and turned to make a three-way conversation. "I was right, then: pilot error *was* a material factor."

"There was no pilot error," he said. "When the door blew out, the burble caused an abrupt loss of lift on that side, so severe it rolled the aircraft and increased the pitch. As this was going on, the tumbling of the unbelted passengers toward the tail—I'm sorry, this is a horrifying image— moved the center of gravity so far aft so quickly that the pitch continued to rise almost to the vertical, where the control system couldn't handle it. At that point the aircraft, falling tail-first, was irrecoverable."

"But then the pilots tried to dive."

"They followed the procedure for a stall."

"She says their reaction was learned in fighter jets."

"She was talking about good airmanship generally. She also says, specifically, that there was no pilot error."

"But how would she know? She's a computer scientist. I'll bet you a year's pay she has never flown an aircraft in her life." What allowed him to get away with twisting facts and making specious arguments—and attacking the credentials of people—was his sincerity. All these false things would pass right through the minds of his audience, who only saw his empathy and conviction.

Or his hair.

"The NTSB are going to come to the same conclusion, Slate. It's on us."

"But these things are never black and white. Are you telling me I should stand up before the world—before the Chinese—and be the first to condemn my product? I don't think so."

This was going to take longer with Slate than usual. Usually, at the first sign of resistance to his opinion, he deferred to the experts. Whether Robin's presence would help or hurt was an open question.

As if he were thinking the same thing—that meta view of a situation that gave him such insight into the motivations of people, and in which his sense of the ridiculous was so active—Slate turned to her. "Your views, Madam Secretary?"

She was looking straight ahead, not at Hilty but at some future beyond him. Beyond them all. Her beautiful eyes slowly filled with tears, making them even larger.

"I think you two are quarreling about something else," she whispered.

"I do too," Slate declared. "Something personal. Our intrepid shamus here has solved an incidental case. How about that, sir?"

"Please don't," she said.

But he was too indignant to hear her.

"What do all those lives matter? You have a chance to settle a score going back to—I don't know—going back to 2009 or so. Why don't I just plead guilty to that, and then we can talk about the problem in front of us."

"Not while I'm here," Robin said, rising from the table. Slate rose as well to embrace—or restrain—her, but she pushed down on his shoulders. "I'm going in. I have other quarrels to hear." Then with a supple twist she swung back to face him, taking his cheeks in both her hands. He was looking up into her eyes, so close that her tears fell on his face. "Whatever you decide, I'm sure you'll do the right thing. That's you, never forget it."

She left the room and the house. He pictured the agent in the shotgun seat elbowing the driver awake and then rushing to hold the door for her, over whom a daze had

[173]

stolen—or would she have put on her work face by then? The car pulled away from the curb. He looked at his watch: 7:06: sunrise, exactly.

"All right, let's have it," Slate said. "Since you're here."

"Which subject?"

"Me. Haven't you learned that by now? Always me." But when he started to speak, Slate put up his hand. "I have to eat something first. There's only leftovers in the fridge. I haven't eaten a leftover since I stopped driving a car. But Robin keeps a shelf of trail bars in the pantry, which she seems to think are as good as food."

He returned in a minute with a bar for each of them. His was something with chocolate. The bar he offered Hilty was called Lemon Zest. Both of them had to bite with their molars, for the consistency was like bark.

Slate's emerging, musing smile: "I stopped you cold at the hotdog place, but apparently you did some thinking later. Well, we've had these conversations before, you and I, haven't we."

"I'm not here about your marriage," he replied. "What you and Julia and Robin decide is none of my business."

"If only that were true. But you know what's best for all three of us."

"I care about your wife's happiness, certainly. And yours. I know that you and Robin have a thing for each other. But it seems to me that you're failing to use one of your gifts, something I've always admired."

"Mmph. Do tell." Though he admired the prospect of praise, Slate couldn't help laughing at this freighted conversation with their mouths full of sticky trail bar.

"Maybe the most important gift of all: you look ahead to consequences. How do you think you're going to feel—down the road—if you walk away from your marriage to Julia after so many years of being happy?"

"Maybe not as happy as we appeared."

"Breaking that incomparable heart."

"Maybe I can live with it. Maybe I *have* looked ahead. I'm sixty-four, Brad. None of my male progenitors have made it past sixty. Don't I deserve, for however short a time I have left, to be as happy as possible? Robin and I click—we always have. I won't bore you with our sex life, but it's transformative, for both of us. Feelings this powerful must be destiny. I know you have questions about how I'm leading the company, what I'm trying to do with the unions. And this accident puts all that and me at risk. But whatever happens, I'll be alive; and so will Robin after Trump fires her. We could go off somewhere—to my house in Thailand, say—and live happily ever after."

"But the wake always follows you."

"I know," Slate said after a minute. "And I'm not sure the stress of it wouldn't kill me—wouldn't that be ironic? And, yes, it would break Julia's heart. Am I really that selfish?"

"What does Robin want?"

"She's afraid. You saw her. Tears. I suppose that should tell me something."

"Painful," he said. He finished the bar with a dangerous gulp, his fingers sticky. The wrapper was on the table, out of place. He balled it up and threw it at the trash can.

"I didn't come here," he said, "to ruin your love affair or make you feel bad about breaking your wedding vows. I'm here officially, as your contractor. But as your friend—or former friend or whatever we are—as an unbiased observer who knows you well, let me give you this advice:

"Don't do it. The cost is too high, and your nature is too sensitive. Julia suspects the truth: you can repair that. But if you run away with Robin, it really will break her heart, and it will anger her too, anger her deeply, that daughter of coal miners. There will be no going back and no possible happiness. All three of you will be miserable—you most of all—miserable and guilt-ridden because the women depended on you to be a man. Don't do it, Slate. Robin wants you to tell her you can't go on. Julia is

waiting, hoping, to be reassured that her nightmarish im-
aginings are only that. Whatever you decide about Flight
72, go home afterwards and stay out of Washington."

There had been a scramble by the lesser chiefs to make
the plane. Those whom Slate chose to accompany him
were Franklin Townes, the CEO of Commercial Aircraft;
Gabriel D'Addario, the chief of Manufacturing and Supply; Nancy Beeman, the chief legal officer; Melissa Trent
Richards of Corporate Communications; and, in place of
Dorothea, himself.

Major Dickerson, the chief financial officer, had wanted
to come, but his appearance might suggest to the audience
that profit, not truth, or justice, or common humanity, had
brought Slate to La Spezia.

The reports from Mike and Emily had been circulated,
and everyone on the aircraft, probably including Roddy
Denton at the controls, had an opinion about the speech.
Competition let rip. In Hilty's experience it was the odd
vanity of speechwriters that the principal shouldn't be
consulted until the speech was ready (although D'Addario pitched his voice to be heard in the forward seats).
Nancy Beeman held the tiebreaker, since the estimate of
legal liability, which was not to leave the aircraft, ran
into the billions. After everyone had their say, Melissa
rewrote the mélange to give it a single voice; Slate's voice,
which she could represent so well.

From Pisa the lesser chiefs and Hilty went ahead.
Within the dome Melissa took charge of the event while he
went around renewing acquaintance. When Slate's car arrived, the scene was set, the lighting and sound were right,
and the cameras caught his expression of sober dignity as
he shook hands with the admiral commanding the naval
base and the head of the investigation.

Wearing black armbands, the CSA team mounted the
dais, which was five steps high and almost underneath
the reassembled nose of the aircraft. D'Addario and

Townes stood behind their chief to either side, with Hilty and the two women in the background.

The work in the dome had been paused. In the silence, without testing the microphone first, Slate introduced himself. The speech that his subordinates had striven to write for him was in his pocket.

It was clear from the evidence, he said, that the basic cause of this terrible tragedy were two failures in CSA's manufacturing and supply chain.

D'Addario straightened his shoulders; Townes gave him a glance meant to be noticed, if not photographed.

The failures were...Slate described them in layman's terms from Mike's and Emily's reports. The explanation carried no spin; it offered no opinions. These were facts, and CSA—he himself—accepted responsibility for them, whatever other evidence might still be discovered.

Behind her Nancy Beeman's clasped hands tightened into a single fist. The back of Melissa's hand just grazed his. A problem for the one, vindication for the other.

On the floor—everyone was standing, Melissa had in-sisted on no chairs—the press was aroused, and even the investigators and local officials were kibitzing.

After a pause to let them finish, Slate continued.

Chance-Stevens-Arrowsmith, he said, had no higher calling than safety. No business interest came close. Safety was their credo every hour of every day. The rec-ord of recent years had been gratifying, but clearly now there was more to do. They would correct these specific failures and any underlying weaknesses in policy or pro-cess or culture that had enabled them. Their employees everywhere were proud of the quality of their work. So they would continue to be. Their customers and *their* cus-tomers could be sure of this. So could the countless people around the world served by the networks of commerce and transportation whose standard of living had been raised so high.

"Ever since the Wright brothers," he said, "it has been a custom in aviation to refer to those who fly as *souls on*

[177]

board. We will never forget that our mission is to safe-guard human souls. Thank you."

"God almighty, wonderful," Townes said.

Beeman turned to Hilty to hide her heaving breast.

Taking no questions, Slate descended to the floor and approached the officials. He shook every hand and heard what the different investigators had done and thought. With his entourage he then went to the other dome to second the work of the morticians and medical examiners. Then to the office of Rear Admiral Acta, commander of the base, to meet some of the grieving families. Grieving and angry, whose anger now had a target. He let the company and himself be apostrophized. He said that he was deeply sorry. He spoke of his regret and shame. He would not demean the dignity of their grief by bringing up restitution, but he gave each person his card. The moment lasted just long enough. The families had heard him with growing respect. Before the session ended, they were sharing stories about the lives of their loved ones.

Outside, sedans were lined up at the curb; the chiefs would return to Pisa to fly home and await developments. Melissa and Townes got into the penultimate car, leaving the last for Slate and himself.

Slate put his arm around him and steered him a few steps toward the water.

Whatever was coming, he preempted it.

"Good speech, Slate. I think you may have saved your own soul. I'm proud of you."

"So my idol faces forward again in the Hilty pantheon?"

One honorable act completed, one to go, he thought.

"Listen, friend," Slate continued. "I need you to stay here and look after our interests—my interests—in the wrap-up. I accepted responsibility, yes. But the NTSB report means a lot to us. Of course it must be completely factual...*but*...but sometimes with these things—we saw this in the Navy—sometimes the findings of fact are colored by the opinions, and I'm counting on you to keep them separate. How much longer do you think all this will go on?" He waved at the mole, where ships should be instead of domes.

"Hard to say. When I was here before, I didn't see any particular urgency."

"Well, that would be helpful too, a little urgency. You won't be surprised to know that the call for heads will start soon. I don't care for myself—yesterday you dented my *Weltanschauung*. Don't smirk—I would have come to it eventually. I really don't care if I stay or go. But the people in those cars do, and I hope we can avoid the wholesale slaughter of crises past. We have a good team. This was one accident. Your legacy will carry on."

"You've got to protect Dorothea," he said. "It would be an awful irony if, having just been confirmed in the job—finally, after four times filling the role—she should pay for my mistakes, most of which she tried to prevent."

"Wilco. I'll see to it. Neither of you made mistakes. Meanwhile, keep me informed."

Townes's face was in the window, looking on.

He watched the cars until they disappeared. Then he walked down the mole and returned to the investigators' dome, where the work had resumed. On his phone were pages of texts from anxious executives. On the news sites *It Was Us!* was the banner headline. On the Dow CSA's share price had dropped eighteen percent.

Pazienza

The air was still, as before a first bolt of lightning. The share price kept falling, he received ever more texts from Chicago, but CSA made no announcements after Slate's surprising disclosure, and as far as he knew no one had been fired.

Under the dome the work went on. The reassembly of the aircraft left almost nothing to the imagination. Nose-on to it, you might even squint and think it could fly again. The Number Two Emergency Door was sealed all around except for a slender gap at three o'clock: this was where the fatal piece should have been, the piece that broke away, perhaps miles before the final plunge. Too far from the crash site to be located and recovered, you would think, except by impossible chance. Yet the investigators were determined to find it. He participated in a video conference to answer the question whether it would have drifted with the current or sunk beneath it. Only when tests showed that it was neutrally buoyant, therefore suspended somewhere in the trillions of acre-feet of the Ligurian Sea, was the search called off.

(Beyond the door the cabin was a mess. Some of the seats were still in their places; others had been hurled into shocking positions. The oxygen masks hung by their tubing like plants that grew downward. In its eerie disorder the cabin was eloquent, a story of disaster. Things fall apart. Here was the end of the world.)

Although he wanted to be home, wherever that was, he owed it to the dead to finish the investigation. Each of the experts had his area of expertise, but if he said so himself, none thought as globally and critically as he did. He understood the accident all the way back to the man on the assembly line who, having argued with his wife that day, had overtorqued a bolt and not reported it—just the kind of human failing that Congressman Hastings

[181]

had predicted. Policy, process, and culture, Slate had said: he felt a pang of regret. He should have done more to save the souls of El Al Flight 72, and there was more that he could do in the future if he were given another chance. But that chance had passed to his loyal deputy.

Pending the storm. He had an idea that his reports to Chicago might influence who would stay and who would go. Well, he would insist on the facts—two of the NTSB investigators were highly opinionated. But if the tone of the report mattered, he would save Slate Greene if he could and Dorothea Billups because he must and leave the rest to—to what? He didn't believe in fate. Even after all this he believed in himself.

Although change was imminent, his days fell into a kind of routine. He walked to and from the naval base, increasingly as low clouds overhung the surrounding hills and one rain shower after another swept across the city. He had a few favorite places for dinner: a lot of pizza, better than he had ever tasted before, but also local dishes like *farinata*—chickpea pancakes—and *trofie*—worms of pasta coated with pesto—and scary-looking seafood so delicious that, once he overcame his aversion, it promised to make him a fish-lover for life.

Returning to his apartment, he would soon be met by Vittoria and Romola with their platter of treats. However hard his day had been, this never failed to lift his spirits. He was superior to all their other tenants: his existence gave them pleasure: they wanted *him* to like *them:* such were their obvious feelings. Romola, her hands flirting with each other, might go on and on about her adventures at school while Vittoria nodded and smiled her approval of the teller of the tale and her audience.

After a refreshing night's sleep in the marvelous bed, he started each day like a native. His breakfast consisted of a tiny cup of coffee and a cornetto, an Italian croissant. Vittoria's favorite coffee house, the Caffeteria Orefici, on

Via del Prione, was no wider than the dining car of a train
and, by the same necessity, just as efficient. In its center
was the bar. On the left, in the working area, one woman
operated the gleaming espresso machine while the other,
a sociable member of Generation Z, took the orders, served
the pastries, and collected the payment, remembering all
the totals despite the distraction of so many friends looking in from the via.

Each morning he would stand at the bar, shoulder-to-
shoulder with the other customers, mostly men, drinking
first the small tumbler of sparkling water served with the
coffee to cleanse the palate and then the espresso or, if he
were feeling homesick, a glass of latte with its crema
styled on top in the image of a fern leaf. Three bites to
finish the cornetto, a few sips to drain the coffee, no more
than ten minutes, and he was gone, leaving a coin on the
bar and receiving a cheerful farewell: *Ciao, grazie mille,
a domani.* They knew him: like Vittoria and Romola they
were pleased to spend time with him: to them he was
more than another tourist. There would be no joy in the
dome—there were few enough human interactions—but
somewhere in his state of mind the pleasures of La Spezia
lingered.

To the right of the narrow shop was a sitting area, with
a counter in the rear and in the front two small tables set
against the wall, each with its two small chairs. Friend
though he was of the establishment, he had never taken
the time to sit there. On the last day of the investigation,
however, a man in a herringbone cap came up to the bar
whose approving glance seemed to know him. Perhaps he
was someone met and forgotten in the early days of the
investigation. He had a singular face, crazed with lines,
out of which his prominent blue eyes looked almost challenging. Yet there was something distinguished in the way
he carried himself, confident and self-propelled, as if the
world would always wait for him.

"Chance meetings may be destiny," the man said in
English, "if we pay attention. Why don't you sit with me?

I am Giuliano Pazienza." He paused. His look inquired if the gentleman might know his name—no matter if not. When Hilty introduced himself, they shook hands and the man went on:

"American."

"That's right."

"Here for the investigation, I would think."

"Yes. My company built the aircraft."

"Very sad. But your chief has defied his lawyers and accepted the responsibility. That has caused a good press here"—he tapped a folded newspaper—"and in Germany and Israel."

Of course it had! And the world's opinion mattered! Here was actual field intelligence, which should be useful in determining accountability. He would find an article in the Italian media and email it to Slate: *Consider the big picture.* He was eager to act on the idea before he went to the dome, but the gravitas of the other man held him in something like a thrall.

"You're well informed, Signore Pazienza."

"As much as I can be. At one time in my life I used to make the news."

"Oh?"

"I was prime minister of this country. Yes!" He smiled to share in the surprise. "In the early Oughts. Briefly, of course, since Italian governments fall with every breath of wind. But I was. What do your movies say? They can never take that away from me."

"It's an honor to meet you, Prime Minister. Do you live here now?"

"In Milano. I am chairman of La Scala."

"The famous opera."

"Yes, and the ballet and the concerts."

"I'm a fan of Toscanini." Having read his biography.

"To be sure. Though he and I were not quite contemporaries." A wry smile. "I was in the navy as a young man. This week I am in Spezia for a reunion of my shipmates."

"It *must be* destiny. I was in our navy for thirty years."

"Thirty years: what rank?"

By magic the title dropped from the aether:

"Capitano della Marina Militaire. Commodoro."

Each bowed to the other, and they shook hands again, two difficult exercises for older men in the narrow space.

Pazienza said, "How is the investigation going, if I may hear?"

"It's ready to wrap up. We know the particulars, as much as knowing is possible. Three minutes of pure terror. The crew did what they could."

"And you are troubled."

"Of course."

"Not just for yourself. Not just for your CSA. It is something else." When he hesitated to answer, Pazienza declared, "Another round will loosen our tongues." He signaled to the young woman, who seemed to be awaiting his pleasure, and presently she brought two shots of espresso to the table. "Your breakfast was quite correct according to our culture. But now, for coffee during the day it must be espresso shots, no milk or sugar. *Cin!*" he said, and they downed the shots together. A fringe of grey hair, curled under the back of his cap, shook with the gesture. "Now tell me."

"Are you sure? It's a long list."

"My life has been full of prima donnas."

So he told him, beginning with Slate: their friendship; Slate's position at CSA, now threatened; his marriage to Julia, threatened by the usual problem (at which the worldly politician nodded). Then Dorothea and his own moral duty to protect her (about which he looked blank). Then Secretary Robin McGill: their history in twenty words and the chance that he might soon gain high office in the government.

Whenever he faltered, Pazienza signaled to the young woman, and they refreshed themselves. The coffee lifted

him high above the tableau of his story, as if once again
the ichor of the gods were coursing through his veins.

"It may not sound like much, Prime Minister. But still:
a nineteen-gun salute! Which would mean even more because I was passed over for flag officer."

"And your wife—you are married?—your wife would
like the nineteen guns also?"

"Well, as to that...."

"Ah, here we come to the heart of the matter. All the
other troubles are mere scratches of the skin. Something
is wrong between you and your wife."

"She was dangerously ill but now is dangerously well."

Pazienza smiled. "Lord Byron."

"Maybe I can explain it best by saying that we have
been together forty-two years."

"Not to me. Regrettably, I have never married."

"What, never?"

"No, never. Thank you, Gilbert and Sullivan. It was a
disadvantage in my work. I was no rake: my colleagues
may have thought I was gay. Not so. I...." After a moment
he signaled to the young woman again. "I need more courage. *Cin!* No, I never married."

"Because...."

"Because I am waiting for the right woman."

"In principle."

"In practice. One perfect woman, the love of my life
since the age of sixteen."

"What happened?" But before the coffee he would never
have been so bold.

"I am a lawyer with a lawyer's caution. Like many people here, I grew up in Genoa. At sixteen I too had a best
friend, a boy named Danieli Scotto. An unworthy friend.
Dani was impossible: he drank, he stole from shops and
homes, he hopped from bed to bed with false promises.
All this was vicariously exciting for me until he fixed his
uncontrollable passions on the girl of my dreams. Of
course she was fascinated by him, as girls are by bad boys.

Almost as soon as I feared the worst, it was worse than
that: she was pregnant. He married her—he did that one
honorable thing—but he continually betrayed her, and the
marriage for her was a nightmare: cruelty and indifference, drunkenness and beatings. She was loyal to him beyond all reason.

"Soon, as quite a young man still, Dani had become a
gangster. I speak literally: he collected debts for a lesser
capo. Genoa with its alleyways is ideal for what cannot
bear the light of day. Inevitably he went too far; he beat
a fellow gangster to death. He was arrested, tried, convicted, and sent to prison. Finally! I thought. Justice
served! Yet it didn't matter to my love's love: she visited
him every week, often bringing their son with her. He
served fourteen years. By then I was somebody in the
government, and I persuaded my chief to persuade the
president to commute his sentence. In some ways prison
had improved him. He stopped drinking. He stopped
breaking the law except for petty crimes hardly worth
prosecuting (I made sure they weren't). He stopped beating his wife after their son threatened to kill him. It didn't
matter: she stayed."

"And you?"

"I waited. I do wait. It's my name: *Pazienza:* patience.
I had my seven minutes of fame in politics, and now I try
to keep alive an appreciation for the beauty of the arts.
Believe me, it's as difficult here as in your country. I have
never given up hope, in humanity at large or in my own
share of it. Three years ago Dani was diagnosed with em-
physema. I have to confess I was pleased that he would
be a burden to her until the end. Once again, it didn't
matter: she cared for him. She would have breathed for
him if she could. He died this year on the fourteenth of
February—*La Festa di San Valentino.* It seemed a sign
to me. Not *yet*—she is as faithful in her grieving as ever
while he lived—but I am sure that someday my ship will
come in." He smiled at the reference; whenever he smiled
his eyes grew even brighter. "Girls have love affairs with

men who frighten them and settle down with men they can rely on. I am such a man. She will see. Until then I will wait.

But if she and the gangster had been married for something like forty years, it could hardly have been a love affair. And she and Pazienza were something like Hilty's age, with hardly enough time for settling down.

Something besides caffeine surged within him.

"How will you know when the moment is right?"

"I follow her life through her son, whom I have known since he was a little boy, before Dani's imprisonment. He too has been disappointed in love. His wife ran off with another man, and then his job took him to the U.A.E. His daughter lives with her *nonna,* here, not five minutes away from this place. I dream of bringing them both to Milano with me."

"What are their names?" he asked loudly, so that the young woman looked across the bar for their pleasure. "The *nonna,* the granddaughter."

"You mean the *nipote.* She is Romola, Romola Mancuso. Her *nonna* is Vittoria Piedmonte."

"She's my *landlady,* Prime Minister! I live in the apartment below them. I see them every day. They bring me sweets."

"How is she?"

"She's wonderful. You must visit her. I'll arrange it."

Pazienza shook his head gently, the way wise men do. "Thank you for your offer, Commodore, but I think it's too soon. I've kept from contact always—even when I was the big cheese. In my fantasies I used to think that she might be won by my title. But she's too good for that. I've never heard from her."

"There is a tide in the affairs of men...."

"I'll wait for another tide, then."

"But you said that our meeting was destiny."

"Yes, Commodore, but for whom? For you, I think. Now that you've unburdened yourself to me, you have greater clarity yourself, correct? Well, sir: look to it!"

The Draft Provisional Preliminary Final Report

He was a few minutes late, which was too bad because the NTSB were meeting about their report. It was not the final report—that would be issued by the board in Washington after the parties named had the opportunity to comment. It was not the preliminary final report, which must be approved by the chairwoman once her staff had wordsmithed it (with, inevitably, the leaking of key findings to key politicians). It was not even the provisional preliminary final report because the investigators now, before *they* approved it, meant to read it together line by line. It was only a draft, but when he took his seat at the table, they had already read to page four, and he felt at a disadvantage.

There were three of them, two men and a woman. In appearance and personality they were as different as chalk and cheese and chisels, but they had the same reading mannerism, each moving a ruler line by line down the page so as not to look ahead all the while frowning to squeeze maximum comprehension from their brains.

Until today they had worked well together. They understood that although he had six years of intimate experience with CSA's operations, he was no longer employed there, and his contract was to investigate causes, fairly and impartially, not to defend actions. Even so, he felt the disadvantage. His frown was different than theirs, and his caution was different. A soft suggestion led to a leading question and then to an open challenge, and his role as their critic was set. Before they got to page five, it was on the tip of his tongue to say that he and they must be reading different drafts.

"Isn't this just *happy* for *glad?*" asked one of the men.

"*Perfect* has no comparative sense," he said. "Something either is perfect or it isn't."

"We the People of the United States, in Order to form a more perfect Union...."

"Yes, but there was no draft provisional preliminary final Constitution."

This drew smiles, but from then on they rolled their eyes at every objection. The obvious errors were conceded to him. What took up far more time were the grammar and diction and even format, about which, though it made them feel petty, they were unwilling to yield. Somehow he had gotten bogged down in minutia, as the old Hilty would have done; leaving him enfeebled before the real problem, the tone of the report, which, CSA having admitted fault already, implied conditions and motives unsupported by the facts.

The very thing Slate had warned him about.

"Turning to the tone," he began.

"The tone," countered the woman at once, "like all the questions of style, is the prerogative of the author. And *we* are the author—we're the ones who will sign our names. We've given you this opportunity to read the draft, at such an early stage—an unprecedented opportunity in my experience—out of respect for you and the help you've been to us. We are under no obligation to act on your extensive comments. I'm sorry if it will make trouble for you with your company. But this is what we found."

"I appreciate the gesture. It's not exactly my company."

But close enough: their sympathy for the awkwardness of his position moved them to copy him with the report. In faux good fellowship he helped them pack their gear. When they were gone and the U.S. corner of the dome was empty except for the Stars and Stripes, he read the report again as the heat rose in his neck.

In Chicago the workday had begun.

"Is it over?" Slate asked.

"We've just adjourned. I've got the report."

"What do you think?"

"They agreed with you. It's all our fault."

[192]

"So much for taking your advice."

"And yet it was good advice. That and the other."

"I know. In the long run. Now I can go to heaven."

"Are you in trouble?"

"What do you get when you cross an elephant and a rhinoceros?"

"Not to trouble you with a detail," he said, "but I have completed our contract."

"Yes. You can go home now. Where *is* your home?"

"Ellifiknow. Shall I send you the report?"

"Yes. No. Send it to the board and the executive committee, every one of them. Say that I told you to. Slate Greene, transparent to the bitter end."

"*Not* the bitter end." But the thought that it might be caused the heat to rise again.

"How are you feeling?" he asked his wife.

"Apparently I'm cured."

"Of course you are. Never a doubt."

"They're going to make a public announcement at the hospital tomorrow. Sort of their version of revivalism: *Our sister is cured!* Hillary says my case will help speed approval for all kinds of gene therapy. Now I only need to grow my hair back and build up some stamina—"

"And figure out the rest of your life and care about it."

"Well, yes. Speaking of which, what are you going to do with the rest of *your* life?"

"What do you get when you cross an elephant and a rhinoceros?"

"I'm sorry?"

"I expect I'll know after the election. Harris is looking good, yes?"

"Seems to be. So you're not going back to Slate."

"Not likely. I just spoke to him. When I pointedly said that our contract was over, you could have heard a pin drop. I asked if he was safe: more silence. If I had to guess

I would say that he and Julia will now enjoy a golden re-
tirement."

"Well, maybe."

"No? What's going on?"

"Julia called me. She's upset. That's all I can tell you.
You can probably learn more in Chicago—you're heading
there now?"

"Am I?"

"To check on the house and console your friend?"

"If they're going to retire him."

"Exactly. Bradford, the election is Tuesday."

"You and I were just talking about it."

"I know we were. If Harris wins—or whatever. If you
really want the Navy job, I hope you get it. But what I'm
trying to say is I won't go to Washington with you. I've
never liked the place and especially I've never liked all
that self-importance, that who-said-what, who's in and
who's out, that secular religious fervor. It's not me."

She meant the call to be about their marriage, then.

"I understand. That's fair. But what's the alternative?
Aren't you at risk for joining the grandmother legion?"

"Great-grandmother legion, maybe. There are worse
things. Weren't you the one who told me to live for others?"

"You have a lot more to offer than free and convenient
childcare."

"Maybe I don't. And maybe I don't need more than that
to be happy again."

"Of course I'm disappointed. Equally of course, I respect your choice. Speaking of which, how *are* our grand-
children?"

"Megan went to school today as a sexy cat, if that tells
us anything—the sexy part."

"Why so?"

"It's Halloween, Bradford. Is it Halloween in Italy?"

"Gosh, I don't know. I'll have to ask. And Blake?"

"Not interested. Or maybe she figures that a seven-month pregnant, agendered, unmarried intellectual who likes to wear overcalls doesn't need a costume."

The Reunion

As a retired officer of a NATO ally, no doubt Hilty had privileges at the officers' club; but he hadn't been there before, and he would rather not have to explain himself to be admitted. During the month, he had been friendly with Rear Admiral Acta, commander of the naval base. It was five p.m., the middle of the Italian working day *post-riposo,* and the admiral was in his office. Hilty explained his mission generally, upon which the admiral anticipated and granted his several requests. Over coffee they talked about the NTSB report. Regardless of the findings, the admiral wondered about pilot error. Hilty knew better than to ask if he would state his doubts in public. The admiral too watched which way the winds blew. Fair or not, the public verdict had already been decided.

Two events were going on at the club: in the ballroom a costume party for the families of the base—indeed Italy did celebrate Halloween—and in the library a reunion of old shipmates: eight or nine well-dressed men in various degrees of hair loss, gathered around a giant globe while they regaled each other with sea stories.

They were delighted to be joined by the admiral and pleased to be introduced to his guest, for whom they switched easily to English when Hilty had run dry after *Bene! Benissimo! Grazie! Prego.*

Standing just apart from them, Pazienza shook his hand with the enthusiasm that recalled their meeting of destiny that morning, along with a half-comic but meaning look not to bring up one particular subject. (Which accorded with his own view, that when you wanted to persuade someone to do something, it was best to let them bring it up.)

They asked about his own service. He sketched it for them, including the Taiwan encore, which moved them from polite respect to genuine interest, since the fate of

Taiwan seemed to be at stake in the American election. Before he knew it he was holding court.

Some time later the Halloween party had spilled into the library, and the admiral had left. Pazienza was standing back from the group again, studying his glass of wine as Hilty eased himself out of the conversation. There had been a good deal of drinking, and one or two of the old hands were more animated than before, but the politician and opera impresario had learned over the years to make a single glass do for an evening. He looked thoughtful—perhaps he had the "particular subject" on his mind—but more than anything he looked tired.

In response to a clearing of the throat, Pazienza said, "Fair warning: there has been no change in the tide."

"I'm about to go back to my apartment. This will be my last night in La Spezia. The report is finished."

"Are you pleased with it?"

"It's factual. If not without bias."

"In all my years in the government I never read an unbiased report. Or at La Scala either. Good luck, then, Commodore. Destiny brought me a new friend this morning." They shook hands.

"A pleasure. Though it will be sad to say goodbye at the apartment after so much kindness."

"You see how kind she is."

"I do. I have. This will be the last time I'll be met with a tray of sweets. I'm guessing it will be Pandolce tonight. Apparently Vittoria doesn't need radiators, her kitchen is always so hot."

He was being eyed.

"An amazing baker. Nothing like her in the States."

"So she was as a girl of fourteen. And?"

"And I'm going to take a liberty now that all my training, my naturally deferential manner, your high position, and the brevity of our acquaintance cries out to forbid: *Giuliano,* friend, come with me. Just for a few minutes. Say hello, break the ice. Don't let forty years of silence go on for another day. In the worst case, any awkwardness tonight will trouble her conscience; she will have to reach out to you to apologize for it, and then at least there will be a dialogue. Think of your career in diplomacy. This is just a first step toward a rapprochement."

"Sir, I will have you court-martialed for insubordination to the prime minister." Then, with that bright smile from the lined face, "Very well, let's go."

"*Spendido.* By the way, Romola is adorable."

"Too much, Commodore. You're overselling."

Pazienza begged the group's pardon for being called away; he would certainly return in time for the dinner. His shipmates excused him and wished Hilty safe travels. It was that easy. In a reunion in the United States, if a VIP didn't pay attention exclusively to *them,* he'd hear some zingers. The Italians, brought up in the Old World, had a deeper respect for status.

It was dark; rather, night had fallen but the Halloween festival was a source of light itself, so brilliant the clouds were tipped with it. Lighted storefronts, torches, lanterns, banks of vertical spotlights like colonnades.

Light and sound. In his piazza muscular men wearing loincloths and helmets with horns pounded on kettle drums until the windows rattled. The beat was primal, deafening. A few pipes raised a piteous melody between the throbbing. Youngsters danced while their parents took photos—Irish step dancing, hip-hop break dancing, Western line dancing: one act following another.

It was good that he led the way and Pazienza must follow. By several signs the prime minister seemed to be losing heart. In the gloomy elevator he whispered that this was a fool's errand. Hilty stopped on the fourth floor, hoping that Vittoria and Romola would be waiting; when they weren't, and when after a few awkward minutes they didn't appear, with the last of his moral influence he took Pazienza upstairs, where the Italian had wished to go all his life.

Romola came to the door, dressed as this year's winner of the Eurovision Song Contest, something between a clown and a vamp. Happy to see him, happy to share her excitement, she smiled at this companion who must be his friend and brought them inside, nearly tripping on her baggy trousers. He presented her to Pazienza, a name she didn't recognize as important either to her nation or to her own grandmother.

Vittoria was on the balcony, overlooking the festival. When Romola slid open the door, the drumbeat assailed them: nothing else could be heard. Feeling Romola by her side, she hoisted her above the railing to get a better look. With the child on her hip, she turned toward Hilty with that smile that was almost loving.

And saw Pazienza.

The next moments were broken and incomprehensible, as if he had found himself in the middle of a barfight. Romola underfoot. A harpy shouting at a startled man. Menacing him, heedless of the child, the child in pain. The woman's hands upon the man, shoving him back, back. He stumbling into the kitchen, she shouting at him through the doorway. Himself, behind her, just managing to pinion her arms. For a moment her resistance, fierce, witless, but instructed by a superior strength. The sudden letting go. Her face wet against his neck, her chest heaving, her hands trapped between their two bodies, restless to strike.

Despite the bedlam outside, peace. Pazienza gone.

They were sitting in her living room. Vittoria had sent Romola to bed, but her door was open and no doubt she was listening. In one respect it would have been easier if she had stayed with them, for the still-offended *signora* struggled to tell her story in English. The steel shutters and the double-glazed windows blocked most of the Halloween noise, but the remainder of it didn't help either.

"I'm sorry to have upset you," he said. "It was my idea to bring him."

"It was a surprise. Seeing his face. Wicked face."

"Why did that make you so unhappy?"

"I am unhappy."

"Yes. You know him. You remember him."

"I know him for fifty years. Since child. But I don't see him. He was prime minister."

"An important man. He told me today he wished that you and he had stayed in touch. He hoped when he was prime minister you might contact him."

"Afraid of him. Evil, evil man."

"*Perché* do you say that?"

"Once I didn't think this. I think he like me. But he do...evil thing."

"Can you tell me? Tell me what he did?"

"I am married. He put husband into prison."

It was getting toward bedtime. Tomorrow he would travel all day, including the extra hours from the difference in time zones. If this was their starting point, he would be up with her until then.

"May I make some coffee for us?"

"Yes; please."

He didn't know her kitchen, but in one of the cabinets he found a Moka Pot, which brewed one cup at a time. In between he had to wash out the grounds and refill the boiler and the basket. Besides missing sleep, he was going to miss his dinner. In the fridge he found a plate of prosciutto and cheese and on top, tucked away hopefully, the tray of Pandolce that she and Romola had planned to bring him tonight. By the time he returned to the living room, the child was sitting next to her grandmother.

"I will say," Vittoria offered, "and she will tell."

"Good idea." Maybe now he would get some sleep; but he would have to be twice as animated to persuade her through her interpreter. "Perhaps you could start by telling me what evil thing Signore Pazienza did. I have to say I was surprised by your reaction."

The child herself was animated, enacting situations and emotions years beyond her. Vittoria, watchful, spoke slowly and in simple language, as if it was Romola's understanding that she wanted.

"He put my husband—my Dani—in prison."

"Can you tell me more about that?"

"Dani was attacked; he defended himself. In Genoa men are strong. He was working for a man who did break the law—this was plain. Dani wasn't always clean hands, but he would never hurt anyone. A tough guy attacked him, and he defended himself. Legal. But Pazienza put him in prison. He wanted Dani out of the way so he could be with me. As if!"

"How did he have the power to put Dani in prison?"

"He was the public prosecutor. He made the charges. He called for the punishment."

"He himself? Did you see him in court?"

"No. Clever man, he got someone in his office to try the case for him. He never showed once. Clever and coward. He never called me."

So even then she must have looked to him for friendship.

"Is it possible he took himself off the case because of the conflict of interest: being friends with Dani, and you?"

But by now Romola herself hated Pazienza for his wickedness, and Vittoria, reimpassioned by her interpreter's tone of voice, said loudly, "No, no, no! I visited Dani in prison every week for fourteen years, bringing little Giulio—I am sorry to name him after the man we thought was our friend—the three of us in the prison visiting room—how I remember the awful tables, the ugly words cut in the wood. Dani told me what this man had done: told me over and over, so many times I heard it. He was convicted of a crime that other prosecutors brush the lint from their sleeves: 'Oh, that's just the life of these men. A tough guy died, so what?' You do the math."

It was unlikely that Vittoria had said *You do the math,* for Romola looked awfully pleased with herself. Perhaps now the adults should carry on alone. But he needed the moral weight of a third person: he had a great deal of persuading still to do. The two versions of the story were unambiguously contradictory. Even if she accepted the other version, how could she forgive Pazienza for the hardship of her life? Even if she forgave him, how could she think of returning his love?

"I see," he said. "I understand. Giulio must be in his mid-forties now, is that right?"

"He is forty-six," Romola answered for herself.

"Do you talk to him often?"

"Every day. My papa."

"What has Giulio to say about his father's misfortune?"

This occasioned a whiteout of Italian followed by a pause for reckoning. Finally Romola answered, "He has never understood his father."

"What does he think are the facts of the case?"

"He believes his father killèd the tough guy on the order of the capo: *la vendetta.* And that Signore Pazienza intervened to reduce the charge."

Another pause, while both women waited for his reaction. He was silent, keeping his eyes on Romola.

"A pardon."

More Italian from Vittoria, quickly interpreted: "My mistake: not a pardon, his sentence was commuted. Fourteen years he served. It should have been a pardon."

"I see," he said after another pause. "I understand. Is it possible that Giulio is right about this?"

Vittoria, slipping her hands between her knees, shifted from side to side as if the Halloween rhythms were in her head. She started to speak then stopped. Finally she said, in English, "I don't want to believe it."

Ƀ Ƀ Ƀ

[203]

"I'm a little lost," he confessed to both women. After clarification, this brought immediate sympathy. He spoke about the job he had left in Chicago, the job he would like to have in Washington, the crisis of his daughter's family in Boston, his wife's frightening illness, now apparently –apparently—cured, and her unwillingness to live with him except on her terms.

"I don't know—pulled in many directions. We've been married forty-two years. Survived long separations in the Navy. Six years ago we almost divorced. Life has been good since then, until these problems." He thought of Slate's lament: "I am sixty-six. The actuarial tables say I have about twenty years left. What should I do with them? I want to be happy."

The two had different opinions on what he should do.

"Marry my grandmother," said Romola, which earned her a swat from Vittoria, who said, "Since you have had happiness, be with your wife."

"That sounds like good advice. How long were you and Dani married, Vittoria?"

"As old as Giulio," she replied with a smirk.

"And happy?"

"Who can say?"

"Well, you can, for one."

"If you belong to your love, isn't that happiness?"

A good question: Was it? Had he ever belonged to Mad, or had it always been that she belonged to him? Had his life ashore been happiness or possession, familiarity, pride?

But he had an argument to make. "If you feel safe, I suppose that's true. If the belonging is not a frightening burden. If you feel that it isn't a sacrifice for you and a selfishness for your *marito*. If the loves goes both ways."

More Italian, with an irritated tone. Romola looked him sternly in the face. "Now you are trying to trap me about my marriage. Shame on you."

"I'm sorry you think so, Vittoria. Perhaps I should be more direct. From Giulio's account of his father, it seems likely that Dani was a violent man and that Giulio witnessed that violence at home. And maybe you did too."

None of them noticed when the drums stopped. He tried to reach her through trial and error: an approach; meeting a rebuff and backing away; another approach. In the silence the conversation lapsed. Romola fell asleep, and Vittoria covered her with a blanket. He and she looked at each other for what seemed a long time without speaking. Although they might change the subject for relief, neither of them was willing to let it go.

She admitted that the truth might be subject to different interpretations.

Rousing himself from his lethargy, he asked, "Shall I tell you what I believe?"

She made something like a seated curtsy.

"I believe that you loved Dani deeply, whatever his faults, whatever his circumstances, and you dedicated your life to him. Now you are dedicating your life to his memory. The first was noble; the second is unfair to you. I believe that the dead have no claim on the living. You are a happy person by nature—happiest when giving your love to another. You have Romola, lovable in every way, but before many years pass she will grow up, and then I'm afraid that you will be lonely.

"Loneliness is not a good reason for trying love a second time. Luckily, you have another reason, a better reason. Yesterday Giuliano Pazienza told me, a stranger, that you were the love of his life, from the age of fourteen, and that he had waited fifty years and would wait even longer for the chance to make you happy."

"By his low trick."

"I really don't think so. I see an honest man, a good man—maybe a little dull but trustworthy—a good man who intervened to help Dani more than once, all for your sake.

"So you have a choice, dear lady. I'm not saying fall in love with Giuliano. If you cannot love him, that would be sacrificing your freedom for nothing. Nor am I saying forget Dani—it's not like throwing a switch, is it."

It wasn't. But she was listening to what it might be like.

"Here's what I am saying. Someone who was once important to you has reappeared in your life. You might be happy knowing him again. Absences are often subject to misunderstanding. And tonight caught you by surprise. Perhaps, you had told yourself what you would do if you ever saw him again. But there was a wound. You are too nice a person not to be sorry. If you feel up to it, I can arrange for you to see him again in the morning."

In fact it was morning already—dawn brightened the slats of the steel shutters. That Hilty ichor was draining from him. Romola the Interpreter woke up wondering what had happened.

As part of the reunion weekend, Friday featured a visit to Porto Venere. Admiral Acta had offered his barge for this, a fifty-foot launch. No doubt the presence of the former prime minister made the gesture a matter of course.

The admiral had intended to go along, but when Hilty had explained his mission in Acta's office yesterday, he decided, "Better not to complicate it, then."

One hour before departure, Vittoria gave her doubtful assent, and Hilty postponed returning to his life in the United States. Pleased but self-conscious, he brought her and Romola, holding hands, through the main gate. They went onboard, to be greeted by Acta's aide, a lieutenant, as well as Pazienza's old shipmates. Uneasy suspense: he hadn't arrived. The lieutenant's orders were obvious: they waited. Finally Pazienza appeared, stepping down easily to the deck. He was all smiles to the shipmates and joked with the aide, but when he saw Hilty, Vittoria, and

Romola he stopped. But in another moment he was kneeling to Romola's level, as adults who had never had children did with children, to say a gentle word, then he rose and shook Vittoria's hand and Hilty's. "This is a pleasant surprise," he said in English. Vittoria said the boat was beautiful.

The weather was ideal for boating, warm and calm under an agreeable sun: November coming in like a lamb. The crew got them underway with relaxed efficiency, and the barge maneuvered through the harbor and past the outer seawall, increasing speed with hardly a drop of spray. The passengers had divided, Pazienza to attend to his shipmates and Hilty to the women. This raised some further doubt—Vittoria looked as if she had been right all along—until Pazienza joined them as they were coming up to the port.

The boat docked, a perfect landing, and the passengers disembarked. The four people now identified as the prime minister's party stood on the quay. Further south the concave shore led uphill to an ancient church on the point, the end of the Ligurian peninsula, which it commanded. To the north, beginning with a row of already crowded bars, restaurants, and souvenir shops, was the frontier of tourism.

"What's beyond the church?" he asked.

"*La Grotta,*" said Vittoria. And Pazienza added, "From there you can *almost* see the *Cinque Terre* towns."

"Romola," he said, "will you show it to me? Maybe if we feel ambitious we'll climb those hills."

"Careful," warned Vittoria. "Slippery."

But perhaps she was speaking of her own life now.

He and Romola did both things and more. He got a lovely picture of her in the grotto backgrounded by the blue water and the terraced hillside leading away to the vanishing point. She was a plain child, but when happy, as now, she looked as if she might one day be a beautiful young woman. They climbed, they hiked, they rewarded themselves with crocks of *trofie* followed by scoops of gelato. In the shops she helped him pick out presents for Megan and Blake. She became maternal when, reminding her of Blake's dilemma, he formed a pregnant belly with his hands.

"Comfortable shoes," she said. "Crocs, in pink."

"Neither pink nor blue," he replied. "A spectrum."

Then he took the time to explain all of Blake to her.

"Crazy," she said. "In Italy females are god."

Running out of the adventurer's spirit, they sat on a bench to wait for the others. The barge moored alongside, and the shipmates drifted back. Once again, the prime minister was late. This time his presumption drew zingers. Someone said *"amore della signora"* with a bite in his voice; for which he deserved the lasting ire of Venus. None of them knew what this moment meant for Pazienza, the culmination of a lifetime of secret devotion. Could any of them boast of such a thing?

Besides the shore route, or the steep paths that he and Romola had hiked, the hillside could be reached by a tunnel, a bore big enough for people and animals, perhaps pulling carts; no doubt dug in older times with market day in mind. The portal was framed with well-mortared small white stones: it made for a dramatic exit.

At last Pazienza and Vittoria appeared, hands at their sides but talking. On the ride back to La Spezia, they and Romola sat in the cabin while he himself mingled on deck with the aide and the shipmates.

Five

The Turnaround

Accountability

Against the dark void over the lake, Slate's mansion was lighted up like Gatsby's party. A dozen or more cars were parked along the turnaround. Without ringing first he opened the door, receiving a blare of voices.

Happy voices, perhaps intentionally so; the blare too high, the laughter too loud.

He was greeted, for everyone knew him, although they didn't know what to make of him now: the former insider who from a distance had helped to turn the inside out. Two of the losers being, as he was quickly informed, Franklin Townes of Commercial Airplanes and Gabriel D'Addario of Manufacturing and Supply.

And who else?

Slate was sitting on a sofa in the front drawing room as the presumed survivors circulated beyond him.

"Is this a celebration or a wake?"

"A bit of both. Relief, regret. But they're drinking like a wake. It doesn't matter how they behave in front of me."

"Because...?"

Slate patted the cushion beside him. He sat. They spoke to each other while they looked out at the room.

"Howard and I settled everything at the club today. Thank you for the draft report by the way; I didn't see a single typo. The result was what you'd think. So Howard and I read the tea leaves. When in doubt, go golfing. All-in-all, a satisfactory day. I birdied seventeen and eighteen. Holed a snake on eighteen."

"But you are...?"

"Sleeping with the fishes. No surprise. While we were on the course I had Melissa Trent Richards draft an announcement to the media and a farewell to the troops. Howard and I did some horse-trading at the nineteenth hole. I remembered what you told me. Your two experts,

[211]

who were only doing their jobs, are safe, though Dorothea wanted to take them down with her."

"With her? She's gone? You fired her?"

"Howard did, actually. He's the grim reaper this time. You can't hold an organization to account for failures in quality without including the chief of quality assurance."

"But that's me, Slate! Me."

"Well, we couldn't exactly fire you, could we. And it's not as if Dorothea wasn't here through it all. Sometimes the obvious answer *is* the answer. And just from a management point of view, whoever replaces me will need a new broom."

"You mean a new team."

"Thank you, Brad. *Semper vigilans.*"

"It's not right. It's not fair."

"I think it is. I should have fired her when you came in."

"I promised her."

"You shouldn't have. Of course I love you for trying."

Yes, they loved each other after their fashion; something like brothers, the only brothers they knew. He wasn't particularly lovable but Slate was, except for his morals.

As they left, his former employees came to tell Slate how much they too loved him. As an afterthought they said goodbye to Hilty as well. Melissa Trent Richards gave him a hug and a sudden sloppy kiss on the lips.

"Where's Julia?" he asked in the silence that followed.

Slate pursed his lips to make a Scotsman. "Ach, m'lady has decamped to our wee home on Arran." He pointed to the bar, where among the bottlescape was Mad's favorite from the island. Hilty poured for both of them; Slate liked his neat.

"Cin-Cin," he said as he clinked Slate's glass.

"What?"

"Why did she go to Arran?"

"Why did she go to Arran? Why did she go to Arran?" Slate stroked his chin. "I suppose, not to put too fine a point on it, she left me. Just imagine: fired twice in one week."

"That's absurd."

"She isn't here, is she? On a night when her husband could use a shoulder to cry on. Irony of ironies: Robin and I, after your intervention, called it off: Julia was gone when I came back to tell her."

"It can't be forever," he said. "It's just a—"

"Christ, Brad, you're not going to say it's a time-out?"

He was going to say a *bump in the road,* but that was clichéd as well. They finished their Scotch in silence. Putting down the glass with what he hoped was decision, he said, "Don't go back to Robin. Don't do anything."

"So you're going to fix my marriage?"

"That's right."

What was another item added to the Entropy List?

Howard Barr lived in a high-rise in Wilmette overlooking the lake. Last year he had lost his wife of thirty years to cancer, and the end of caregiving had been no relief when the ordeal was over. Life went on. For years he had been Slate's loyal deputy. Now, suddenly, he was all-powerful.

When Hilty pressed the button, Howard answered at once, and his voice was strong and alert, as he himself had always tried to sound when called late at night.

He was still dressed in golf togs.

"What time is it in Italy? You've been up for—how long? Twenty-four hours?"

"Something like that."

"You did good work out there. Come in, sit down."

"Thank you. The facts spoke for themselves."

Howard eased himself into his chair. He was a big heavy florid man. On the golf course he took vicious swings and wanted his opponents to die.

[213]

"And the public reaction has spoken for itself. In 20:20 hindsight, Slate shouldn't have accepted responsibility as early as he did. But that was just like him, wasn't it, and I don't suppose it changed anything. Our announcement made the network news tonight, and already the comments are turning positive. I expect Monday's share price will recover somewhat. —But you never cared about share price anyway. You're here about something else."

"Yes sir."

"An appeal—not for yourself, you wouldn't do that, even if you still worked for me."

"No sir."

"You can't save your friend. He's got to go."

"I understand." He understood too that the saving of his friend had taken a new path.

"Then who? Not the aviators?"

"Howard, I want you to spare Dorothea."

"Too late. She was part of the announcement."

"Melissa can manage that. The issue in the accident was quality, yes, but that was *my* responsibility. Dorothea was acting under my supervision, carrying out my instructions. I'm the one you should hold accountable. The public doesn't know that I left before the accident: they think I was on a leave of absence. So fire me now, publicly. No one gets hurt."

Howard put his hands on his meaty thighs as if he were preparing to get up. And do what? Strangle him? Hug him? Show him the door? Settling into his chair again, he asked, "Have you seen Joshua Hastings's speech on the floor of the House today?"

"No sir."

"I'll send it to you: you'll want to put it on your wall. A ringing endorsement of our *former* chief of quality assurance, who left us under mysterious circumstances: you! Typical of us that we pushed out the one person in CSA who was actually improving things. The only possible solution is to reappoint you. Don't gag: he convinced me, the board, and a great many of our investors. The public loves you, everyone wants you back, even the Chinese have asked about you, and whoever the next CEO is will understand the landscape. You're too big to fail, Brad. We need you. And I'm guessing that when the election goes against Harris next week, you will need us."

Howard was full of fire now while he himself felt hot and cold. The argument was so plausible, so easy to accept. It would solve so much. If he wasn't to have the thing he wanted more.

"I gave Dorothea my word," he said softly.

Howard shrugged. "Shit happens."

Shit happens! What insight!

He rose while Howard looked at him, apparently unwilling to exert himself further. These people wanted what they wanted, and they had been pampered so long that they expected it to fall into their laps.

The Boxes in His Apartment

In the Navy he had often traveled on short notice, by ship, airplane, helicopter, or boat, from one need to another—traveled without thinking about it or feeling it much, always on the go; but now he was sixty-six, and the pressure of events and the jet lag had caught up to him. Instead of returning to Boston on that Sunday, he slept till noon in his nearly abandoned house in Northriver.

Better rested, he watched the speech that Howard had sent, whose email enclosing it, after pointing out its two million views, repeated the hope that he would soon come back to CSA. After the way they had parted, this was merely proforma and certainly insincere; having no regard for the moral position. *Nothing is lost save honor,* and so forth and so on.

Though if anything could persuade him to change his mind, it might be this speech of Joshua Hastings; this unsolicited, unexpected, disinterested high praise.

Speaking on the floor of the House, Hastings cited him only in parenthesis. His main purpose was to warn his colleagues of the folly and greed of defense contractors.

As a Progressive he was reluctant of course to question progress, but his colleagues should consider whether our fabulous machines had become so advanced as to pose a threat in themselves.

Take for example the recent tragedy of El Al Flight 72. The CEO of the company that built the aircraft had acknowledged that two hundred and three innocent persons died because of failures in the manufacturing process. What he didn't say, but what was obvious from the type of failures, was that CSA had tried to do too much—in striving for perfection had created vulnerability. As with war, as with energy, as with food, so with transportation: perfection was not the enemy of good enough: it had become the enemy of itself—and of us.

Life was infinitely variable: beyond data, beyond rules, beyond machines. To save ourselves (and a million other species) from extinction, the very nature of progress must change. Only the ethically-guided, imaginative, and flexible human brain could be entrusted to save human souls.

One person had understood this. Behind his heroic attempt to change the corporate culture at CSA was a keen insight into the magnitude of the problem. He was beginning—just beginning!—to make a difference when tragedy struck in the Ligurian Sea. Characteristically, knowing that he might put his own future at risk, he joined the team of investigators in Italy, where his searching honesty soon found the dreaded answers.

Hastings's speech went on at length, giving examples from his years of drilling into the minutia of testimony. And then the peroration: "No doubt in response to the loss of Flight 72 the system will twitch: platitudes will be mouthed, blame will be fixed, heads will roll. But that should be no comfort to us. Here is another warning. Time is running short. Either we change our habits or the Earth—far more enduring than we can ever be—the Earth will twitch and start over to evolve a different form of intelligent life. On a personal note, I hope that Mr. Bradford Hilty of CSA will be enabled to continue his efforts to help us learn this lesson."

Watching the video—more than once—he was tempted to reverse his decision to sacrifice himself for Dorothea Billups. Truth be told, it wasn't just morality, honor, and fairness that had moved him: it was also conceit.

Until now he hadn't really considered what he was giving up. A job he loved. Growing success. Admiring colleagues. Real wealth for the first time in his life. And that intangible thing that had proved so satisfying: the power to act on his beliefs. All this came from being the chief of quality assurance at CSA. If he did nothing now but be grateful for this second chance, his life would carry on.

[218]

He could find some happy resolution with Mad. He could help other members of his family. He could do further good in atonement for the good that he had left undone.

As much as he would like to be an assistant secretary of the Navy, it wasn't for him; this job was for him.

Ah, but time was indeed short. When he and his sailors had chased submarines, they might get a sniff, but if they were late going to datum—the starting point of the search—their quarry always escaped. He was sixty-six. Slate Greene, at sixty-four, wanted to improve his remaining life by changing wives. Misguided as that was, at least it was doing something. What would he do?

On Monday he flew to Boston.

Self-discipline was one form of doing something: instead of going at once to Wellesley he returned to his apartment in Beacon Hill. When he opened the door he nearly fell over a packing box, one of many. A river of boxes filled the entrance and turned the corner into the living room. Books, pamphlets, small artifacts from the kits of Civil War soldiers, reams and reams of photocopies, and on the dining room table a careful ledger of time sheets and expenses: without supervision William Carney had faithfully continued to work.

But in his own indiscriminate way. Hilty tried to get a sense of the collection. It was massive. It was too much. How would he ever carve a narrative from it?

The next morning, election Tuesday, they had agreed to meet. The weather was auspicious: clear, calm, and dry; no winds of change were blowing. At the main entrance of the library people came and went, while on a sidewalk leading to the McKim Building a line of voters waited. The law allowed electioneering up to fifty feet from the polling place. For every Trump sign there were five of Harris. Surely Democracy would be saved today, and in gratitude she would choose Mr. Hastings's hero to serve her.

[219]

The Turnaround

William Carney was in their carrel, already at work. Documents were stacked on the desk and on the floor. It had been exactly a month since their last meeting.

"Hello, Sergeant," though Carney wasn't in uniform.

"Yes sir, Cap'n. Help you?"

"But you've *been* helping me."

"Yes sir."

"Amassing a trove of documents to select our narrative from. When I opened the door to my apartment last night, I was overwhelmed."

"Sir."

"Deeply impressed."

"All right."

"If you hadn't left such an accurate record of your time, I'd think I owed you more money."

"Money for work." Carney stood. Picking his way among the documents, he backed from the carrel, which brought the two men, one tall and white, one short and Black, face-to-face.

"Before you go," he said, "Can I get your advice?"

"Sir."

"Not about all this."

"All right."

So he told him about Blake's pregnancy. Carney didn't need to know about her questioning—he might be prejudiced; the point of the story was that the father of the child didn't know or didn't care to know.

"Shouldn't he be held accountable?" he asked.

"You think because I'm Black I'm an expert on fathers that abandon their children?" Carney, scowling, looked just like the faces in the *cartes de visite* of the soldiers.

His heart felt like a tomato being squeezed. Sharing his problems had helped him connect to Vittoria. This here was a mistake, a case of self-plagiarism.

"No, no, not at all, William. I'm just looking for another point of view, and I respect your judgment. I know you're a father to your boy. You can picture my granddaughter's

[220]

situation even though it isn't yours. I'm inclined to approach the young man and his parents too. What do you think?"

The face relented to a degree.

"You going to tell her first?"

"No. She wouldn't like it. Won't like it."

"Tell her parents first?"

He shook his head.

"I don't know, Cap'n. Where I come from *accountable* means going to jail, maybe getting shot. White people have it different: shake hands all around and put some more in the trust fund."

"I suppose that's true. I'm not going to shoot him."

Carney's sense of humor: "Maybe if you confront him his people will shoot you."

"I just want him to help raise the child. It might determine whether or not Blake can go to college."

"And you want me to care about that? I put myself through college cleaning hotel rooms."

Here was an interesting detail. But not for now.

"Quite right. I was just hoping for your thoughts. I know we come from different backgrounds. I was just hoping each of us could look over the wall."

"But that's this whole story, isn't it," Carney replied. "The Black soldiers led by white officers and fighting without pay—without decent uniforms at first. You think either side could look over the wall, despite what they were fighting for? The Glory regiment? That's liberal white people feeling better about themselves. You think your history is going to know my ancestors?"

"It's a challenge, but that's what I want. I believe that we have the ability to understand each other. If I don't get there, it's because I'm not a good enough writer."

Carney ran his hand across the top of his head; the darker shadow of his hair had receded; a gold class ring caught the light.

[221]

The Turnaround

He said, "You know: all this research I bring you and you reject three-quarters of it? *That's* the history—those details. I don't care that General Truman Seymour walked into a trap at Olustee. I don't even care that the Fifty-fourth saved the day there covering the Union retreat. That's old news. We're always rescuing you white people, starting in 1619. Soldiering, why it's like picking cotton. I care what it means to have a suppurating wound and a racist doctor ready to hang a tag on your toe when he could save your life with a little effort—if he thought it worth saving. I care that Black enlisted died of dysentery at *three times* the rate of their white officers. I care that none of the officers of the Fifty-fourth—not one—gave up his pay when the Black soldiers refused theirs. I care that the soldiers sang their Negro spirituals even as they marched to their death. You want to talk about Jim Crow? Show us the real soldiering."

"Is that what you do at the memorial?"

Carney smiled: a hit, a palpable hit. "No sir. That isn't real either. I found a market—a poor market—and I sell what I can to make a living. Just as I take a jury award from a fool doctor's malpractice. Just as my wife works beneath her education at Amazon, hoping for an opportunity. I know you want my respect, Hilty. My stamp of approval: Bradford Hilty, humanitarian. I do respect you. I believe you when you say you want to write an honest account. So go ahead, sir. Dismiss three-quarters of my work if you want. I'm just as likely to be wrong as anyone. But don't dismiss my intention. Open your mind to it. Apply your imagination to the facts. Make the reader *see* those men's lives—and mine."

"I'd rather not have to imagine yours, William," he said after a moment. "If we got to know each other, I could see it firsthand, and maybe we could help each other."

"Maybe so." But he didn't seem inclined that way.

Election Night

The polls on the East Coast closed at seven. The Nichols family, with Hilty and Mad, watched the results from their basement theater. This being a special occasion, family members brought down their favorite snacks instead of dinner. Before the first state was called, Hilty had each person put their prediction in an empty carton of cranberry juice.

"Cranberries are red," Phil observed. "Not a good sign."

"The carton is printed in blue," observed Megan.

"Too close to call," he said, though the Churchillian foreboding had been with him all day.

Notwithstanding the importance of the decision, he hoped it would come early. He was so tired he would sell Harris out for a full night's sleep. The first hour, if not promising, was at least unsurprising—of course New England and the northern Atlantic states would go for her. The analysts droned on and on about the swing states. This cohort, that cohort: shortly after nine he awakened to find the family grim and grimly satisfied, as people were when hurricanes killed those who stayed in their homes. At breakfast he opened the juice carton. Only Megan and he had predicted that Harris would win, and his prediction, of course, was a lie, just to keep up morale.

Sarah and Phil went to work, the girls to school. Mad and he held the postmortem.

"Is this really our country?" he asked. "Did I really serve thirty years to defend his idea of the Constitution?"

"Everything is turned on its head. Committing crimes, if you get away with it, is admirable. It's the *Zeitgeist.*"

"After the 2016 election they told us how stupid we'd been not to know his voters. No one made that mistake this time. We know them, *ad nauseam.* It's not only them: reasonable people, some of them highly educated, have bought into his self-delusion, wanted it for themselves. What we were stupid to miss was that elusive, messianic power of the great huckster. That appeal to the viscera. That hateful speech that feels so good. *You've been cheated, make them pay. My revenge will be your revenge.* Well, they got what they wanted. And they're going to regret it. The huckster is in charge now."

"Apparently without you," Mad said, serving the sting with a smile.

"I don't think I could be a part of Trump's government if he begged me to take the job."

"No danger there"—a second hit, superfluous.

Although he kept going, he was surprised to feel the loss. He could have done a lot of good in that job, and perhaps it would have been good for him—certainly he would have enjoyed the distinction. Joshua Hastings's speech continued to garner views. Without (much) self-delusion, he thought it fairly described what he still wanted to achieve in the world and what he had to offer. Few people were better than he of holding things together.

One fewer item on the list, anyway.

He didn't expect Robin to phone him.

"So I'm out," she said. "Apparently I didn't make a good enough impression on President Trump when I had the Pacific Fleet."

"I doubt that."

"But it's true. His name for me in his inner circle was 'the hottie in Hawaii.' A young thing with an offensive familiarity confided that to me by way of consolation. An aide to McMahon or Lutnick, the transition team leaders, I don't know who. The only notice I'm to get, apparently."

"And a backup plan?"

"I'll serve faithfully until noon on the twentieth. After that I haven't a clue. I've never been unemployed before,

Brad, and I'm actually rather poor. You wouldn't know of a multinational defense firm looking for a CEO, would you?"

"That would be perfect. And since my fantasy is that Slate becomes SecNav, you two could swap, like Kekich and Peterson."

"Like who?"

"Mike Kekich and Fritz Peterson, two pitchers for the Yankees, who swapped wives something like fifty years ago. The world was scandalized but not them. All four were friends, before and after."

"Did the marriages last?"

"Peterson married Kekich's wife, and they made a go of it. Kekich and Peterson's wife split up."

"Is this the world's most ingenious segue, even for you?"

"I wish I was that smart."

"It wouldn't have worked, would it. It was more than— the physical attraction: I truly believe he's the man I'm supposed to be with. But we wouldn't have survived the guilt. Julia Greene is a very nice person."

You might feel guilty yet, he thought.

"And if the job swap doesn't happen?" he asked.

"When that doesn't happen I'll move south. Leo and I have a gentleman's agreement that if I ever stop chasing rainbows, he will make room for me to spend time with Nestor, our son—you remember him, of course. They live in South Carolina. He's in high school now, playing two sports, so it wouldn't be fair to move him. I expect I'll become that Yankee mom in Charleston.

"But of course my little problems are not the purpose of this call. I'm sorry that I gave you false hopes, Brad. I was so sure we would win, especially when the president withdrew."

"I admit it had its appeal. Nineteen guns."

"One for each headache."

"The Honorable Bradford Hilty."

"As if you should care about that, since everyone knows how honorable you are and always have been. I've seen you in three life crises, Brad: your one thought is always to do the right thing. So it was when you and Slate ate all my trail bars."

"God, they were hard to get down. No good deed goes unpunished. Anyway, you are kind to call, and for my part watching you has always been an exercise in admiration. I wish you great things as a Southern Yankee."

"Thank you, friend. Goodbye."

"Oh, Robin, one more thing?" It felt essential that she not hang up.

"Yes?"

"I want to ask a favor. I don't mean a horse-trade, you're leaving all that behind, so feel free to say no. It's personal, for me. *Constitution's* schedule says she's going into drydock at the end of this month."

"Correct. Thursday the twenty-eighth. Would you like to ride along?"

"Yes, please. And could I bring something like a dozen guests? I know that's a crowd. It would mean a lot to me."

"I am writing the email as we speak. SecNav Guest Cruise for my particular friend and his friends. Crystal Schaefer is her skipper. There's no one more accommodating. Goodbye, Brad."

Veterans' Day

Commander Crystal Schaefer was more than accommodating. He had hardly hung up with Robin when she
called him. Commodore Hilty was already well known to
her, for the Naval War College had done a case study on
his brilliant stratagem with the Taiwan destroyers. And
he was in Boston now? Excellent! Of course he must come
for the turnaround—bring as many guests as he liked.
Might she ask a huge favor? Would he visit the ship himself, have lunch, speak to the crew? Any day would suit.
The duty here was so particular, she looked for opportu-
nities to remind them of their connection to the fleet.

"You never know when we will need another frigate,"
he said, and she laughed and agreed.

Monday was Veterans' Day. The library was closed,
and Carney expected a lot of visitors at the memorial.
Hilty stayed home and made yet another attempt at the
boxes of research. Just after breakfast he was turning
through a piece of Lincoln's correspondence with Horace
Greeley:

> If I could save the Union without freeing
> any slaves I would do it, and if I could save
> it by freeing all the slaves I would do it; and
> if I could save it by freeing some and leav-
> ing others alone I would also do that—

when his phone rang with an unrecognized number. He
let it ring and ring then at the last moment picked it up.

"This is Howard Lutnick," said the voice. "Please hold
for President Trump."

He hung up.

Moments later he checked the area code: 561, Palm
Beach. Mar-a-Lago was in Palm Beach. In a year so im-
probable, could the impossible have happened? He called
the number; it devolved into a series of clicks. His face

[227]

aflame, the cords rigid in his neck, he told himself to remain calm, but Lincoln's argument to Greeley was nothing but a blur. He sat. He got up and paced the floor.

The phone rang again.

"This is Howard Lutnick," said the voice. "Please hold
for President Trump."

"Hilty, if you ever hang up on me again, I'll have the
IRS audit your taxes until you die. And then your family."
It was Trump. He had never liked his voice, that effeminate monotone rapidly speaking hateful things, but you
couldn't avoid it, he was everywhere. And he was here,
now.

"But you hung up on me, Mr. President," he lied with
a grin in his own voice as his heart knocked in his chest.

"Did I? Lutnick, you asshole, we hung up on him. Listen: Bradford: I have a job for you. Not a cabinet seat—
I've given all those out already, the fastest appointments
in history. But an important job just below that. As assistant secretary of something for something. Where was
that, Elon?" In the background a thickened voice that
might have been Musk's said a few words. Trump went
on: "Defense or State or something like that. But your
thing is quality, right? And after twelve years of Obama
and Biden, God knows we need quality. It's a quality job.
Interested?"

"Flattered certainly, sir."

"Of course you are. You're a famous guy now, Bradford. Welcome to the club. You *want* to belong to this administration, which is already the best this country has
ever seen. I need an answer by the end of today. Appropriate, right? Veterans' Day and you the famous veteran.
Elon, why aren't we making him Secretary of Veterans
Affairs? Right, that's going away. Well, Bradford, do as I
say—strictly as I say: you know loyalty is important to
me—do as I say and I'm sure you'll move up, maybe to a
Cabinet chair. So you'll tell me today. And because I'm so
confident you'll say yes, and because we're showing the
country how efficiency in government really works—just

like the hotels I'm building all over the world—wait until you see the ones in Greenland: spectacular views of the glaciers crashing into the sea—we're going to start the vetting process now. You're not committing to anything—you'll sign the NDA by the close of business, remember?—but just to get the ball rolling. I can't wait to see you at our first cabinet meeting, Bradford. Lutnick will walk you through the security check. Don't let me down on this or you can expect that IRS audit."

Presumably Trump then handed off the phone call so he could offer someone else a fabulous job. The greatest multitasker the world had ever seen. Another series of clicks led finally to Lutnick's voice.

"So glad you're doing this, Bradford, and I can't wait to meet you. I'm personally vetting all the candidates the president deems his top tier. It's simple. I'm sending you a text now. Please click on the link and follow the instructions. We need you to ID yourself by verifying some personal information and uploading a camera shot that we can compare with a known picture, which we have from that impressive testimony of yours before the House subcommittee. The whole process takes about ten minutes, and if you run into any problems—but we've never had any before, Elon's programmers wrote the code—but if so, the phone number at the bottom of the page will reach me directly. Directly! Good luck, Bradford. As the president said, you'll be part of the greatest administration in the history of the planet."

The form was easy to use, and some at least of the data had been populated already. He picked his Northriver address out of a list of possibilities. The transition team already knew his date of birth and years of naval service. He provided his SSN—apparently no longer sensitive—and the identity of one of his savings accounts so a few cents could be transferred in and out for verification. Uploading his picture was similarly straightforward but a little disconcerting because his selfie was represented on the form as a cartoon character. But ten minutes was correct: he received the usual congratulations by email.

Of course he wouldn't take the job—Trump didn't even know what job it was. Or did he? Did Musk? Here, literally dropped from the aether, was the answer to the fundamental question. He would be an assistant secretary after all. Or better! But in that man's administration? But why not? Reckless heads of government needed sane advisers to limit the damage. But really?

Unable to possess his soul in patience—his parents' catchphrase—he lay down to sleep off the excitement.

Thirty minutes later he sat up with a start.

More than a few cents had been transferred.

The representative at the bank didn't seem alarmed.

"The transfer looks completely regular, sir."

"But it wasn't, of course. Where to?"

"A bank in the Bahamas."

"In the Bahamas. Would the transition team for the president-elect use an offshore bank?"

"We send money there quite often."

"But the amount. Wouldn't such an amount require extra scrutiny."

"As I say, it seems completely regular. Your identity was verified by multiple factors, including biometric, the highest level of security."

"I'm telling you I didn't authorize the transfer. And I'm me—you have verified my identity for this phone call."

"That's true. Thank you for verifying your identity. Is it something you might have done and forgotten?"

"The amount!"

"Yes, it's a large amount. But we send amounts many times larger than that every day."

"Read the amount."

"One hundred eleven thousand, one hundred eleven dollars and eleven cents."

"Eleven eleven eleven eleven. And what day is today?"

[230]

"November eleventh." The representative sounded less confident.

"The armistice," he said, "that ended World War I, and which Veterans' Day commemorates, went into effect in the eleventh minute of the eleventh hour of the eleventh day of the eleventh month." An inspiration: "What was the *time* of the transaction?"

"Eleven a.m. Oh I see."

"You see. You see that someone has stolen one hundred and eleven thousand dollars from my supposedly secure account with you."

"I don't have the authority to say that. But I'm sorry for your loss."

"It's not my loss, sonny, it's your bank's loss."

"I don't have the authority to say that."

As he had learned during the Taiwan transit, he had a heart murmur—not really serious but he needed to watch himself. This wasn't doing that any good, and the angrier and more frightened he became, the less effective he would be (though dropping dead during this phone call would certainly get action). He asked to speak to a manager. The manager passed him to a senior vice president, who must have been trained both in finance and legal. The transfer was irreversible, she said. The extent of the bank's liability would have to be determined. When he reminded her of the bank's promise, widely advertised, of fraud protection, she prevaricated. What, then, should he do? She answered with an incident number, as if he were having a password problem, and advised him to contact the FBI.

In forty-two years of marriage he had never needed to confess such a foolish mistake. A phone call wouldn't do: he drove at once to Wellesley.

The household was in an uproar Everything was wrong. Blake was insisting that she would raise the child, and Phil and Sarah were arguing about it. Katie and Megan had hugged and made up, but Taylor, from her worldly vantage, was condescending to them in their innocence, being particularly cruel to Megan. None of these things seemed important.

Always quick to understand, his wife was uncanny with bad news. "How did this happen?" spoken calmly, merely introduced the coming unpleasantness.

"Obviously I made a mistake. I was incredibly stupid. Every time I hear something like this, I think the victim ought to be shot. If it's any consolation, I still think so."

They would come back to that point.

"How did they do it?" she asked.

"The FBI special agent"—perhaps his being special would mitigate the stupidity—"said it's a well-organized sophisticated gang, probably based in Russia. Maybe even the Russian army. Experts in deepfakes. Among my other mistakes I didn't record the call. He said it would have been easy for them to impersonate each one of them, Trump, Musk, and Lutnick."

"And you thought you were important enough for Trump to call personally?"

"I know. Delusional. I just wanted it."

"And you didn't stop to ask yourself what you were doing when you gave them your personal data? Our bank account—our biggest account? Not even a flicker of a thought that this might be a scam? Did you look at the URL? Haven't we been warned about this kind of thing—like forever?"

"Yes, incredibly stupid."

"Then to upload your face? Ye gods, Bradford, what will you be like when you actually go senile?"

"I'll be lovably senile, like a lap cat."

But it was too soon, far too soon, to try humor.

"I mean it."

"Well, for one thing, you won't have to worry about my moving to Washington."

Humor of any kind: she shook her head in wifely disgust.

The murmur of raised voices came through the ceiling.

"Can we afford it?"

"Yes. It hurts, of course, but...yes."

"Because forget about getting the money back. Not from the Russian army, not from our bank."

"Realistically, no." But at least the conversation was moving toward closure.

"So tell me this." She pointed to the ell of the sectional, and he sat. They were in the smallest of the living areas, which Mad by spending time here every day was trying to turn into the Nichols family room. "If you go back to the company, could I buy here? Would we have enough?"

"I'm sure we would. Especially since I don't plan to go back except, actually, tomorrow to put the house on the market."

"Your childhood home."

"It was never the same. Hubris."

"Where will you live, then?"

Do you mean I won't be living with you? he thought. He shrugged, giving her no doubt a feckless smile.

They reflected upon the vagaries of life.

"So you're not going to be a resident nana," he said.

"Bad for them, bad for me. I want some place not too far away: convenient but I wouldn't feel on call. If *you'd* like to live here, we could switch places, and I could go to Beacon Hill."

"Like Kekich and Peterson."

"Like them. Only two of them didn't make it."

"On the whole I'd rather be like Hilty and Hilty," he said, which earned him the glimmer of a smile.

They settled in for the evening, and the bruised family members left them alone. She wanted to know about Slate; she seemed to know all about Julia. He invited her onboard *Constitution* and asked if she could persuade the whole family to come. She asked if Robin would be there, and when he said no she nodded as if the outing might be all right, then. He didn't tell her about anyone else he planned to invite.

In the morning he touched base with William Carney, already at work in the library carrel. The piles of research were if anything even higher than before. It had rained yesterday, discouraging visitors to the memorial. At noon Carney had given up and gone home.

"How was *your* day?" he asked, the first interest he had shown in Hilty's life.

The phishing scam, besides revealing his monumental stupidity, would have required at least alluding to the size of the loss; either of which might have made Carney doubt the project. As much as he wished for a friend, their relationship was fragile. He fell back on banalities.

"I did have two things for you, William," he continued, trying not to rush. "I've been thinking about our last talk, about your ideas for the direction of the book, and I want to explore them with you. I have to be gone the rest of this week, but next week we can review the whole project, not only the scope of the history but your role in writing it. Does that interest you?

"And the other thing: an opportunity has come up for me and some guests to ride the *Constitution*—'Old Ironsides'—on one of her cruises in Boston Harbor. I've already met the crew, who are enthusiastic about history. They'll be wearing their 1812 uniforms. Will you come? And your wife and your son?"

"My wife has to work."

"Of course. But your son might like it, don't you think? It would be kind of a field trip, so I would think his school would excuse him."

Just then a man asleep in the adjacent carrel woke up and started shouting about his faith, and after this interruption Carney never did give him a yes or no.

The Peripatetic Hilty

In Northriver he interviewed three realtors, who took amusingly different approaches to winning his business: one marshmallow now versus two if he waited a while versus all the remaining marshmallows if he waited until the end of the experiment. He chose the two; the house, aggressively priced, would be listed in the spring. Until it was sold the furnishings would remain. If the weather was warm enough, the realtor would fill the pool and hire some kids to swim there when showing the place.

After signing the contract he drove to Slate's house. Despite all the changes, the staff seemed in full force and as busy as usual. Frank Mastrangelo, the butler, directed him to the back, as he had done so many weeks ago when Hilty had been looking for Julia; when Slate and Julia had been together and Slate had stood astride the corporate world and the house had abounded with guests.

Indian Summer was over; all the pumpkins had been gleaned. The sun was cold, the air was crisp, and the yellowing grass, after the early morning frost, was crunchy underfoot. At the back of the lawn his friend, standing on a strip of artificial turf with the stub of a rubber tee in front of him, was hitting golf balls into the lake.

A waste of time. But Slate had time to waste now.

He took up a caddy's position. Using his driver, Slate hit it fat, and the ball barely made it to the water. Then he topped the ball, which ran down the bluff and stopped on the sand.

Leaning on the club: "It's official, Brad: I'm snake-bit."

"*You're* snake-bit? I just lost 100K to a phishing scam."

A disbelieving but believing smile, he being Hilty.

"Oh?"

He explained the circumstances.

A grimace: "You should have suspected the timing. It would have been too soon for you. This morning Trump

[235]

just announced his secretary of defense: a co-host on Fox news would you believe it?" Setting another ball on the tee, he hit a banana slice.

"Your timing's off. Try a lofted iron to get your rhythm."

A seven-iron went relatively true, but hitting it from so high a tee was cheating.

"That's more better," Slate said, despite this. "Any chance of getting the money back?"

"From the Russian army?"

"Good thing you're a rich fella. You know, I've always thought that cyber attacks should be an actual casus belli. There should be an international protocol against it, like weapons of mass destruction. If the president had any balls, he'd warn once and bomb twice."

"Which would be perfectly reasonable except that we and our allies are the worst offenders."

"That's what I'm saying: ban it completely. Not that I care, but it's bad for business." That wry grin.

"How are you holding up?"

"How am I holding up? I'm hitting golf balls into Lake Michigan, for Christ's sake. How do you think I'm holding up?"

"Or you could just answer the question after I've shared my own misfortune with you."

"All right. Since you asked—and thank you for asking—I'm riddled with regrets. We shouldn't have ruled out pilot error, Brad. First, because we still can't be sure, and second, because it was too soon. I should have ignored the NTSB, ordered my own review, and accepted responsibility—if in fact we *were* responsible—when the agony had passed. I'd still have a job, and you and I could be making meaningful changes now to fix the problem."

Except that the *I* had summarily fired the *you.*

"I think you did the right thing," he said quietly.

"I don't know. We're talking about regrets, which allow for short memories. I regret that I'm never going to be with the love of my life. Is either of those things true: the love of my life and never? I don't know. But I feel I've given up a high probability of happiness for a low probability of saving a compromised marriage. Only a fool would make that choice."

"Well-reasoned except for the guilt."

Another seven-iron; this time a snap-hook, the ball, drunk with sidespin, staggering toward the neighbor's beach.

"Let me ask you something," Slate said. "You talk a lot about reason and logic. Clearly you think that you think. But do you really?"

"I try to, according to my lights."

"My problem is I haven't actually done much thinking, maybe ever. All my decisions, through both careers, were instinctive and quick, mental reflexes. If something had to be thought through, I simply made sure that I trusted the source and that it didn't seem foolish. Instead of thinking I used my personality. Now, facing the future, and when I have time to think, I find I don't know how. I start down that path and something distracts me—too easily, I want to be distracted. When I'm alone like this, I'm not conditioned to think, and there's no one around to use my personality on as a substitute."

"You're describing the exercise of command," he said. "But in between snap decisions commanders reflect. I've always seen you as thoughtful, Slate, sometimes surprisingly so. I told you that in Washington. As far as both Robin and Flight 72 are concerned, I believe your mental reflexes, as you call them, were exactly right."

"Very convenient, since you advised me on both."

"Even so."

"So is Julia happy? Happy with *her* decision, leaving me. Rational as it was," he added dryly.

"In part that's why I'm here."

Pointing with his club: "You see how the cloud shadows fall on the lake?"

"Yes, they're beautiful."

"And then you get a mass of clouds together and it parts and sunlight pours through the cut, like a broad beam from heaven. See it lighting up that sloop, how white the sails are? What's that condition called, that phenomenon?"

"Crepuscular rays of the sun."

"That's it. And the green flash, something you said you actually saw, and you wouldn't lie to me about it."

"On the way to Taiwan. I saw it."

"The one thing about a zealot like you, you wind up knowing a lot: things the rest of us don't care enough to learn. Are waterspouts dangerous?"

"You bet they are."

"You said Julia's why you're here."

"I said in part."

"Give me the other reasons first."

"There are two of them. First, I want you to come to Boston to celebrate Maddy's recovery. *Constitution* is turning around in the harbor. We've all been invited by Robin, though she won't be there. Two weeks from today."

"Robin won't be there."

"Correct."

"Might I expect to meet someone else of interest?"

"You might."

"All right, then. Certainly for Maddy. I'm curious about the person of interest: make sure you send me your guest list. Now tell me the other reason you're here that isn't about Julia." He smiled. All his chaffing belied his hope.

"If, as I remember, the private jet is part of your severance package, I want to borrow it, and Roddy and crew. I need to visit several places in Europe before the turnaround and there isn't much time. It would be convenient to have dedicated transportation."

"Might I expect Scotland to be on your itinerary?"

"You might."

Slate picked up the driver again. He placed his feet, checked the alignment of his grip, waggled the club, did his forward press, swung fast and hard and dribbled the ball off the tee.

"Maybe I'm thinking too much now."

"No, it's your timing. Timing is everything. You're starting your downswing before you've finished your backswing. Think of fly-fishing: that lovely moment of suspense just at the end of the back-cast. The proper golf swing is like that: one...two." He swung an imaginary club.

"Okay, Mr. Know-It-All: you do it. One shot. If it's good you can have the plane."

"You want me to hit one shot cold, with the biggest, heaviest club in the bag?"

"Hot or cold shouldn't matter if your theory is correct."

So he took the driver, swung it a few times, and hit the ball, saying to himself "one...two" and willing that vicious acceleration as his hands went through the hitting zone. The ball started low and climbed, kept climbing as if self-propelled, faithful to its name, driving itself into the air and carrying into the distance, upwards toward the cloud-cover probably on its way to Detroit. He could retire from golf now on the memory of that one shot, taken unrehearsed, proving his excellence.

Slate laughed. The world made sense now.

After they had cleared the coast, the co-pilot slipped out of his seat, and Roddy invited him to take the controls. Slate had often done this; Hilty had always declined, just as in the Navy, for it set a bad example. As soon as he put his hands on the yoke, the numbers started changing. He didn't know where to look, let alone what to do. Some vestibular sense told him the airplane was losing confidence, like a horse with its rider. And the rider in himself. A red light glowed, in response to which his hollows sweated. Yaw was the pedals or was that the yoke? The throttles were speed, or were they lift?

With one or two subtle motions Roddy brought instant calm. He fixed the altitude so Hilty could concentrate on

the heading. This was surprisingly easy, not unlike steer-
ing a ship. His hands held the yoke with his fingertips,
and he was able from time to time to take his eyes off the
compass.

They were flying through the night taking the stars
with them as they consumed a stratum of moonlit clouds.
Roddy's profile in the twilight of the instrument panel
had the relaxed vigilance of the expert.

"Admit it, Brad: this is more fun than driving ships."

"I admit it. Every ship-driver would rather be a fighter
pilot. Maybe it's our primal desire for wings."

"To slip the surly bonds of Earth."

"Safely. Slate thinks the crew of Flight 72 could have
recovered the aircraft. What do you think?"

"Slate's wrong. It was our fault, totally. The flight
crew, that attitude they were in and the response of the
computer—they were goners."

"They had thirty-six thousand feet to figure it out."

"Let me have her a mo." He pulled the yoke, at which
the clouds disappeared, invisible hands pushed Hilty into
his seat, and a didactic voice intoned, "Stall, stall: lower
the nose, lower the nose." They were falling, then; the terror of pointing up and falling down. His guts in his throat,
strangling him. All the wet places again. But Roddy
brought them back to level flight, throttling up a bit as if
he were clearing his throat.

"Pretty uncomfortable, right? Now, imagine the case
when the cabin pressure is gone, you've had to secure
your own air supply, the plane is inverted, the center of
gravity has slammed into the tail, and the airframe is
breaking apart: what you have is a great many separate
objects that happen to be sharing the same trajectory."
He was going to say more, but the cabin door opened and
the co-pilot and the flight attendant were asking, in the
faux calm of aviators everywhere, if he needed anything.

"Another cuppa wouldn't come amiss, guys. As I was
saying," he continued. But he had finished: the company
was at fault, Hilty had been right all along.

The silence, like the flight, settled into routine. There was no sense of motion—certainly no sense of going six hundred miles an hour. Up here the engines were a whisper. He was sitting at an increasingly intelligible control panel with an unchanging picture above it. The slightest touch on the yoke held them on course.

The co-pilot, bringing coffee, checked the nav display and left again.

"So," Roddy said. "We're going to Glasgow, right?"

"Right. I'm taking a ferry to the Isle of Arran."

"To see Julia."

"I'm hoping to be there for dinner, depending how much more time we lose to aerobatics."

Roddy smiled. "While we stand down, admire the pictures at the Kelvingrove, and be ready for wheels up on Saturday. Just a small question about that: where are we going from there?"

"Paris, I hope. With Julia. I've made reservations for her at the George Cinq for Saturday and Sunday. With luck we'll return to Paris on Monday to take her to Boston. Maybe with some other folks."

"Return on Monday because we will have gone to...."

"Not sure yet. Milan. Or Pisa. Or both. Or neither. I'm writing this script as the actors play it."

"Gotcha. Improv. I don't think crew rest will be a problem, but we might have to build in another day. We could always include you as part of the aircrew in that calculation, but then we'd probably wind up in South Africa."

"Nice shot. The score is tied."

"Actually, that was a hint, you being a tad off course."

"Whoops." But he recovered something of his self-respect by setting the course dial and punching in the full autopilot, as if actually flying the plane had been child's play.

"D'you think Julia will come with us?" Roddy asked.

"I hope so. If she's already having second thoughts. I've learned through bitter experience that people are seldom convinced by one conversation."

"A tearful scene, an epiphany: those things don't stick." Roddy turned to look at him, as the light of the instrument panel crossed his cheek. "Something I don't share much: ten years ago my wife left me for another man. The affair sneaked up on her, it got physical, and she lost her head. I think in some ways she *had* to leave me to justify her mistake. Anyway, it was sudden: I came back from a job, and there was the note."

"No warning of problems?"

"None. I thought we were good"

"What did you do?"

"I waited. I kept asking myself, What's the big picture here? What are the odds they make it? After about five months the guy left her, and now she wanted to come back. I wanted it too, no question. I liked her, and we got on, until she lost her mind. But I waited. We did it by the book: counseling, meetings at neutral sites, casual evenings out. It took two years. I didn't sleep with her until both of us were sure about reconciling. That part was no picnic, let me tell you, figuring out sex again with a woman who couldn't help making comparisons."

"And through all that time apart...?"

"I was celibate. That might surprise you, given my reputation for *joie de vivre.* But loyalty's important to me. I think that Slate and Julia have the same value. Maybe they can build on it. If this helps when you talk to her."

He did arrive at Julia's house—Slate and Julia's house—in time for dinner, despite an accident on the A727 outside of Glasgow and a headwind and opposing tide in the firth. The drive up to Lochranza from the ferry at Strathwhillan required some concentration. Night had fallen, the coast road was dark, and the land all around was dark, with a few pinpricks of light in the fabric.

[242]

Julia's house was in the middle of a loose crooked line of properties above the shore road. Each had its parcel of land, irregularly shaped and sized, though they were not on Slate's scale of wealth. Bigger houses loomed on the inland foothills, distant from each other, not to mention the castle on its peninsula jutting into the loch, but the Greenes had chosen this house as a *pied-à-terre* in the flush of an idea that village neighbors would be an added pleasure. He wondered if she regretted that now. Perhaps her neighbors respected each other's privacy.

As soon as he rang, with a few quick steps she opened the door, and before he could greet her as he'd rehearsed she pulled him into the house, kicked the door shut, and hugged him hard, pressed her bones against his.

"Oh—so kind!" she said against his shoulder.

The moment took a moment. Her breathing slowed while her eyes remained bright and fixed on him. She led him to the living room, through whose windows the castle looked like a backdrop in a play. "Sit by me," she said, gently pushing him into place. But after she too had sat, close enough to touch him, she was amused that neither of them knew how to begin.

In his experience people in such circumstances, before they said what they really wanted to say, often resorted to the weather or logistics.

"I made reservations for us at the inn," she said. "On Friday nights they put on a dinner—fixed menu, usually a choice of seafood or mutton, all beautifully cooked. And you'll stay here tonight, Brad?"

Was she ardent? He was awfully aware of her. The reason that had brought him—his grand plan—was just beyond his thought, a word on the tip of his tongue.

"I'm so glad you're here," she continued. "I was wishing for a friend, but that was like a message in a bottle. But it crossed the ocean and washed up and you found it, didn't you. Where? In Boston?"

"For now, anyway." This led to a long report about Mad's health, Blake's dilemma, Megan's friends, Sarah's

[243]

job, and Sarah and Phil's marriage. And William Carney and their research together. He confided in her what the people concerned might have thought too personal. A good listener, as she had always been, she followed along, laughed or shook her head at the right moments, and understood him when he wasn't quite clear; and her questions added savor to the point of his stories. In fact she seemed to pay him the highest compliment of all: her interest in his life took her out of her own troubles.

They went to dinner, strolling around the corner of the loch. Beside the heavy door of the inn was an elegant sign that said *No Vacancy.* The dining room was full, which felt like a version of privacy in which couples might tell their secrets. Because he had always liked her, because she had once been unappreciated by the great world, including her husband, the prospect of hearing her secrets now gave him a heady feeling.

"At this point," she said, sensitive as a cat, "we're going to solve all the problems of my life, yes?"

"Why not? We've already solved mine. I'm actually here with a specific proposal."

"From him?"

"No. From me."

"I assume he knows you're here, though."

"Particularly since I borrowed his plane."

"What's going on with him?"

"When I saw him he was hitting golf balls into the lake."

"Maybe that's his next career: the senior tour."

"A high percentage of them didn't make it to the water. His timing is really bad."

"Tell me about it," which gave them both a laugh.

"I take it his girlfriend will be out of office soon," she said. "That's convenient for them."

"I've spoken to her. Actually, she called to tell me that the dear leader wouldn't be offering me a job either. And that's another story: remind me to confess the stupid thing I did. Oh, yes: senior citizen stupid. But Robin. She said she's moving to South Carolina to be with her son." He looked at her. "They're not together, Julia. They've made a decision, both of them. I do think it's over."

Eyes bright with tears, she shook her head quickly.

"I know you've heard that before."

"Oh yes: half a dozen times."

"So what now for you?"

"So what now for *you?*" she asked. "You're not exactly attached either."

"Roddy told me a story on the plane, wrapped around a kernel of advice. Maybe advice for both of us. I don't know if you remember but you told me the same thing in Taiwan: think about the big picture."

"Oh, I hate that advice! It always turns out to be foolish. Self-defeating. Life is a succession of small pictures. They only make up a big picture when you look back. Here's better advice: if the small pictures aren't making you happy, don't wait."

"If you have that luxury, I suppose."

"I do. I own this house. He's already conceded that."

"And the pain? Yours and his?"

"Each of us is responsible for our own pain. I've had enough of mine. Slate is an attractive man, but judgment-wise he chases even more pitches out of the zone than that friend of yours, the shortstop with the hair—"

"Dansby Swanson."

"Dansby Swanson, there you go. Did you ever think when we were watching that game—the only ones from the company watching it—"

"Those suck-ups."

"That we'd be here now?"

"It's been quite a year."

"This place is mine, and either the condo in Antibes or the house in Thailand—I get to choose. It's disgusting, really, it's a moral outrage, all this wealth actually makes

[245]

me unhappy. If the guillotine were still standing in the *Place de la Concorde,* I'd send myself there."

Her lovely hand had formed a fist. It wasn't the wealth that bothered her.

"And I'd add your name to my knitting."

She smiled, the way people did at clumsy attempts to lighten the tone.

"My proposal, Julia." he said.

"Oh yes, I'm listening."

"I want you to come with me to Paris. For the weekend. There's someone I want you to meet—I think I can arrange a meeting—and a new life for you to consider. If you like it, you'll be so busy and, I hope, happy that you won't care which of your houses to choose."

By now they were walking through the village. On the shore road people passed them in both directions, recognizing her with a nod, a smile, a noncommittal greeting while giving him a longer look.

He described the plan with its uncertainties...its potential rewards. In the worst case she'd have had a weekend in Paris.

"A new life. Truly a new life?"

"A new interest that would, I think, exactly suit you."

"And this would be with Slate?"

"If both of you want that." He looked into her face; her eyes lensed with tears. "Foolish or not, I believe in the big picture. I'm guessing you still love him. No doubt that's an act of sainthood, but you aren't one to stop loving when there's pain."

"Over and over, Brad. Scar tissue on scar tissue."

"And if you decided to do this, and it worked out, you'd be different together. But there would be room for that, and the important point is you might both be happy again. You shouldn't let the pain you feel now dictate your judgment."

"How much pain am I supposed to take?" she cried. They were on her doorstep. "How many times humiliated?

You know the most worst part, Brad? It's not the discovery that he's been unfaithful. It's not even the agonizing days when I think he's been unfaithful. It's when it's all out in the open and he's so remorseful and promises the affair is over and won't happen again. And I believe him. *That's* humiliating."

"Yes."

"Will you come in?" she asked.

"I—I don't know, really."

"Shall I tell you what's going on? All my neighbors are waiting to see if you're coming in. Let's do what the best writers do: postpone their gratification. Do you remember way back when, you asked me to read the diary of one of Robin's sailors to see if it proved that she had committed adultery with him?"

"Yes, of course. And did it?"

She laughed. "I don't remember. I wish I could say that it did, that you can still report her for it, but I really don't remember. What I do remember is thinking, 'Stupid me: here's a far better man than your husband, sitting in your window while you lie on your bed, and he's half in love with you already. Show a little skin, get him over here.' Do you ever think about that visit? Could you see the pulse in my neck? How tempted I was?"

"It was in the air between us, maybe. Or I thought so. But I wasn't sure. And I wasn't—I didn't—I wasn't—"

"Dishonorable. Faithless."

"Audacious or desperate enough, to take a chance. Afraid of ruining my life. Not that being with you would have been anything but pure joy. Looking back all these years, one thing I regret is that I often confused ruining my life with changing my life. And what's worse, that I didn't want *any* change because it would require extra work. Can that be true? My big picture is that I'm lazy?"

She was calm again. He had accomplished something; perhaps simply the time elapsed had done it. "Won't you come in?" she asked. "Whether I go with you tomorrow, it's late now. Shouldn't you stay here?"

She said something else then, under her breath. Something like *You can sleep on his side.*

Don Quixote had fallen into a well and was calling up to him with a thready voice. Twice he counted his breath to seven and back. To her it might look as if he were summoning audacity, or desperation, or even cruelty; a little cruelty would suffice for both of them.

"It was a hundred and eleven thousand and change," he said. "What I lost in a phishing scam. I thought I was talking to Trump."

The doorstep was certainly conspicuous. He felt her neighbors' eyes. Possibly she did too, possibly she wanted a scandal, some definite end with Slate. In the future he would be embarrassed by his fantasies and alarmed by his candor. When passions cooled, self-control was more valuable than audacity. They had come to an intersection, not a junction. Hugging her quickly, and with the brush of a kiss, he turned away and went to his car.

There was romance enough in his predicament: the the last ferry had gone and the office was closed. He parked in the waiting lane, under the lights, in case being first in line would increase his chances of success with her, and hung his sports coat on the rear view mirror as a window shade and pushed the seat flat for a bed.

In the morning Julia's car pulled up behind him.

Children with Children

After a bumpy flight, Roddy Denton dropped off most of his passengers at Logan and continued to his home field near Chicago. It was Monday; *Constitution* was scheduled to go into drydock on Thursday. Hilty settled his guests at the Park Plaza hotel, just south of the Public Garden, and walked to his apartment in Beacon Hill to sleep.

The next afternoon he was sitting in his car in the parking lot of Wellesley High School, partly hidden beneath a linden tree still dropping a few yellow leaves. From this spot he looked across a broad, handsome turnaround to the entrance. What high school was entered from a turnaround? But a caution too: although no security was visible—nothing to detract from the tone of invulnerable privilege—his car was probably on camera. But audacity in the service of others was readily forgiven.

There was no bell: shortly after three p.m. children and some adults began to stream from the entrance. The children were all beautiful, being both children and the offspring of wealth. The adults came in all sizes and shapes and apparent distinction, which need not depend on appearance. That nice-looking, well-dressed woman could have been a teacher her students would remember for the rest of their lives, who took an interest in them beyond school hours, encouraging them to aspire greatly...or she could have been a dunce with good connections. That short fat man with the greasy face might know more about organic chemistry than a Nobel laureate.

Among the stream and yet apart from it, not speaking to anyone, Blake came out, gravid of belly, leaning back slightly and duck-walking to compensate for her burden. He shrank in his seat. She looked as if she might cross the turnaround—sharp as she was, she would remember his rented car. But her way was blocked by several limos, and if she suspected anything the pregnancy was too

[249]

much to act on it: she turned to follow the sidewalk out to Seaver Street, along which she could duck-walk home.

The departures dwindled. He waited. He would wait until dusk if necessary or until someone sent him away. Probably most of the students still inside the building were kept by an afterschool activity, like football or orchestra. Hannah Brigand played the violin. Blake had boasted that Hannah was sure to get into Julliard, which, adjusted for youthful enthusiasm and ignorance of the true size of the world, meant that he was about as gifted as other aspirants who would go on to ordinary careers.

(Careers that included fatherhood.)

A student with hair to her shoulders and wearing a beret at a jaunty angle and a kilt over her slender hips came out carrying a violin case. At once a midnight-blue sedan with tinted windows pulled up to the curb, and she opened the back door and got in. Here was telltale camera footage: the sedan and his own car following it, scattering the yellow leaves.

The sedan entered Route 9 and a couple of exits later took a side road up to a development on a hill.

All professions required their apprenticeship. A real investigator would have known that the entrance to the development would be gated, and a pro would already have obtained the gate code. The sedan proceeded while he stopped and pretended to consult a road map. Wending its way along the contour of the hill, it turned into a driveway. As the student got out he made sure which house it was then drove to the gate.

"Yes sir?"

The gate was opened not by a code but by a guard in a booth.

"My name is Bradford Hilty, and I'm here to see the Brigand family—Mr. Brigand if he's home already."

"Would you be on my list?"

The shortest path through authority was to be candid.

"No sir, and the family doesn't know me. I'm here on a matter involving Peter—or I believe he's called Hannah now."

"Let me check for you." The guard picked up a phone and spoke to someone, nodding his agreement while he kept his stony eyes on the visitor. Putting the phone down, he said, "Could you schedule an appointment, sir?"

"I'd be happy to do that, but then of course they'd ask what I wanted, and my news is best delivered in person. This matter involving their—son—is time-sensitive. I say *son* although I know he's transitioning. I just don't know the right term to use, it's very confusing."

This was rewarded with a gleam of sympathy. The guard probably hated transgender women athletes and had voted for Trump.

"I realize you need to protect the residents' privacy. I'm not a solicitor or anything like a threat. I'm a retired naval officer, a captain. I've commanded ships and squadrons. Served thirty years. Peter—Hannah—is in an awkward situation involving a member of my family, which I would like to resolve as comfortably as possible for everyone and before nature takes its course. If that's any help for an explanation."

"I hear you," said the guard, without the *sir* but without the state trooper face either. "Only Peter's home right now—I don't know what to call him either. His parents work late. If you want to come back tonight, I'll let my relief know."

"I can do that. But I'd be sorry to get either of you in trouble. I'm happy to talk to Peter alone, unofficially."

"Let me ask if he'll see you."

The wait was longer than the first time. Finally the guard signaled that Peter had picked up the phone. A short conversation ensued. The guard nodded, put down the phone, and smiled as if he himself had been admitted. The gate opened.

As he was about to drive through, the guard called, "A lesson for all of us, don't you think?"

[251]

To reinforce the legitimacy of his visit, he parked in front of the house. The door was opened by Peter. The scene that followed was something like the reveal in a whodunit: the surprise, the guilty look not unmixed with relief, the confession that needed to explain itself.

Few things were more pleasing to him than when one success left time for another. From the Brigands' house, waving cheerfully to his friend in the security booth, he drove the short distance to Wellesley College, where he appeared, again unannounced, at the office of the dean of students.

Audacious from audacity's success, he asked for the dean, who as he could see was sitting in her office, probably waiting for the five o'clock whistle. As commodore of the Taiwan squadron, he had gained admission to the very president of Panama to obtain clearance for his ships in the face of some malign Chinese influence. Compared to that, a dean of students hardly twitched the needle.

He gave the assistant his calling card, one from his service days, engraved nicely in Garamond. This was a good time to be from the military. In five minutes he was sitting with the dean.

"I have an unusual request," he began.

"Oh, you wouldn't believe what people ask for," said the dean, whose name was Margaret Holbrook, an overweight woman with a breezy manner; exuberantly so.

"It's a bit late in the day. Thank you for seeing me."

"It *is* a bit late. Luckily for you, I need to update my spreadsheets. But let me send my assistant home, as I've worked her like a draft horse since the start of the term."

She didn't bother with the door. A few loving words, the assistant's insincere protest, and Holbrook shooed her from the office. When she returned, her face wore the self-satisfaction of a good deed done.

"Now to your unusual request," she said.

"My granddaughter, Lisa Nichols, is applying for admission to the next incoming class. I'm not here to lobby for her—"

"I wouldn't listen to you if I thought so. Go on."

"She has serious credentials and is personally impressive. If your admissions people don't accept her, she'll do very well somewhere else. She won't need financial aid, not that that's important to you. And she lives here, which would be convenient for her—possibly good for the college as well, if you're interested in local admissions."

"And yet you aren't here to lobby for your granddaughter. What's the problem, sir?"

"She might be applying to you as Blake Nichols—she's been questioning her gender."

"No problem there. What?"

"She's pregnant with no identified partner, as yet."

"Good for her! And a bit of feedback on the gender question, I would think." Holbrook's eyes were merry.

"It's a long story."

"You're not going to reward me for my time by saying how a questioning young woman got pregnant—"

"By another young woman, transgendered."

"Excellent! They have the right to play on our teams, so why not impregnate us? But you aren't here about that either. You aren't here to cheat the admissions process. You know you're speaking to the dean of students. You don't know, and neither of us can consider the fact, that my son is also a naval officer—"

"Is he, by God! What ship?"

"*Theodore Roosevelt.* He flies F-35s."

"I was onboard *T.R.* just a few years ago!"

"Well, there you are. And now we'll disregard all that pleasantness and you'll get to the point."

"Blake—we use her questioning name—has chosen to carry her baby to term. There's a controversy within her loving family about whether she should raise it herself or give it up for adoption. She would be a splendid mother, no question about it. The controversy is whether she can raise the child and continue her education. She told me she conducted an informal survey of the Wellesley campus and found no single mothers here."

"Then I would fail her for her sloppy research. Perhaps I should append a memo to her admissions file."

"She did say the survey was informal."

"I have always taken that word to mean cursory, superficial, slapdash, sloppy, biased."

"There's nothing superficial about Blake. She pulls and pulls on a string until she gets to the end of it, counting all the knots as she goes."

"Once again you're making the admissions case. Let me state your real request. You would like Blake to meet someone here who's been through this experience, the baby and the education, and who will convince her that she can do both; for I see that's what you and at least one of her parents want. Very well: unusual request received. Let me mull over the possibilities. For your information, and hers, out of twenty-seven hundred students here, we have thirty-two single mothers, including fourteen among my first-years."

Her eyes gleamed with that same self-satisfaction, perhaps including the satisfaction that a well-informed female had once again corrected a misinformed male.

"One of the advantages of our small college is that the dean of students *knows* her students. I am thinking of two or three excellent candidates. If you quote me on this I'll deny it, but I'll see to it that the child is adorably cute."

"So kind!" he exclaimed. "This is everything I was hoping for. Thank you, Dean Holbrook. I'm thrilled." He was. Besides that other breakthrough, the family would now know the facts. And praise him for arranging this help.

ᗷ ᗷ ᗷ

If you're still in Wellesley please come here now read the text from Sarah.

It was late. Besides tired, his audacity had left him ravenously hungry. Waiting for him in the apartment were all the ingredients for the omelet he delighted to make, self-levitatingly light and melt-in-the-mouth delicious, which he could toss into a perfect half-moon from the skillet. Heading into Boston by the most direct route, he turned around.

The tires on the gravel sounded judgmental. He rang the bell, opened the door, and went inside. Sarah met him in the hall and silently led him to the smallest of the living rooms, where the family, all but Megan, were sitting on the ell-shaped sectional. Blake was sitting on the long side, opposite which a dining room chair had been placed. Sarah sat beside her and beckoned him to the chair. Mad and Phil had squeezed together on the short side. None of them were taking advantage of the comfortable back cushions.

Sarah said, "I think Blake should go first."

Blake said, "I'll speak later."

Sarah said, "We had an unexpected visit just now. Hannah Brigand and their parents. Apparently you've decided to inform the Brigands of Blake's pregnancy."

This was one of the many occasions he had found in life when it was better to breast the flight of arrows, shield high.

"I called on Hannah at his home. While we were talking, his father came in. I didn't meet his mother."

"Can you tell us what was said?"

"I can. I said that my granddaughter was pregnant, that we knew the date of conception, which coincided with the date she had been intimate with Hannah, and that I was confident a DNA test would confirm him to be the father. He had been frightened from the moment he opened the door to me; now he looked really scared. We went on from there with that assumption. I said that of course—"

[255]

"You bullied them!" Blake cried.

"No. I spoke to him in a friendly way throughout. I said that of course I was interested in helping you, Blake, through this challenge, but in terms of his own life too it would be better for him to live up to his responsibilities. At that point his father came in, and I repeated the story. I have to say, he took it well. If his first thoughts were of an abortion, as soon as he heard you were seven months along his attitude changed. I'm not sure how you left it with the three of them when they came here. We can talk about that in a moment."

He leaned forward on the hard dining room chair.

"Since I feel a charge of treason coming, let me offer my defense. Phil and Sarah, you're not going to like this, for different reasons, and I won't sugarcoat it. Blake will have this baby, and then she will need to get on with her life, like so many parents of unplanned children. She has enormous resources behind her, from both families. I'm confident Hannah knows that his life too will change now, though perhaps not how much or how thankful he will be.

"Four of the five people sitting in this room think that Blake should raise the baby. Four of the five—a different four—think that she should continue her education without any gap. I say four, Blake, because I have learned in these past few months, including that difficult time when you, despite your condition, were so helpful to Nana and me—I have learned to read your character. You have ability; you have ambition; you won't settle for less than your full potential. But even more important, you have a generous heart. You will not be able to give up this child without lasting pain and guilt. You will not. You will not.

"As sure as I am of these things, I saw the situation stalemated and the clock ticking. Who could end it? Look at the five of us: my advantages are time, desire, distance, and experience—years of experience serving with sailors."

An open cadence: the others looked at him to confirm he had finished then at each other to see who would go next. Both Sarah and Phil started to speak, stopped, then stepped on each other:

"If she keeps it she'll be poor for the rest of her life."

"If she gives it up she'll be sorry for the rest of her life."

They sat back, insistent and dissatisfied.

Mad said, "You guys sound like an opera duet."

Sarah scowled; Phil grinned.

Blake saw nothing funny. She had a young person's account to settle with an elder. In the silence she took her chance:

"Pop, you have betrayed my trust."

"Yes I have."

"Yes you have. You *knew* I didn't want to tell Hannah. You had no right to go behind my back to them, and no right at all to talk about my sex life. Fuck! I don't want their help raising my baby. *You betrayed my trust!*"

Mad said, "He has admitted that, dear. We don't need to dwell on it."

"But he did! How am I ever going to trust you again?"

"You and I will have to work on that," he replied. "But is that really the question tonight? Raise your baby? Where's the crib? Where's the stroller? Certainly your family has the right to help you."

"But you have no right. No right at all."

"I agree with that," said Sarah.

"I appreciate his help," said Phil.

"Things may look different soon," he said.

"Not as far as you're concerned. I'll never trust you again." At this declaration she nodded emphatically.

"So be it. I'll be sorry if that's true. For now, please, can we talk about the immediate problem? I'd be interested to hear what Hannah's mother said."

"She said she knows someone who performs late-term abortions," Sarah replied. "That was her contribution. Apparently she forgot that she was speaking to a couple of physicians."

"They're not advocating that, certainly."

[257]

"No," said Phil. "As soon as Hannah and Roy showed that they were appalled by the idea, she retreated. She'll go along. Roy seems almost pleased—I would guess it has something to do with his feelings about his son's gender quest, or maybe he wants to be a grandfather himself. As far as Hannah is concerned, he said he was ready to be involved."

"I don't want them involved," Blake said.

"Them? Which them?" he asked.

"Them them."

"She means the family," Sarah said.

"No, I mean *them:* Hannah. But I don't want them involved either."

"As Pop has suggested," Phil said, "you may change your mind about that with the first midnight feeding."

"Are we going to have him live here?" Sarah asked.

"Them!" Blake cried.

Having settled nothing, the adversaries went to their own places to continue the conflict in their thoughts.

"Here we are again," said Mad, "looking for lost balls."

"That sounds like the title of your future memoirs."

"I'm not the one who needs to set the world straight."

"You'd be good at it. And it needs setting straight."

"No shit. So how did your shuttle diplomacy go?"

"After constructive talks, a proposal is under review by the several parties concerned."

"Which means?" These days she had little patience for his joking pedantry.

"Ellifiknow. We'll see who crosses the brow on Thursday."

"And in domestic politics?"

"You mean...?"

"Yes, Bradford, us. Now that you're not going to be a member of the next administration, and now that we are one hundred thousand dollars poorer—"

"Plus change."

"Plus change, what proposal is on the table?"

"To live!" he said. "And to feel alive. The last time we spoke, you were interested in buying a place close to Blake but not too close."

"And I still am. What's unclear are your plans."

"Correct. My golden parachute is exactly the same as Slate's except for the five houses, the club membership, the dedicated airplane, and—oh, yes!—the tens of millions in severance."

"That said...."

"That said, I am happy to settle in Boston. I need to discuss some changes in the history project with my assistant, but I think it has potential, and most of the material I need is here. The part of my plans that's unclear is whether we want to live together."

"True."

"You weren't willing to go to Washington with me. I understood that. All the same I wonder if you would really prefer to live alone."

"Yes, that's the question."

"And?"

She shook her head. "Still unclear. I'm happy I'm going to live—I feel that. But how? Would it be a mistake, do you think, to look for a place we could both enjoy?" Her slight emphasis on *both* reminded him that his childhood home, with its unhappy memories for her, had been decided by fiat. "And then we could make up our minds whether...together or apart...."

"But then we'll just keep postponing it."

"Maybe."

"Our last good years before *we* need help. I really think we should face it now, Mad."

"But not tonight, at least. Not everything can be fixed just when you want it."

He received this in silence. They cleared the table and loaded the dishwasher. The first sound of water when the dishwasher started was oddly comforting.

[259]

"Have you heard from the FBI?" she asked.

"Not a word. It probably takes a while to drop an agent into Russia and steal the credentials of their account in the Bahamas. As I told you before, the loss doesn't affect our decision on where to live."

She smiled mysteriously.

"So what will happen now, with Blake?" he asked.

"Ellifiknow. I don't share Phil's optimism about Roy. He seems like the crafty type, or maybe I just don't trust billionaires. I wouldn't be surprised if he lies in the weeds and helps us decorate the nursery, then after the baby is born, suddenly he appears on the scene with adoptive parents in tow."

"That would be one solution, certainly."

"But terrible for her."

"Yes."

"For what it's worth, I agree with what you did. Blake will forgive you."

"That's good to hear," he said.

"Do you need to get back?"

"I should. I'm still fighting jet-lag. See you Thursday?"

"Yes. See you then."

Old Ironsides Underway

Onboard *Constitution* per custom, liberty had expired on Wednesday, the day before sailing, at midnight, and on Thursday at six a.m. the ship's bosun walked among the lumpy hammocks on the berth deck, divided into male and female compartments, shouting, "Reveille, reveille. All hands heave out and trice up. I come with a sharp knife and a clear conscience."

Presently the crew appeared on the spar—or main—deck, their hammocks, rolled and tied, over their shoulders; to be stowed, numbers out, against the bulwarks as splinter shields. In theory, had they not heaved out and triced up when called, the hammocks would have been cut down while they lay inside them; but with such a well-trained crew, of course, that would never happen.

For an hour they polished brightwork and priddied the wooden deck, giving everything an extra touch, for today was a special day. Being about four hundred short of their wartime complement, and with the advantage of Dr. Franklin's discovery, they used electric buffers instead of holystones. After this they went below for their breakfast.

By nine a.m., clean and presentable, fed, mustered, inspected and instructed for the day, they had shifted into the dress uniform of the period.

At nine-thirty Captain Schaefer in her own dress uniform, complete with scraper—her hat—worn fore and aft in the Nelson manner, appeared on deck, and the executive officer reported to her that all hands were present or accounted for, that the ship was ready for visitors, and that preparations for getting underway were in train.

Moments later a minivan stopped by the brow, and a tall man organized his family for going onboard. It was Bradford Hilty, wearing a herringbone cap. The crew knew him from an inspiring talk he had given. The petty officer of the watch rang the quarterdeck bell, four strokes in two groups of two, and announced, "Captain, U.S. Navy, Retired: arriving." At this the bosun and four sideboys took their places by the brow in two lines facing each other.

While his family waited Hilty came onboard, pausing to salute the colors at the stern then holding a second salute as he strode through the passage of sideboys, themselves saluting, while the bosun piped his four-noted *twee!* Honors rendered appropriately, he beckoned to the others, who followed his example but with hands on hearts instead of saluting and with no side honors. As they pooled on the quarterdeck, Captain Schaefer went among them. Blake felt self-conscious, but Nutmeg the Cat, in Megan's arms, onboard by special permission, got most of the attention—the smiling eyes and exclamations of "Ah!" and "Look at the kitty!" and "So cute!" and, from the bosun, "Always good luck to have a cat onboard."

While he waited, Hilty, feeling the November breeze on his cheek, glanced at the light chop in the harbor and read the ebb tide on a buoy. They weren't going to sea, only as far as Fort Independence. The stable deck would be unlikely to make anyone ill, but the guests, as he had advised them, might well be cold. None of his hopes would be realized today if teeth were chattering.

A car came up, and the three Brigands got out. Hannah didn't look like Hannah anymore. He, she, or they had had a haircut and was wearing boy's clothes. Mr. Brigand corrected the sailor who was checking off the guests to say that his son was named Peter—Hannah had been a misunderstanding. Peter's face was soft and full, androgynous, but presumably that would change when the estrogen left his body.

All this was surprising, to say the least, and the one most surprised was Blake, who didn't know how to react. A Peter unsexed offended her progressive values; on the other hand it was good that her child would have a father. Finally she hugged him, saying, "I don't care, it's your life," for nothing mattered more to her than kindness and tolerance. At this there were smiles among the two families and none brighter than Phil's.

It was nearly time to leave. VIPs, fully aware of their importance, always boarded at the last minute. The most important of them arrived now: Former Prime Minister Pazienza. Because none of the Navy directives covered his title, Captain Schaefer, taking proper initiative, had him announced as "Italian Government, Retired" with eight bells and eight sideboys.

Pazienza, naval officer though he had been, didn't know whether to salute or put his hand over his heart. Hilty should have briefed him. Moreover, his hands were busy holding those of Vittoria Piedmonte and Romola Mancusa, both of them delighted and astonished.

"Bradford, my friend!"

"Prime Minister, my friend!"

With a silly grin Pazienza pointed to their matching caps; Hilty's had been a gift in Milan. Since they had been in each other's pockets for nearly a week, the greeting was a little enthusiastic, but since it encompassed all the excitement, joy, and satisfaction of those days, and, more than that, the culmination of forty years of hopeful waiting, it felt just right. Hilty had shuttled between Milan and La Spezia to bring them together. Pazienza, of course, was willing, and Vittoria had acknowledged and finally overcome a long, bitter misconception about her late husband's—and her own—loyal friend and benefactor. If this wasn't yet love, the idea of love was allowed.

Other friendships were swift in the making. Romola was thrilled to meet Nutmeg, and Megan was thrilled to meet a girl from a foreign country who was nearly her own age and full of wisdom. Vittoria's gentle amiability won over Sarah, Blake, and Mad. Mrs. Brigand had studied in Rome when Pazienza had been prime minister; having heard all the stories about Silvio Berlusconi, she began to tell one of the most scandalous. "Dear lady," Pazienza said, "the president believed that scandal was a precondition for greatness." To which Mad observed, "We have someone like that over here." To which he himself was tempted to confess that that person's voice was easily imitated. But with this audience the story of his feckless act would make him not sympathetic but ridiculous.

The Special Sea and Anchor Detail was set. The pilot arrived with two Navy tugboats, one of which was made up on *Constitution's* port quarter to act as her propulsion and the other with a line to her bow to pull her away from the berth. The crew were at their stations, and the mooring lines were singled; wire slings had been shackled to the brow, and a crane was standing by to lift it. At this point Captain Schaefer made a mistake. With a glance at the commodore to say that they were running out of time and couldn't wait for his remaining guests, she ordered the brow removed.

Just then another car came up the pier, and Admiral Slate Greene got out, alone. Quickly the pattern on deck rearranged itself. Uncovered, Slate came across, hand on heart, and the bosun *tweed* and the sideboys saluted. The captain hastened to welcome him, perhaps a little red-faced about her mistake, for here was someone who had once stood at the top of her chain of command and who for all she knew might still be influential.

"Where's Julia?" Hilty asked him as they shook hands. Slate only shrugged.

Schaefer gave him another look; the crane operator was waiting. Apparently Julia wasn't coming, but he had one last guest to hope for. "May I borrow this?" he asked the watch officer, reaching for his spyglass. At the foot of the pier a soldier in Union blue, with a woman and a child, was seeking admission from the gate guard; and apparently was getting a hassle about it. With a quick salute to the quarterdeck and the colors, he left the ship, ducking under the slings even as the brow began to rise. A laboring diesel stopped, a voice shouted at him from the cab. He went on, stepped on the pier, and hurried to the gate, a little short of breath.

The soldier, of course, was William Carney, and he was upset. In the presence of his family the gate guard had insisted on searching his Civil War knapsack. The guard was white.

"Did you search everyone?" Carney asked.

"I am authorized to conduct random searches."

"Random. Have you searched anyone else?"

"You have a weapon." This referred to the Enfield 1853 rifle-musket, which had not been fired, probably, in more than a hundred years.

Carney looked up and saw his employer. Even so, he said, in a loud voice, "Then we'll just go home, then" and turned away from the gate. His wife looked both angry and frightened; the boy looked uncomprehending.

"I can vouch for him, officer," he said while catching his breath. "He and his family are on your list. They are my guests and the guests of the Secretary of the Navy. My name is Hilty."

"I know he's on the list. I just want to be sure of that pack. He could be carrying C-4."

"And *have* you searched everyone, officer? Cars have driven onto the pier, mine and others. We weren't searched. I repeat, I know him and I do vouch for him and his family."

"Yes sir."

But Carney seemed to have had enough.

"This was a bad idea."

"William, it's a glorious day," he said privately. "The weather is fine this close to Thanksgiving. We are celebrating my wife's recovery from a nearly fatal illness, who herself is in a celebratory mood. My daughter and her family are here—I've told you the story of my grand-daughter—and the father of her child. And there are some interesting and influential people for you to meet, which is always worth something. Please join us. The guard made a mistake."

"No mistake."

"Yes, you're right, and I'm sorry. And embarrassed. Here's another example of the injustice that you and I will be writing about. But now he's changed. Please join us. Your son will be thrilled by the ship."

The brow had been set back in place. Of the crowd on deck, some were looking away from the incident, but his own people were curious and sympathetic. Perhaps this watch too would make trouble...but the officer complimented Carney on his period uniform, gesturing to his own, and with a glance at the lock mechanism of the rifle-musket assured himself that it couldn't fire. The crane removed the brow.

Getting underway was about as ordinary as rising from a chair. Captain Schaefer, conning from the foretop, spoke to the XO on deck, and the pilot said a word to the tugs. The last line came in, the tugs began to open a wedge of water between the ship and the pier, and the underway flags were broken from their respective masts, spots of color beneath the lowering grey sky. Since no sails were set, these were plain to see: the captain's commissioning pennant, swirling in the breeze like a scrawled signature; the frigate's call sign—NAPJ—two-blocked on the signal hoist; and alongside it Code Hotel, meaning that a pilot was onboard, toward which every pilot always glanced to be sure it was flying.

"No commodore's pennant," Mad said to him, partly in fun, partly in nostalgia. At some point in their forty-two years of marriage, she had learned to accept the fact that wives and ships each had their place in the heart of a sailor, though not necessarily at the same time.

"No, nor admiral's flag. Old retired fuds like Slate and me should have a flag with a horse grazing in a pasture."

"But maybe, thanks to you, Slate will race again."

[266]

"We'll see. I'm sorry Julia's not here."

"Where is she?"

"He won't tell me. I brought her to Chicago, hoping something good would happen."

"Life doesn't work that way, though." When he didn't answer, she prompted him: "Does it."

"No, Madeleine. I understand that not everything can be fixed just when I like. But if you were Julia, wouldn't you want to be associated with the Paris Ballet?"

"It does sound wonderful, sign me up. I'm not sure she wants to be associated with it through her cheating husband, however. And she might be thinking that she could do the job herself."

"She probably could."

"Don't worry, she knows the effort you made"—with a meaning glance that might recall his earlier infatuation.

That's not why I'm disappointed, he said to himself.

The tugs had hauled the ship into position. Sailors cast off the one at the bow, which moved out in company. Since *Constitution* displaced considerable weight—1,576 tons—the tug at the quarter leaned on her throttle. The ship surged, but the higher speed canceled the following breeze, so that the diesel engine sounded as loud and unpleasant as a jackhammer, and its acrid exhaust filled the quarter-deck. In a body the passengers moved to the starboard bow, as far as possible from the nuisance, breathing clean air with an inspiriting needle of salt. Ahead of them the horizon belonged to the open sea, but of course they would turn around before then.

"Just spectacular," Roy Brigand said to him. "Did the Navy teach you all these ropes?"

"I can tie the knots and splice the lines—so can Maddy, after so much exposure, and maybe my children. I know how to command a ship. I can sail a boat. For the in-between parts I would have to trust my crew. Do you sail?" But of course all hedge fund managers did.

"Never. I don't care much for unstable environments."

"And yet you trade in Bitcoin."

Brigand enjoyed this. "Maybe it's compensation."

"But that's the question. *Is* it compensation?"

"Very good. I surrender to your—what?—to your superior weight of metal. You know, when I came home on Tuesday and you were there with Peter, with this news, I might have fainted. It's been an interesting couple of days. Lots of changes. You can see that Peter has decided he's a boy. As far as the baby is concerned, we're all in— my wife too. Whatever the young parents decide about getting married—it's nice to see them so comfortable with each other today—but whatever happens in that respect, I'm sure Peter will be an active and responsible father."

"On our side we want Blake to continue her education." Which was true at least by a majority vote.

"Oh, we do too. Both of them. Wherever Peter is accepted for music school, they can make their home. Of course, I'm hopeful about New York—the Julliard—but that would be winning the lottery, wouldn't it. I've brought in a number of first-class violinists to evaluate his playing, and I still don't know. The Curtis in Philadelphia would serve. The imprimatur is so important, isn't it. Maybe I should make a donation?"

He was rather an effeminate man, with a soft voice unsure of its footing. It was probably more vigorous when talking about money.

"For our part," he said, instead of *on our side* a second time (though Brigand seemed like the type to have read Fowler on elegant variation), "we think a school in the area *here* might be a good choice. Of course there's Wellesley— none better than that, right? It would be convenient if Blake and Peter went there, don't you think?" Giving him back his tag questions.

"I suppose so. I haven't looked into their music program."

"Or for Peter maybe the New England Conservatory or Berklee College. But I've always thought that serious musicians, like journalists, should get a well-rounded education first: it enriches their understanding, *n'est-ce pas?*"

"I can see you've given some thought to this," Brigand said and went over to join his son.

Holly Brigand was continuing to instruct the former prime minister and the love of his life and the love of his life's granddaughter about Italy. Of the three only Vittoria looked happy. He gave a glance in Slate's direction, over by the starboard bow chaser, and presently he and Pazienza joined him.

In Milan, reunited with Vittoria, Pazienza had undertaken to come to the United States to speak with Slate about leading the Paris Ballet, of which he was an influential director thanks to his position at La Scala and his distinguished résumé before then. Hilty, after giving Slate and Julia time together, had proposed the idea to Slate, who seemed open to it, so that only a little personal chemistry would be needed to close the deal. (At Julia's request, he had met with Slate alone: as much as she liked Paris, and the ballet, she wouldn't commit to join him.)

This was now the meeting. Rank had its privileges, one of which was to speak first. Pazienza filled his lungs with the bracing air.

"You know, Admiral, in its way this ship is just as impressive to me as those magnificent buildings along the Washington Mall. The so-called iron sides: indestructible! Imagine what damage this very cannon must have caused to the *Guerriere.*"

"I agree with you, sir. Although I believe in that battle mostly broadsides were fired, not this bow chaser. Isn't that right, Professor Hilty?"

"If I knew I've forgotten," he replied, an untruth justi-
fied by the end in sight. "Slate, the prime minister is one
of us: served as a lieutenant in the destroyer *Audace.*"

"*Audace.* That must count for something."

"I was quite a junior officer," said Pazienza.

"Hilty makes me feel like a junior officer every day."

"When you need it." But the threesome was awkward:
they would have done better with one fewer or one more,
especially if the one more had been Julia.

He said, "Since I've broached this idea with you both
independently, I wonder if it wouldn't be useful now to
talk about the Paris Ballet."

But at that point Megan and Romola brought Nutmeg
over for the men to admire. The cat was draped across
Romola's shoulder like a big baby whose head no longer
needs to be supported; like the baby whose belly you
couldn't resist smelling. Who is perfectly content to be
passed around and adored. Pazienza, who had cats at
home, tested his potential as an aviator, laughing at how
relaxed he was when inverted. He offered him to Slate—
in its way this was the employment interview. But Slate
had never owned or liked any animals: Mad had once said
it was the only charmless thing about him. He shook his
head, the revulsion obvious in his face. Pazienza gave the
cat to its owner instead. His limpid blue eyes, normally
so inviting of good fellowship, were unfathomable.

"What's bugging you?" he asked Slate.

"The best-laid schemes of mice and Hilty often go agley."

"I have no author's pride in this. But it does seem that
destiny is offering you your wife back as well as the perfect job to end your career with."

"I don't like him."

"Why not?"

"I know why," said Mad, joining them. "Envy. You
won't be the smartest man in the room anymore."

"Not true. Your husband cured me of that long ago. Maybe I've become the thing I detest: resistant to change. I do like Paris. I do like the ballet. I speak passable French."

"Your wife would love it," Mad said. "Maybe that's the problem."

"It's not a package deal," he said. "If you and Julia work things out, she could join you. She and Pazienza hit it off."

"Which makes me part of the package."

"Why isn't she here, Slate? Come on, you can tell us: between us we have more than thirty years' experience with your marriages."

Bending over, Slate removed the tompion from the muzzle of the gun and shined a penlight down the barrel. A small gesture, performed in a crowd, yet it brought over a warrant officer to see what the admiral found. "Looks good, Gunner," Slate said, giving him that easy approval from one professional to another as he snapped the tompion back into place. "If you two insist on knowing: Julia is afraid of how I'll react, and I have to say I'm not so sure myself."

"You're not saying...?"

"No, don't worry. It's not about Robin. I'm over her—or she's over me would be more accurate. Or we're both afraid of the wrath of Hilty. But it's something to think about, isn't it: Paris, where having a mistress is *de rigueur.*"

"I'm sure Julia is far too loyal to become someone's mistress," said Mad, pleased by her wit.

"Thank you, dear. Actually, it's the culture I worry about. A thirty-five-hour work week? Life isn't just about pleasure. I'm afraid I won't approve of their commitment, they'll resent my superior American attitude, and then I'm sure to crash and burn—publicly."

"They're serious about their ballet," he said. "You'll have so much to learn—the difference between a *dégagé* and a *jeté.* If you show interest, if you give them that Slate Greene attention, you'll be a great success."

"Listen to him: he sees one dance and he's an expert."

[271]

The Turnaround

"But back to your marriage," Mad said. "Did Julia come to Boston with you?"

"She did. Then last night over dinner we started to talk about Paris and she turned into an ice sculpture in front of me. We have separate suites at the Park Plaza. I don't know where she is now, but she sent me a note not to wait for her."

"So it's not really Pazienza you don't like."

"He's all right for a lawyer. I can't see him going out on a limb for me. Too much the politician."

How little he knew.

The diesel revved to a higher pitch. With the tide running and the wind astern, the frigate was moving briskly over the ground while being set toward the shore. They passed the long wharf, where in 1863 the Fifty-fourth had embarked in the steamer *De Molay* for the war in the South and for glory. That part of the waterfront was now a giant conglomeration of masts and cranes; of ships with blocky lines and tall sheer rusting freeboards.

"Ugly now," he said to Carney, "but we can imagine the regiment lining up to go onboard."

"The officers to the wardroom, white linen and silver."

"Well, yes."

The Carneys, standing apart from the other guests, though polite to those who approached them, were clearly not thrilled by the outing. Tamara Carney, serious and watchful, kept Dree, their son, who was seven or eight, close by her side. Dree himself seemed intimidated by the strangeness of the ship, the masts and rigging, the orders and the smells, the basic idea of traveling on water.

"Your husband and I were talking about our project," he said to Tamara.

"Oh yes?" The same politeness as the others received.

"Do you remember what you told me, William, about our showing the real soldiering?"

[272]

"I remember."

"Well, you convinced me. Instead of the military history, which anyone could write, I want to concentrate on the social history. I want to make the reader feel their sacrifice, and why they made it, and how much has been lost since then."

"Uh-huh."

"You've done the research, most of it yourself. Now I thought we could write it together. Co-authors. Submit it for publication together. Share the royalties."

"Uh-huh. Whose name goes first on the title page?"

"Ooh, too much," said Tamara, hands on her chest.

"Of course, Mrs. Carney, the ship's beginning to work a little: sit here." He helped her to a carronade, to sit with her head between her knees. As queasy as she felt, she muttered how embarrassing. Actually the harbor was flat, except once in a while when the frigate seemed to shift its weight over an oncoming swell: a fractional movement, no more than a suggestion. He and her men tried to shield her from view.

The ship was coming up to Fort Independence: a squat, one-story pentagon with embrasures where office windows might be expected. The auburn granite was pleasant to see above a lush esplanade, still nearly green in this grey month, and beneath a grass-topped roof nearly brown. The Stars and Stripes were flying from a pole on the north side, and behind the embrasures was a saluting battery. It was customary during turnaround for *Constitution* to fire a 21-gun salute to the fort, which would return it.

The executive officer came up to check the line of fire. Tamara Carney, feeling in the way, started to rise from the carronade, but the XO said, "No, you're fine, ma'am, we'll be firing from the gun deck," and she bent over again with beads of sweat on her forehead.

The escorting tug took up a new station on the bow, ready to help bring the ship's head around, and the tug on the quarter slowed them to bare steerageway. The sea was close: waves rolled under the bow. A flight of terns passed up the side and wheeled to port with their racking cries. Then the world was hushed. All the guests were now gathered to starboard, nervously expectant, as people were when they thought the phone would ring.

The gunner walked by the bulwark, speaking into his radio. "If I weren't such a fool I wouldn't be here," he said. "Fire one."

Directly below them a twenty-four pounder spoke. The blast was like being slapped for something you didn't know you'd done. Smoke issued from the gunport, and the deck rumbled to the recoil as it might if the ship had gone aground. But these were normal sights and sounds.

Everyone reacted according to their nature. Over many years of practice he himself had learned to brace for the report without showing it.

"I left my wife and child and everything I hold dear," the gunner said. "Fire two."

Nutmeg escaped to the deck, clawing bloody furrows in Megan's soft white skin; with a few balletic bounds he leapt to the rail and was gone before the gunner could say *Fire Three.*

At once and automatically, like Russia after Sarajevo, Megan jumped overboard, arms wide and legs scissoring to enter the water.

"You stupid!" Blake yelled after her, and jumped.

In the moment of recognition differential, while most of them stood in shock, Dree Carney climbed on the rail, assessed the drop, and jumped.

Time has stopped, as it must in the moment of death: the last perception. He is standing on the extreme edge of the deck, the rail behind him, and is giving himself to the air as Phil to his right and Peter to his left are also jumping. A giddy feeling, like belonging at last, like a line of daredevils over a drop. The surface rises to his teeth which are bared in a grin, and he exhales a stream of bubbles—the last breath—that no doubt contains a giggle.

But the water is cold. Colder than the giddiness. Numbingly, mortally cold. The cold is inside his skin already, freezing his bones, icing its way to his heart. His exertions won't keep him warm before he freezes solid.

The water all around him, thrashed into a grey turbidity. The heads of people he knows, loves. Men, children. If he weren't so cold he'd be able to name them. He must concentrate. Life rings and safety lines rain upon him. Annoying and, more important, counterproductive to his being here to have to keep ducking. "Stop it," he croaks, but of course they won't, even if they can hear him. This is what people do in emergency: make things worse.

Who is in the water? Who needs saving? A muster is needed, sorted by order of entry. Nutmeg missing. Megan being tended—Phil, Phil Nichols, her father, putting her into a life jacket. Blake: Blake? There, and Peter Something with her. The little black boy is missing.

He reaches down to untie his shoes. The water is really cold—has he noticed that before?—and his fingers are growing numb, and like an idiot he has doubled the knots. He manages, the current takes them, which some diver will find one day and wonder what story they tell. The ship looms overhead. There is a commotion on deck. But have they not trained for this, that nice young crew? Do they not know to lower a boat?

He is called, called from long ago, to dive beneath the surface. Using his arms mostly, for he has never been good at the frog kick, he impels himself lower. A small figure is suspended in the murk, as behind a screen. A churchman once preached the comfortable doctrine that the dead live on with us behind a screen. Swedenborg. Good God: and *this* is to be his last thought on earth, this useless thought? He swims and swims. At one time he was a powerful swimmer, except for that frog kick. Up, out, together, down; only *together* is so hard. There! It's the boy—Dree—below him still, slowly sinking, his arms adrift like tendrils. Better they shouldn't have come. A tragedy, and all his fault.

He struggles downward, the boy just out of reach. A burst of swimming doesn't get there, and probably he won't have a second chance. The earache alone will kill him; crush his skull. Submarines have a crush depth. His pounding heart fails to send heat to his muscles, which somehow keep working. Racehorses run after their hearts have exploded.

He is down to the boy, whose arms are active, who if he isn't careful will latch onto his neck to sink them both. Acting between thoughts, like a prisoner between sweeps of a searchlight, he pins Dree from behind.

He swims him up, regretting his technique: up, out, together, down—or just kick like hell. His heart and his lungs are bursting; in the suffocating cold it must be possible to get a cramp in the chest. A stomach cramp less than thirty minutes after eating is just a superstition. Higher, higher—lighter, lighter—he pauses beneath the surface until a swell passes over them, and then a final kick and they break into the air, the lifegiving air, warmer than his blood. Dree gasps for breath; gasps and coughs out water—alive! He pulls him, unresisting now, onto his back and tows him to a life ring.

But the cold. The cold is shrinking the periphery. In the Norwegian Sea the life expectancy from exposure is three minutes or less. When he took his ship up there he closed the weather decks for safety. Someone has thrown a line around him and is pulling it tight, towing him to safety. What sort of knot would that be? But the pressure hurts. A slip-knot, perhaps. A cowboy's lasso is a glorified slip-knot. The bight of it shrinks to nothing, to darkness.

Entropy Concedes the Fight

He was lying in a bed. A woman was standing beside him. He didn't know her: a doctor, a nurse, a technician, someone in scrubs. But he had an obligation to present to her his winsome, long-enduring character, cheerful under adversity. He was hooked up to a monitor, which repeated the same reassuring chirp: *alive, alive, alive.* The horse needle that someone had driven into his arm had been replaced by an inoffensive and lifegiving connection to the back of his hand. A curtain—blue and yellow wildflowers in a green meadow—had been pulled around him.

"Hello there," said the woman. "I am Cecilia Freeman. You may not remember me, but I was just inside your heart."

"Apparently it's still working," he said, surprised by his mucoidal voice.

She liked that. His heart *was* working. He was lying in the cardiac care unit of Mass General Hospital. He had had a heart attack. When she said this, the chirp quickened. No, she went on, it was probably a mild one. By the early signs no damage had been done. But in addition to the mitral valve prolapse—the murmur—which of course he knew about—two of his coronary arteries had been ninety percent blocked—that's what brought on the attack, that and being a hero!—so she had gone in with a catheter through a small incision in his leg and cleaned them out—an angioplasty—and put a stent in each artery. All successful and safe. The stents should keep the arteries open for many years. With moderate exercise and a healthy diet, and with cholesterol meds and blood thinners, he should be feeling well—better than well, full of beans—very soon.

"In fact"—here she sat on the bed and thumped his chest, at which both of them looked at the monitor—

"sitting here I see a youthful sixty-six-year-old man who, if he takes care of himself, should live to a ripe old age."

She liked telling the truth, and her skill was another source of pleasure, and her self-confidence helped bring out her kindness and optimism.

"I feel full of beans already. Who knows about this?"

"Of course your family knows. They were on the ship. Dr. Nichols and Dr. Hilty-Nichols teamed up to save your life, I think."

"And the people who went in the water?"

"Why don't you ask your wife about the details. She's right here."

She pulled back the curtain to reveal Maddy's small precious self, sitting in a chair.

He had been spared a roommate. His room was not much bigger than the bed, but it had a window, now dark. No one else was present.

"What time is it?" he asked.

"Nine-thirty."

"Same day?"

"Oh yes: they wheeled you right into surgery."

"We've got to stop meeting like this."

"I'm sorry?"

"Last time you were in the bed and I was the visitor."

"Except no one said I would live to a ripe old age."

"And everyone else?" After a victory Hornblower always asked about the butcher's bill.

"Everyone's fine. Pazienza had a slight case of hypothermia, but they warmed him up with one of those space blankets."

"Pazienza went in the water?"

"He saw that you were in trouble. Didn't hesitate. But Slate beat him to it."

"They both went in?"

"After you rescued the kid you were going under. Slate pulled you into the air again, and both of them held you afloat until the ship's boat came around. Then, on deck, you stopped breathing, and the doctor's right, Sarah and Phil saved your life."

"I need to thank them."

"They'll come by tomorrow. You may see a particular gleam in Sarah's eye. Besides her heroics, she received the news today that her surgery coach gave her high marks."

"So she's—"

"Back on track. Ready to conquer the world. Someday she'll see this struggle as a good experience."

"She will. And Slate?"

"Slate. That's been your life, you two, looking out for each other. He and Pazienza are now thick as thieves. They're off tomorrow for Paris. Pazienza told me that the job was Slate's if he wants it, and he does. He told me he'd do it for free except that the ballet folks should believe that he's highly valuable."

"They'll find that out. Whatever the artistic equivalent of a share price is, the ballet should be bullish. But I expect they have a union. And they're artists. He'll have to learn their culture and take a softer approach. Julia could guide him, if she goes."

"That won't happen soon. You can't just reassemble the pieces of a marriage. Though I have to say she was concerned enough to bring him dry clothes from the hotel. Maybe. Who knows?"

"I'd like to see her. I feel responsible for suggesting—"

"She's returning to Scotland tonight. Sends her love and is happy you're going to live."

"You and I could visit her there."

"Well, we could. Let's see."

"And the girls?"

"Both fine. Megan needed some stitches in her arm."

"Poor Nutmeg."

"Poor Nutmeg was recovered lying across a life ring. When the sailor handed him to Megan he was purring."

"Interesting. I've never known a sailor to purr."

"The cat. Really, will I have to put up with your sense of humor for the rest of my life?"

"Apparently so, since we're both going to live to ripe old ages. Let's see. Are Blake and the fetus purring?"

"That was a sight. Blake and Peter. The boat recovers them, they're standing on deck dripping wet, about three feet apart facing each other, and all I could think of were those formal steps in a Japanese Kabuki dance. Enjoy your seat: it's going to be a long performance."

She might have added that he was the one who had brought the dancers together. Well, he and she were going to be a long performance too.

They fell silent. Dr. Freeman returned with a nurse. While the nurse added some medication to his IV bag, she listened to his chest. The vital signs on the monitor looked good, but she wanted to hear the living heart. AI be damned, people would always have better judgment.

He dozed. When he awakened Mad was sitting as before.

"I need to get out of here," he said.

"Tomorrow, I think. Maybe Saturday."

"I have to go back to Chicago."

"Yes, all right, when you're better."

"I have to see Dorothea. In person."

"There will be time for that."

"It's a question of honor."

"Well, if that's all it is. But I doubt if she's going anywhere. Meanwhile, someone else is actually waiting to see you."

"Ah: I forgot the Carneys," he said.

"The boy is fine. He can't swim, but he sure can hold his breath. They went home and brought him back to thank you in person."

"I didn't think I'd get to him. William and I are going to write this book together. About the lives of the Fifty-fourth, not their battles."

"I know, you told me. It should be a best-seller. You already have outstanding name recognition."

"How so? The white man who rescued the Black child?"

"Not quite: the man responsible for the only two-gun salute in the the the history of the Navy."

"Funny. Yet I don't think I was responsible."

"Yet you always go on about perception being reality."

"All right. And yours? Your reality?"

"What do you mean?"

"Have you learned to care about things?"

This went home: her sweet face was thoughtful, perhaps troubled. She stood and turned back to the chair as if she would bring it closer to his bed. Instead, she came to the bed herself, reached over, and put her hands on either side of his face. Leaning in, looking up through her grizzled eyebrows to meet his eyes, she said,

"When you disappeared in the water I really wanted to see your head again."

The next morning he was moved to a single room in the general ward. Ordinarily he would have been released to go home, but Dr. Freeman wanted him watched for a day or two. He didn't object. The bed was warm, and the room was warm. Not just that, but it wasn't clear where home was. He was waiting for his family to invite him to live with them, but no one brought up the subject.

About mid-morning, when all his visitors had gone, a man in a business suit sat by his bed.

"Do you remember me, sir?"

"I should. You look familiar. I can't quite place you. My heart. They say short-term memory."

"Special Agent Jason Hubbard, Boston office of the FBI. I took your report about the phishing scam."

"Oh yes. Sorry." Especially since he had spoken to Hubbard twice on the phone as well.

"We've made some progress in the case."

"Your agent survived the op in Moscow?"

Hubbard smiled a tolerant smile; he must hear jokes like this all the time. "Actually, the Russians didn't do it, the Chinese did. I won't go into methods and sources, but it appears that you were specifically targeted in revenge for your participation in the Taiwan crisis."

"Good Lord. That was six years ago."

"They have long memories."

"So, the money? Any chance...?"

"I can't promise anything, but your case now falls un-der U.S. law. My office can testify that this was a political act by the Chinese government. You can sue them and collect, if you win, from assets frozen in our banks." This he said with another smile, either for the victim's good fortune or in his own self-satisfaction in closing the case.

"Hah!" said Hilty. "The last item on the list."

"I'm sorry?" asked the special agent.

About the Author

Thomas Corcoran entered the Navy in 1972 and retired in 1993 as a captain, having served during the Vietnam War and Operations Desert Shield and Desert Storm. He commanded two ships and was selected for command of a destroyer squadron. He lived in Navy ports on both coasts, including Norfolk. Besides sixteen years of sea duty, he served in the Pentagon as Special Assistant to the Chief of Naval Operations and as Military Assistant to the Secretary of Defense.

Hilty Defeats Entropy, the third in the series about this quixotic character, is his sixth published book of fiction.

He writes about the 54th Massachusetts Infantry Regiment, both as soldiers and as men, in his novel *Decoration Day.*

www.ingramcontent.com/pod-product-compliance
Lightning Source LLC
Chambersburg PA
CBHW061945170626
46813CB00006B/2537